BATTLETECH

ESCAPE FROM JARDINE

FORGOTTEN WORLDS, PART THREE

BY HERBERT A. BEAS II

BATTLETECH: ESCAPE FROM JARDINE
By Herbert A. Beas II
Cover art by Tan Ho Sim
Interior art by Doug Chaffee, Harri Kallio, Chris Lewis, Duane Loose
Cover design by David Kerber

Printed in USA.

Published by Catalyst Game Labs,
an imprint of InMediaRes Productions, LLC
5003 Main St. #110 • Tacoma, WA 98407

CHAPTER 1

Blake foretold that the day would come when all fighting ends and we—the believers of his Word—would emerge as the saviors of all humankind. The victories would come for us "one world at a time—then one House at a time—until we control everything". Mankind, it is said, will do so willingly, inviting us to rule.

But ruling requires sacrifice, and to end all fighting, we must be prepared for the greatest of sacrifices. On this day—the Third Blessed Transfer—Terra, and the Inner Sphere with it, will see a new dawn in one last, great conflict. The war that will, truly, end all wars. Our victories shall indeed come one world at a time—then one Bloodhouse at a time—until we destroy the greatest threat mankind has ever faced.

Then, and only then, will we prove that we alone have earned the right to lead our people to a new, everlasting, Golden Age...

—Excerpt from "The Master's Promise"
(authorship and date unknown)

FOREST OF SHROUDS
JARDINE (HERAKLEION)
FREE WORLDS LEAGUE
2 NOVEMBER 3067

Kona was a magnificent beast, a credit to her species. Weighing in at a mere two hundred and twenty kilos, she was lean, almost wiry, beneath a fine coat of reddish-brown fur. But her muscles were as powerful as myomer, and even with an extra ninety-five kilos of harness, rider, and saddlebags, she could tear across six meters of uneven ground a second at a sustained run and barely make a sound while doing it.

Right now, she was clawing through soil and undergrowth at a frantic nine meters a second, her breath blasting through bared fangs with a savage grunt at every pounding stride. Within her massive chest, her oversized heart hammered away, powered as much by primal fear as it was by the exertion of her mad sprint through the forest.

In the saddle above her—his body crouched forward, one hand clutching the reins for dear life, and the other grasping the handle of a rifle easily five generations older than himself—rode Elike. Like Kona beneath him, his heart raced, and his breath came in ragged, low grunts. Like the *tabiranth* he rode, his eyes scanned the wild forest ahead for threats, obstacles, dead ends, and as one, man and beast plotted their desperate course through the foliage.

Like Kona, Elike knew the terror that urged them onward.

Unlike Kona—as he heard and felt the thunderous crashing behind them—Elike realized no amount of speed the animal could provide would save them from their pursuers.

In spite of his own fear, he dared a glance back. Smashing through ancient trees and snapping centuries-old vines like cobwebs, a titan of metal chased them. Fading from scarlet at its bulbous head to black at the broad metallic feet, the lumbering giant stood easily as tall as six men. Upon one shoulder sat a boxy missile launcher, while the right forearm carried a weapon so large it mimicked a heavy rifle in human hands.

Intellectually, Elike knew of these BattleMechs from the ancient wrecks that littered the forest and the clearings around the City of Hope.

But facing an operational one—for *real*—was something well beyond the hunter's twenty-two years of experience living in the wilds of paradise.

Even so, at the first thumping sound of the approaching war machines, his raw instinct had taken over.

Run!

The BattleMech lifted its left arm, bringing a smaller laser weapon to bear. Elike felt the beam's blistering pulse slice the air just overhead and ground his teeth. A tree ahead exploded into steam and splinters that showered him and Kona, ripping through the flesh of man and mount alike.

Elike shoved his rifle into its saddle sheath—its power would be useless against the armored skin of the monster behind him—and seized the reins with knuckle-whitening tightness.

Other parties had encountered Hope's 'Mech patrols and lived to tell the tales, but to Elike those were just stories for the night lamps. This was no patrol. Somehow, deep down, he just *knew* it.

But others had survived them. *How?*

Another blast, this time directly ahead and into the ground. Elike's eyes registered the blue-white flash, and he felt the prickling sensation that set his and Kona's hair on edge only after the earth erupted in hunks of superheated soil and rock.

Kona's instincts took over, and darted them around the blast. Elike felt the *tabiranth* buckle, almost stumbling to one side as she lost her footing on the underbrush, but before they could go down together, the animal pounded the earth with all four legs and propelled them over a fallen trunk he'd not even noticed until a millisecond before.

They were airborne for only a second, leaves whipping Elike across the face as they brushed too close to a tree. Kona let out a low growl as she landed. Her gait faltered, and Elike knew from the stride and the breeze that they'd lost speed.

And still the 'Mech thundered after them, shouldering through the trees and sending branches flying.

Suddenly, it occurred to Elike—possibly their only chance! All he needed to do was get his bearings, remember where to go, and guide his wounded beast to the right spot.

...And hope the Guardian now hunting the hunter would continue to enjoy his game of cat-and-'Mech until they got there...

Phantom Adept Tau Iukini Moakay frowned as he tracked the Wayward scurrying through the woods before his *Griffin*. More than once, his crosshairs flashed gold over the mounted rider, begging for the simple caress of the firing studs that would unleash enough megajoules of raw energy to slice through the man and his majestic *tabiranth* in less than a heartbeat.

But more than once, Moakay found, he simply could not take the shot.

Deep down, he burned with shame. He was one of Apollyon's Chosen, the Master's most blessed. A lifetime ago, he had sacrificed his frail legs in the name of Blake, and the Master had rewarded him with true legs that never tired and never felt pain. His frail muscles had been enhanced with the true strength of myomer bundles that would never tire and would never flinch. Within his skull, he could hear his true conscience—the clipped chatter of his team, the orders barked quickly by Precentor Sigma Lucille as the rest of the Level II turned toward the Waywards' camp, entrusting Moakay with this straggler's fate.

And yet, he could not kill this Wayward!

There was little question why, he knew; the Waywards were not the enemy he had trained for. Indeed, they were not his enemy *at all*. The man now attempting to flee from him on his magnificent cat could have been part of the Chosen himself but for the act of fate or poor judgment that now sent him fleeing into the woods beyond the City of Hope. And it was with that in mind that Moakay had grown up on Jardine, and trained to be one of the world's guardians, to help fulfill the Promise one day—all so that the Wayward might return home and share in Blake's blessings.

This was no sub-human Clansman Moakay now targeted; he was as much one of the Master's children as Moakay himself!

But fate, and cruel necessity, now dictated that this man die for the sins of his tribe.

"And it is my solemn duty to be your executioner..." the adept muttered.

The click in his true ear told Moakey his true conscience had heard him. A metallic taste filled his mouth.

"Is there a problem, Adept Moakay?" Lucille asked with just a hint of malice.

Mentally, Moakay stood at attention. His vision cleared before he even realized he had lost his focus. "No, sir," he snapped back at once, his voice instantly transmitted through his conscience. "The Wayward has simply changed course and is heading further east."

"He is undoubtedly trying to lead you away from the camp," Lucille replied. "Perhaps toward more of their EMP mines. Do *not* play with him, Adept! Take your shot!"

Moakay allowed his eyes to close for only a moment. Lucille was right; this was foolishness. When he opened them again, he felt his resolve returning, and swung the crosshairs around to meet the fleeing Wayward.

At least this way, it will be quick...

"Yes, Precentor," he said to his conscience. To the hunter, he added, "Blake's mercy be with you."

The crosshairs flashed gold, and he fired.

The bright crimson beam sliced through the hunter's body just as he executed a hard turn on his animal, trying to drop behind a fallen tree that sprang up in his path. Meant to carve military armor, the laser found no obstacle in the flesh and bone of the man they struck, and the body all but exploded from the heat.

The beast fared little better as excess energy sliced its body in half. Its hindquarters flashed away, leaving its head, half its torso and two fore paws to tumble forward and vanish into the brush.

But the horrific deaths of the rider and his cat were the last things to register in Moakay's mind, for at that moment—just as he began to slow his *Griffin* to a halt—his entire universe suddenly dissolved into a burst of electric-blue light, and it felt as if the hand of God Himself had suddenly reached out to crush his chest...

TRIBE ENCAMPMENT
FOREST OF SHROUDS
JARDINE (HERAKLEION)
FREE WORLDS LEAGUE

Mikeke had read the pages of this old tome a dozen times before, but for some reason he could not explain, he always found himself drawn back to it time and time again. It was a classic Star League-era piece of science fiction, written long before the Fall, about mankind encountering an alliance of intelligent alien beings that seemed hell-bent on ending all life in the galaxy. The story, he realized, was probably a retelling of any number of even older fantasy tales; even in the centuries before man left Terra's blessed soil, his kind had wondered if they were alone in the universe.

These stories amused the tribal chieftain, in a way that tugged at his cynical side. For all of pre-spaceflight Terra's certainty in discovering new civilizations among the stars, humanity's fiction on the subject overwhelmingly presumed that any such civilizations would set its sights on genocide. Even in the glorious days of the Star League, it seemed, the storytellers fixated on the possibility that overpowering agents of death lay just beyond the boundaries of explored space.

Mikeke often wondered how many of these creative thinkers would have been surprised to know that man would breed his own genocidal alien menace—with nary a strand of non-human DNA required?

He was just about to reach the chapter in which humanity's warring factions put aside their differences to unite against the common foe when the sound of running echoed from the outward cave entrance. Without so much as a rap on the threshold beams to grab his attention first and await permission to enter, Ravid burst through the curtain.

The chieftain raised his head to see a look of panic on the young hunter's face. Seeing also that Ravid's age-worn gyroslug rifle was in his hands, rather than slung over his shoulder, sent a foreboding chill down the older man's spine.

"Mikeke!" Ravid said breathlessly. "It's Guardians... Dimke radioed in! He says they're heading this way! 'Mechs and armor!"

The book fell out of Mikeke's suddenly numb fingers, completely forgotten. His mouth went instantly dry, and a second chill shook him. He was out of his chair before he even realized it, reaching for the rifle affixed to the cave wall behind him, and the bandolier of magazines hung beside it. His old hunters' instincts came back to him with a surge of urgency.

"How many?" he snapped. "How close?"

Ravid's eyes remained tense. "Two kilometers at most," he replied. "Dimke counted five 'Mechs, maybe two squads…" He swallowed hard before adding, "They're *his*!"

Mikeke wished that information surprised him, but instead it only made his heart sink further. There was only one complete Domini formation left on Jardine he knew of, but it was the only one that needed to be here. First Pilipo's disappearance on a hunt, and now this!

Any hope left in his mind that this could be just a random patrol vanished like smoke.

"They're coming for the Lost ones," Mikeke said flatly. "But we won't be spared."

"Couldn't we just *give* them to him—?" Ravid started, even though the words clearly pained him. It was the kind of thought Dimke would have uttered.

"That wouldn't stop them now." He closed his eyes and bent his head for a moment. "May Blake have mercy, for his Guardians won't."

He looked up to find that Ravid had bowed his head as well, silently praying with him. Mikeke checked his rifle, assuring himself its magazine was loaded. Ravid's eyes came back up the instant he moved. The men locked gazes.

"Find Alahni, Ravid," Mikeke told him. "Tell her to take the Lost to the city, through the secret pass. I would send you with them, but—"

"My place is with the tribe," Ravid finished for him. It was both an acknowledgment of his duties, and a vow not to run, in one determined statement.

Mikeke nodded. "Try not to panic her, but tell her to stay with Uku and his people until we call her back; tell her you will catch up, if you must, or she'll try to stay. Moze and I will send as many of our kin through the deep tunnels as we can spare. But you, I, and the rest of our hunters will need to delay the Guardians for as long as possible if they are to have any chance to survive."

Ravid nodded, but said nothing. He knew, as well as Mikeke did, that the Shrouded Forest Tribe had already seen its last sunrise.

Sending Alahni away with the Lost was merely a way to ensure that its memory survived.

THE SANCTORUM
CITY OF HOPE
JARDINE (HERAKLEION)
FREE WORLDS LEAGUE

With the hood of her robe thrown back, the delicate curves of Lamashti's head and face could be seen in all their glory. Not one strand of hair or bit of stubble marred her scalp; even her eyebrows were bare and pristine. Her porcelain skin was absolutely smooth, and free of all but the tiniest wrinkles—save for those that formed slight crow's feet around the reddish rims of her eyes. It was as though her entire visage had been sculpted and polished from a single piece of unblemished ivory.

The lighting in the communications chamber had been muted for her benefit. Her true eyes had just received their final upgrades a week before; cosmetic modifications made to give them an *almost* natural appearance—save for the silver discs that replaced iris and pupil alike. That personal choice in aesthetic, combined with her flawlessly smooth skin, lent Lamashti an otherworldly appearance. But for now, in the wake of the surgery, she found it better to shield her eyes and reduce any glare in order to avoid too much strain while her frail flesh healed.

These final modifications had come after her Ascension, after she rose from the ranks of the Manei Domini's elite Ghost operatives to the rank of junior Precentor. Now, she possessed the very best in true vision, true hearing, and true speech—abilities so finely tuned even her commander could scarcely compete.

To the mere Frails of the Inner Sphere, Ghost Precentor Sigma Lamashti would seem supernatural, almost telepathic for all intents and purposes. Her true vision could sense electromagnetic wavelengths from gamma rays through infrared as easily as any other human being could see in visible light. Her true ears could not only detect sound waves at greater range and distance than normal people, but could even eavesdrop on radio waves. And her true voice, capable of modulating to the very same ranges as her ears, gave her the means to communicate to others even when she appeared to stand mute.

At this moment, however, Lamashti's eyes were closed, her true voice silent at all frequencies. She focused her mind completely on the sense of true hearing now, studying, memorizing, and assimilating the recordings of radio transmissions sent by the DropShuttle that had brought two misguided Frails to her homeworld. Her mind studied every nuance and inflection in the feminine voice that made those calls to distant, unseen allies. She picked apart the foreigner's accent (Lyran, likely raised in Donegal's Eastern Hinterlands region), assessed her vocal tones (tense, but far from panicked), and mentally mapped her vocal range (contralto, *fascinating*!).

Unfortunately, none of the terms this woman used in her recorded transmissions felt stressed enough to Lamashti's extra-sensitive ears to suggest code phrases or special cues to her colleagues. If there were any special commands hidden in the messages, they were hidden so well, and spoken with such discipline, that even one of the Domini's best intelligence operatives would miss them.

Something Lamashti knew to be impossible.

Ergo...

"Nothing, my Precentor," she said, knowing her master still stood nearby (precisely 2.6 meters to her forward right, and facing her).

Her silver eyes opened, but the visual confirmation that Apollyon stood nearby was unnecessary. He had not moved a muscle for the past ten minutes. His arms remained folded together, tucked into the sleeves of his red robe. His hood was pulled back as well, leaving his bronzed scalp bare, and allowing the dimmed lighting and blue-green haze from the comm center's nearby vid screens to glimmer upon the metals of his prosthetics.

Apollyon nodded, almost solemnly. He had not truly expected to find codes hidden inside the intruder's mayday, but that was hardly the only reason to have Lamashti analyze the message. "Can you mimic her?"

Lamashti favored him with a crooked smile. It was hardly worth saying, but she immediately re-modulated her true speech, and replied in the foreigner's voice: "Brooklyn Stevens. At your service, *Herr* Precentor."

Scoring the name of the woman, and even that of her crew's JumpShip, came from a careful analysis of her wrecked shuttle, rather than the mayday transmission. It was a wise enough move of this Frail to omit such details in case of hostile eavesdroppers, but clearly she had not thought it all the way through. Or lacked the training of a proper covert operative.

If Apollyon smiled at all in recognition of Lamashti's resourcefulness, it was imperceptible even to her true eyes. He merely nodded again. "It'll have to do," he said. "Perhaps, with some properly timed interference, we can make a call just convincing, yet garbled enough, to make up for any lack of known keywords."

"A challenge," Lamashti replied.

"May Blake reward our efforts, then," he agreed. "I will leave you to compose the message, Ghost Precentor Sigma. Feel free to broadcast when ready, using the same frequencies as her distress call; it would seem unlikely that they would reserve a secondary channel for further such hails. In the meantime, I will be at the 'port, seeing to our shuttles."

CHAPTER 2

My Dearest Tyler,

I don't care what the vid-games tell you; driving an actual BattleMech is even more awesome than it seems! Oh, I know you don't really care for them, but this 'Mech-obsessed culture we live in has all but assured that half of these IE missions will call for us to either retrieve some walking junk-heap dating back to the Camerons or drive one of their armed WorkMechs into a dig site.

The new guy assigned to us, Tibor Mitternacht, apparently has some tech skills and knows the ins and outs of 'Mech operation. He's ex-military, he says, but doesn't go farther than that. His accent tells me he's Lyran-born, though. Anyway, he was so impressed with my handling of the clunky old DiggerMech here that he decided to convince one of the 'Mech jocks in our attached security detail here to let me at the helm of an actual BattleMech!

It was a smaller model. A Commando, *they called it. They make them on Coventry, and I'm told its one of the lightest machines they still use in the LAAF today. Anyway, I just have to say that even though it was described like the runt of the litter, there's a genuine thrill in piloting a walker that moves with such fluidity. I've heard the MechWarriors talk about how much more refined and flexible their rides were compared to the civilian variety, but until I put that* Commie *through its paces, I didn't believe it!*

I tell you, it was like learning to drive on an old farm tractor, and then being handed the keys to a Hurricane

Windracer with all the options! Well, except in this case there are also missile launchers and lasers mounted on it that you can use to blow your way through the typical Donegal City gridlock!

Tibor says I handled the thing like a natural! And while he may just be saying that just to get in my pants (Men!), the Commando*'s owner did say I managed a pretty good shots-to-hits ratio for a "dirt digger."*

—FROM THE COLLECTED WRITINGS OF DR. BROOKLYN STEVENS
(CA. 3060)

FOREST OF SHROUDS
JARDINE (HERAKLEION)
FREE WORLDS LEAGUE
2 NOVEMBER 3067

By Brooke's estimate, the three of them had traveled through at least four kilometers of jungle when the sound of distant thumping reached them. Tibor was the first to hear it, pausing abruptly and raising a fist as his old training kicked in. Brooke, standing just to his left, caught the motion and stopped short herself. She had just begun to ask what was wrong when Tibor put a finger to his lips and made a sharp hissing noise.

It was that noise that told Alahni, walking ahead of them, that her charges had stopped. She turned around, and Brooke caught her gaze. The young Wayward's eyes were wide, showing the same fear as when Ravid had found them back at the encampment and urgently told Alahni to lead "the Lost ones" to the city. Tibor's alert stance registered in Alahni's expression as well, along with his repeated gesture for silence. The girl's face grew whiter as the first *thump* finally resonated across the earth.

Followed by another.

And another.

"'Mechs," Brooke whispered. She turned slowly, trying to get a fix on the direction, until she noticed Tibor had already locked onto that: behind them. "Following us?"

Tibor held his breath and closed his eyes for a moment. "No," he muttered back. "I don't think so. Not yet, anyway. But it's more than one..."

Brooke listened again, and realized she heard it too. The distant pounding was not synchronized; it was irregular, like competing drumbeats. She narrowed her eyes.

"The Domini don't send their 'Mechs into these forests on patrols," Alahni said, her voice low, tense, nearly cracking.

They're looking for us, Brooke thought.

She looked back at Alahni, unsure what to say at first. But before any words formed, a sound like distant thunder interrupted the distant footfalls.

"*Scheiße*!" Tibor spat.

There was no need to explain that noise, or the other brief rumbles that quickly followed. Alahni's face paled, and Brooke saw true terror and heartache in the young woman's eyes.

"*No!*" Alahni shrieked, tears welling in her eyes. "For the love of Blake, *why*!?"

The girl had taken two steps forward—back toward the camp—before she even knew it. Instinctively, Brooke reached out and grabbed her by the arm. Alahni strained against her grasp, crying hysterically.

"Alahni, *don't*!" Brooke shouted. "There's nothing you can do for them!"

"Jesus," Tibor hissed. "I figured they knew something was coming when they rushed us out of there, but *'Mechs*?"

"We just wanted to live in peace!" Alahni whimpered, her face now pressed into Brooke's shoulder. Brooke held her awkwardly, and looked over at Tibor. "We were no danger to them!"

"It's..." Tibor started, but his voice trailed off.

"It's us," Brooke finished. "It's our fault, Alahni. I'm so sorry..."

Alahni pushed herself away from Brooke, breaking free with surprising strength. Brooke held her breath, braced for the tirade, but while the look on the Wayward's face showed rage and fear in equal measure, the words that came out were heartbroken.

"*Damn you all*!" she screamed.

Suddenly, she was gone, darting into the brush before Brooke could stop her.

Tibor blinked. "Crap! There goes our guide—"

"Come *on*!" Brooke snapped back, already breaking into a sprint. As she, too, lunged into the woods, she called Alahni's name.

With Tibor on her heels, Brooke raced almost blindly into the woods. The trees and underbrush were thick in this region, shadowing the landscape, giving her little time to watch her steps. Low-hanging branches raked across her face, and she nearly tripped more than once.

Ahead, she could hear the rustle of the leaves, accompanied by infrequent sobs. Behind her, Tibor's labored grunts reminded her he was in no shape for a foot race like this.

They'd been running for almost a full minute when she heard him fall. Hard.

"Son of a—!" he growled, then abruptly stopped.

Brooke came to a stumbling halt, looking back to find him on his knees. For a moment, she almost didn't see what he was staring at with incredulous eyes, so entangled was it in the undergrowth.

Then she recognized the powerful, clawed forelegs of a reddish-brown *tabiranth*, connected by half a torso to a large feline head that stared at her with sightless eyes, its fanged mouth agape. How Brooke had missed the massive carcass in her charge through the woods defied her imagination, but as Tibor pushed himself up, she noticed he'd actually tripped over the remnants of a riding saddle.

"Poor beast," Tibor muttered, his eyes beginning a sweep even as he gasped for air.

"It's fresh," Brooke said, her own voice low and breathless. "One of them came through here. "How did we miss them?"

Tibor was shaking his head. "Dunno," he answered, "but we better find the girl, before—"

The scream cut off his reply, and his eyes snapped in its direction. Brooke spun around, following the sound as well. With only a moment's glance back at Tibor, she bolted off toward it.

Seconds later, they found themselves bursting out of the undergrowth and into a swath of broken trees and fallen branches. The broken cover and the forest canopy still made it difficult for Brooke to home in on exactly where she'd heard Alahni's cry, and her footsteps faltered as she instinctively slowed to survey the path ahead.

Until Tibor jogged past her, clapping her on the shoulder as he went.

"This way!"

Brooke fell in behind him now, quickly beginning to realize what she was seeing. The ruined foliage, the unmistakable scent of freshly split wood and churned soil—all told the tale. But there was something more, a sound, so deep and so faint that she almost couldn't sense it over the sound of her own footfalls, ragged breathing, and pounding heartbeat.

Ahead, she saw Tibor clambering over a short hillock, and felt a moment of surprise when Alahni suddenly emerged from beyond it to embrace him.

She's safe! Thank Bast she's safe!

Relieved, Brooke's stride slowed as she reached the hillock and ascended it, her feet slipping a little as she found the soil beneath looser than expected. The deep hum in her ears was rising, but over the distant sound of more gunfire, she'd almost forgotten about it.

Until she saw what lay just beyond the rise.

There, sprawled awkwardly on the forest floor, lay the massive hulk of a BattleMech, painted in foreboding shades of red and black.

**TRIBE ENCAMPMENT
FOREST OF SHROUDS
JARDINE (HERAKLEION)
FREE WORLDS LEAGUE**

With an ear-shattering pop and a flash of electric blue light, the sleek, humanoid form of a 25-ton *Nexus* came to a sudden, lurching halt. Smoke billowed around its right foot, and its arms tensed to the sides, locking into place as if frozen in shock.

Feeling the ripple of hot air and the tingle of the electro-magnetic pulse, Lucille's head snapped around in time not only to see the BattleMech crash-land on the forest floor, scattering brush and earth in all directions, but also the twitching death of at least two more of his own troopers, whose bodies soaked up too much of the pulse themselves.

Adept Jorg, the closer of the two, clutched at the helmet of his power armor and howled in enraged pain. A flash of light inside his visor and the abrupt end of his scream told Lucille the man's true eyes had exploded. A heartbeat later, the suit itself flew apart as the rest of Jorg's body followed, showering the field with shrapnel, bone, and gore—small chunks of which even reached Lucille's battered Achileus.

Adept Sonia's own self-destruction was lost beneath the falling hulk of the *Nexus*. Her true voice, likely destroyed when the EMP struck, never even uttered a sound.

Lucille felt his jaw tighten and released his rage in an incoherent snarl.

These frail Waywards had gotten lucky—*too* damned lucky—since this hunt began. Already, Lucille had lost two BattleMechs and five armored troopers to their EMP trip-mines and salvaged weapons.

That the nomads knew who they faced and had modified their weapons to deal with them was hardly an excuse! That Lucille and his men had already killed over twenty of their misled kind was little consolation! The hunt should *not* have been going this badly!

Another rocket-assisted shell exploded against his armor's flank, tearing through to find the flesh within. The pain barely registered to Lucille; he simply used it to determine where the shot came from.

With a battle cry roared through his external speakers, he lunged toward the shooter. Closing the distance in a fraction of a second, he tore through the brush and the fallen tree the Wayward had used for cover. The hunter was male, with long black locks and a scarred, stubbled face. His dark eyes widened and his mouth opened to say something even as Lucille punched through his frail chest with an armored gauntlet.

Lifting the gurgling, blood-soaked Wayward high, Lucille flung his corpse into another hunter—this one a woman with flowing brown hair, flimsy flak armor, and an elephant gun.

The body struck the woman dead-on, knocking her to the ground and sending her weapon flying. Still snarling through his speakers, Lucille stomped toward her, incidentally crushing the male Wayward's forgotten gyrojet rifle beneath one of his meta-shod feet.

Though clearly dazed, the huntress struggled to free herself from the weight of her companion's body. She gasped as Lucille towered over her, stabbed the muzzles of his Mauser 1200 toward her, and painted her forehead with the steady beam of the rifle's targeting laser.

"Where are they, Wayward?" he demanded. "Where are the Lost ones?"

She opened her mouth to speak, but by that time, Lucille was already pulling the trigger, unleashing a burst of laser fire that transformed the once-pretty young girl into a smoking mass of exploded flesh and bone.

Answers were unnecessary; this entire camp would burn the moment he could account for the intruders personally.

A voice spoke in Lucille's ears just then; strong, confident, but devoid of any real emotion. "East flank secured, Precentor," the warrior said. "We count a dozen kills here, all Waywards."

"Blessed be," Lucille replied. "A number have fled into the caves below. My troopers will move in to flush them out while you and the other MechWarriors hold the topside perimeter. Maintain thermal scans to track any others, but remember to engage all hostiles with minimal overkill; we'll need something to conduct tests on in the event you should catch the off-worlders."

"Understood, Precentor."

"No obvious damage. And my eye's getting a heat glow from the engine, so it's clearly operational," Tibor said, admitting for the first time that his implant was working again. "Terrain doesn't seem too rough for 'Mechs here, so I'm guessing he must've triggered one of those EMP mines."

Brooke put a cautionary hand on Tibor's shoulder and looked around. He caught her gaze for a moment and twitched his head toward the fallen *Griffin*'s bubble-shaped head. The transplas armor that gave its MechWarrior an unparalleled field of vision was polarized for glare, but it looked as if the Domini had tinted it as well—with what looked like a highly reflective form of dark, metallic green.

It was also lying sideways against the soft earth, quite intact. The 'Mech had come down on its right shoulder, trapping the right arm beneath it, while its left hung limply across its mid-section. The legs had locked almost perfectly straight, forming a neat V-shape behind its half-twisted torso.

And so far as Brooke could see, not a single hatch was opened.

"The engine's rebooted," Tibor said, "but the thing's still down, and the canopy hasn't blown. I'm betting the pilot's still inside; probably took too much feedback for his implants."

"The Blakists were in a rush to catch the tribe off guard," Brooke mumbled bitterly. "Didn't even bother to pick up their toys."

Then the crazy idea hit. She rolled it around in her head for a few seconds before finally catching Tibor's gaze. "Can you hotwire it?"

"The machine men can merge with their 'Mechs," Alahni muttered. Her voice was still tiny and distant.

Brooke turned to her, perplexed.

"The controls," the Jardinian continued, utter defeat written all over her face as she stared back through puffy, unblinking eyes. "They need special implants to work. No neurohelmets or manual systems are needed, so the Guardians remove them."

"*Scheiße*," Brooke whispered. *So much for that idea, then...*

Tibor leaned against the machine's cockpit until he was practically pressing his nose against it, and cupped his hands over his eyes to block out all daylight. Suddenly, mere seconds later, he burst into a coughing and gagging fit, and stumbled back from the machine, collapsing into an awkward sitting position on a mass of churned up earth and roots. Brooke took a step closer as he covered his mouth for a moment and stood back up, still fighting an obvious urge to retch. When he removed his hand, he revealed an expression that was at once shaken and...*pleased*?

"Well," he said after one last cough, "*this* one must've missed that memo. I'm seeing standard system controls in there. Throttles, panels, and displays, all lit up. I wouldn't even need to hack it. But it looks like the *Arschloch's* cyberware betrayed him all the same."

Curiosity got the better of Brooke, and she also peered through the tinted transplas—only to regret it instantly. Now it was her turn to blanch.

"Thank Bast for small favors," she croaked out between coughs. She clambered to the side of the BattleMech's head and yanked on its emergency latch. There was a hiss of air as the hydraulic release complied, parting the cockpit seal enough for her and Tibor to grab onto and pry open.

The stench that hit them was unholy—a mix of burned metals, ozone, and human waste. Both explorers turned away for a moment to gasp for fresh air. Brooke glanced over to Tibor and nodded, then turned to face Alahni, who now stood behind her. Though still horror-stricken, the look in the Jardinian's eyes also betrayed an eagerness to see what lay within.

"You will probably want to look away," Brooke told her. "This won't be pretty."

"What do you—?" Alahni started, then her entire body recoiled and her face twisted in a look of revulsion as the odor reached her. "Oh, *Blake's blood*!"

"Close enough," Tibor darkly quipped, as the young woman twisted herself away.

Brooke joined him and suffered a new gagging fit at the sight. In her career, she had seen many corpses, of course, but this may have been the first time she saw one that looked like it had both imploded and exploded at the same time. Blood was everywhere, painting much of the control systems, splashing and pooling along the right side of the canopy and—almost certainly—the lowermost areas, which she could not make out for all the shadows. Bits of bone, shrapnel, meat, and other unidentifiable tissues clung to surfaces all over the chamber, some wetly coming loose even as Brooke and Tibor forced the opening even wider.

At the center, still buckled into its seat, still clad in the tatters of what once had been a pristine cooling suit, was a sagging, skeletal...thing. The pilot's body was twisted as close to a fetal position as its five-point harness allowed, and its limbs looked compressed, as if they began to shrink while they curled inward. More blood dripped slowly from several tears in the suit.

But the most disturbing part was the head. Still attached—but only barely—and still inside a neurohelmet of first Star League design, it was remarkably intact. The MechWarrior had been male, and Brooke guessed by his skin tone that he shared the same ethnic heritage as Alahni's people. But his eyes had sunken completely inside their sockets, vanishing somewhere deep inside the skull, while his jaw hung open crookedly, blood painting the lips, chin, and right cheek a bright crimson. It was a rictus of incredible, soul-crushing agony—one that told her the man had *suffered* in his final moments.

Good, was the first thought that struck Brooke as she realized that, and allowed herself one final shudder of revulsion.

She pressed on the body's harness release, which sank into the chest of its collapsed torso. Something inside the cooling suit made a sound that reminded Brooke of the time she once tripped into a steaming mud bath. Thankfully, the release popped before she had pushed her hand all the way through the squishy, spongey remains.

Together, she and Tibor heaved the vaguely humanoid sack of pulp out of its seat and hurled it into some nearby brush. In the process, the head had separated, ensnared by the neurohelmet that was still wired into the consoles. After pulling the chin strap upward, Brooke gave the helmet a shake; the head slid out like a single hunk of canned meat, thudding against the forest floor. Tibor kicked it into the same brush as its body.

Glancing back in, Brooke sighed in relief. Protected largely by the suit and the head's apparent failure to explode, the cockpit seat and the interior of the neurohelmet were mostly clean. Lacking the suit would be a problem, but not insurmountable. She handed the helmet to Tibor, then set herself to clearing the spattered blood from the cockpit displays and controls, wishing she had a bundle of rags to do this with instead of her bare hands.

Alahni had turned back, but now stood a few extra meters away, staring at the Lost ones in bewilderment. But it wasn't until Brooke began shedding her clothes on the forest floor that the girl found her voice again. "What are you *doing*?"

Brooke froze for a second, her eyes meeting Alahni's. Standing in the open in just her undergarments, she suddenly remembered that she had an audience (beyond Tibor, at any rate), and the gooseflesh spread quickly over her arms and legs. A soft snort from him deepened the flush she felt burning at her cheeks, but it also shook her out of her momentary pause.

"Y-you two will need to stay put," she stammered. "Trouble, is your radio implant working?"

"Fortunately, yeah," he mumbled as his hands continued working the insides of the helmet. "Both it and the eye are a bit fuzzy, but they're working."

"Then I'll tune a private channel to you," she told him as she put her boots back on.

"Okay," he replied, handing her the helmet. "But I'm with Alahni here. Just what *are* you doing?"

"Something stupid, maybe," she said as she climbed into the cockpit, feeling for all the world like someone who was now modeling one of those tasteless "Sexy MechWarrior" costumes that become so popular every October. Despite the awkward angle, she managed to leverage herself into the seat enough to refasten the harness around her torso.

She kept her eyes focused on the harness, then the control displays, afraid to look at either of her companions—especially the young Jardinian.

"But I'll be damned if I'm letting these monsters get away with this slaughter scot-free," she added. Secured into the command couch, she reached up for the canopy handle, before finally meeting Tibor's judgmental gaze. Any one of a thousand things could go wrong at this point, but she shoved those doubts away.

"If I don't make it back," she told him, "tell Tyler I'm sorry..."

With that, she shut and dogged the hatch, turning her attention to completing the *Griffin*'s restart sequence and recalibrating the neurohelmet to her own neural patterns.

Outside, Tibor gathered up her discarded clothes, and guided Alahni to a safe distance.

A few minutes later, the 55-ton monster rose from the forest floor once more.

LEOPARD-CLASS DROPSHIP _KAYLIN_
PIRATE JUMP POINT
JARDINE (HERAKLEION) SYSTEM
FREE WORLDS LEAGUE
2 NOVEMBER 3067

Lenard Bryce, executive officer of the _Kaylin_, straightened up from the comm station just as Captain Anton Hara floated his way through the bridge hatch. Hara's malachite eyes caught his within moments, asking their question silently.

Bryce was just about to respond when he noticed the second man trailing behind him. Instead of speaking right away, he flashed his captain a frown. _Why, in the name of all the heavens, did that IE slug have to follow him around like a lost puppy?_

Hara acknowledged Bryce's ire with a sympathetic roll of his eyes, and the subtle shrug that communicated his own non-verbal comment: _What are you gonna do?_

If the exchange of expressions even registered to Nathan Bellamy, the liaison assigned to Hara by Interstellar Expeditions, he was damned good at hiding it. Before either man spoke, he nudged himself sideways with a gentle shove against one of the bridge rails. The maneuver almost made him look graceful, had he not misjudged and began a tumbling spin he was forced to stop by grabbing one of the ceiling rungs.

Not for the first time since they had been saddled with the man did the ancient words "landlubber" flit through Bryce's mind, leading him to favor Hara with a cock-eyed smirk.

Hara didn't even bother looking back to see what Bellamy had done _this_ time. Instead, he broke through the white noise of bridge systems and air circulators with a simple question: "This just came in?"

Bryce nodded. "In the clear, sir," he reported. "It's slightly garbled, but it tracks back in-system."

"Let's hear it, then."

Bryce nodded again, and tapped on the panel in front of him. The senior comms officer for the bridge was off-shift at this hour, likely asleep in his cabin. Bryce had been on solo watch when the transmission came in. Though the message from the dark took him by surprise, the monitors had faithfully recorded every word as it came in.

And now, the voice of Doctor Brooklyn Stevens crackled once more from the speakers in playback, faint and distorted by random bursts of static:

"DropShuttle Magellan *to* Sacajawea— *Guys, it's Brook— We're still here— Trying to repair the ship— We think we'll be able to— When we're ready, we'll try to sig— But fuel is limited— We'll need telem— Not send anyone else! I repeat: do not— Still unsafe—"*

The transmission ended with a sharp *chirp.*

Hara's eyes, closed throughout most of the playback as he focused on trying to hear through the signal noise, opened again, and met Bryce's.

"That's all we picked up," Bryce told him. "If there was any more, it's likely something blocked it out; maybe even the planet's rotation."

"The channels used?"

"Standard IE distress frequency. Looks like another case of her crew still using their old employee handbook."

At this, Bellamy sniffed. He now clung to the ceiling rung nearest the comm panels, his wide form casting an imposing shadow. Had anyone actually been seated here, Bryce noted, the poor soul would probably feel claustrophobic with three men surrounding the small, free-standing podium of a station.

"Did the *Sac* respond?" Bellamy asked, pre-empting Hara's next question.

Bryce raised an eyebrow at the man, but directed his answer to both of them. "Not yet, so far as I can tell."

"Are we sure they heard it?"

"It's unlikely we would've heard anything they didn't, Mister Bellamy," Hara said flatly.

"Indeed," Bryce said. "So, judging by the content, Doctor Stevens is reporting that she's still alive and well, trying to fix her shuttle, and trying to get telemetry for a return trip."

Hara nodded. "Sounds like low fuel, which would make sense if they'd burned much of the way in, or suffered a leak from whatever damage they took. She doesn't want to make escape velocity, only to have to waste whatever's left in the tank on course corrections."

"And yet," Bellamy said, "Captain Pohl has not replied. For all Stevens knows right now, the *Sacajawea* might not even be here."

Hara sighed. "Technically speaking, Pohl doesn't have to reply...yet."

"It *does* sound like Stevens plans to signal again when she's ready to launch," Bryce agreed. "Telemetry info sent now would be useless if it takes her several days to make repairs."

"Or her friends are watching what they say around us," Bellamy offered.

"Or just around whoever else may be watching," Bryce countered. "She did warn them not to send anyone else, after all."

"Whatever the case," Hara said, "it lets us know to expect something sooner, rather than later. If Stevens is planning to make her escape, it seems she intends to do it as quickly as possible, and she's telling her crew to get ready for when she starts."

"Then *that* is when we should be ready to strike, Captain," Bellamy said, betraying the hidden edge Hara had warned Bryce about.

TRIBE ENCAMPMENT
FOREST OF SHROUDS
JARDINE (HERAKLEION)
FREE WORLDS LEAGUE
2 NOVEMBER 3067

As he stepped through another *tabiranth*-hide curtain into a chamber that appeared large enough to be a communal barracks, Lucille spared a moment to admire the Waywards' resourcefulness. Fiber-optic light channels, hewn wood structural supports, woven rugs, ancient-yet-well-maintained firearms, EMP mines on triplines, and all manner of portable energy devices (likely scavenged from Hope itself), all worked to provide maximum habitability within their earthen enclave without giving away their presence to the world outside. Just like their brethren in the city, these Waywards valued their invisibility; clearly, the lessons of the Malu Tribe had not been lost on them.

It was a shame they still had to die.

Just because two off-world Frails entered their midst.

As quickly as the warring surges of pride and regret washed over Lucille, it was gone. Mercy was not the way of the Master's Hands. The mission was paramount. Although these Waywards were not the enemy they had been made to fight, the Manei Domini had only one ultimate function. Everything else belonged to those who were *not* monsters.

The shoulder of Lucille's Achileus armor scraped a furrow into a curved, earthen wall as he swung about, scanning a small side chamber for signs of life. Two corpses—still cooling toward ambient temperature in his thermal-augmented view—were all he saw. Each had been penetrated by no less than four shots, and left propped up against the wall.

His HUD flagged them as a navigation point labeled "*Null.*" The flag told him what he already knew from the bodies' hand-made hunters' garb and deeper skin tones. It also told him his troopers were still minding their job and inspecting their kills to confirm that these weren't the off-worlders they sought.

"Precentor!" a voice harshly snapped in his ear—Adept Quang, the MechWarrior commanding the *Nexus* he left to hold the perimeter above. "I have a contact approaching."

Lucille's eyes narrowed. Quang's tone hinted at his confusion. He keyed the warrior's channel directly. "And?"

"It appears to be Adept Moakay's *Griffin*, sir."

This time, it was Lucille's turn to sound bewildered. "*Moakay?*" he repeated.

His mind raced. There had been no time to confirm that the *Griffin*'s pilot had survived his fall. Indeed, after the squeal of the warrior's comms going dead amid a roar of unspeakable agony—followed by his machine's IFF winking out while chasing that Wayward hunter—Lucille simply presumed Moakay had suffered a fatal run-in with another of these Waywards' damnable mines. After trying to regain contact several times, it was Lucille himself that ordered the *Griffin*'s last known position flagged for later investigation, certain they would find only a dead husk of both man and machine there when this was all over. The odds certainly did not look good, after all.

It *was* possible he had miscalculated. But that would make Moakay the luckiest Domini in this entire operation.

And Poltergeist Precentor Sigma Damien Lucille did not believe in luck.

"Adept Quang," he barked, "hail that BattleMech at once!"

Though Brooke had recognized and adapted to the main control systems quickly enough, the cockpit of this *Griffin* was much different than any BattleMech she had ever driven before. For starters, it was all so *brand new*; save for the smears and spatters of darkening red and black left by its previous occupant, the various boards and panels looked pristine. Even the smallest retaining screws gleamed amid the cockpit lights, as though they had been machined only yesterday.

For another, it was remarkably cool; where many combustion or cell-powered WorkMechs rarely required cooling vests to operate, and could accommodate a pilot just fine by leaving the windows open, the act of merely walking a fusion-driven BattleMech in springtime conditions tended to require a refrigerant-lined vest to prevent a sudden onset of heat exhaustion when waste heat filled the nominally sealed piloting compartment. And yet, even at a mad run through a rainforest, this cockpit was only a balmy twenty-nine Celsius, according to one of the secondary displays Brooke found no reason to doubt.

Then there were the electronics, some of which she scarcely understood. If the HUD was to be believed, she was getting updates on the positions of all known battlefield units in the area—friend and foe alike—in real time, rather than via periodic sensor sweeps. Hell, it took her several minutes to even realize the targeting sensors were in passive mode to begin with, the changing of which only made the flow of information more dramatic, as she suddenly found that all those friendly icons had names and 'Mech designators ready to go. It was only after wracking her brain over memories of Star League-era engineering that she realized what this meant. But since there was no way she could imagine anyone driving a heavy, well-equipped command vehicle into these thick woods, it had to be one of those much more recent C^3 computers she'd only read about before now.

After that came her mental inventory of the 'Mech's capabilities—something she felt she'd "cheated" on a little bit by running the diagnostics. Extended-range particle projector cannon, large LRM launcher, two extended-range medium-size lasers, and a Guardian electronic countermeasures suite—a combined amount of equipment nobody could have crammed into a frame like this during the Succession Wars, but might have in the days of the Camerons (if all of it even existed back then). And all put together perhaps as recently as last month by the self-proclaimed protectors of mankind's knowledge.

So, basically, what Brooke was driving right now was the single most advanced hunk of military hardware she'd ever *seen*, much less commanded.

Inwardly, she knew she would probably feel more impressed by all of that if she wasn't seething with rage right now. That, and possibly the fact that she was also struggling to ignore the overwhelming stink of blood, remains, and excrement she probably couldn't have scrubbed out of this thing without a power hose and a dozen liters of bleach.

Opening the few cockpit panels she could to ventilate the foul air accomplished next to nothing, but she'd done it anyway. Because of that, she also heard the snapping of branches and the thunderous footfalls of her captured 'Mech as it plowed through the foliage toward the nearest "friendly" marker on her tactical display.

She was breathing through her mouth, hissing through bared teeth, when that marker blinked, and a click sounded in the left speaker of her neurohelmet (the only speaker that apparently still functioned).

"Inbound *Griffin*, identify at once!" commanded a male voice, his accent nearly identical to that of Alahni's tribe. "Adept Moakay, is that you?"

Brooke bowed her head a little, as every muscle in her body tensed. Ignoring the hail, she lined herself up until the *Griffin*'s targeting reticules projected onto her HUD hovered over the brackets surrounding the still-unseen 'Mech. The battle computer flashed the target's identity as "*2M: NXS-Quang.*" Beside the brackets appeared a range reading: 300 meters... 270... 240...

"Inbound *Griffin*," the target shouted again, but never budged. "Halt and identify yourself! This is your final warning!"

Brooke snarled and shoved the throttle to maximum. The reticules flashed red, then gold, as the distance readout fell past 200 meters.

At about 120 meters, the foliage suddenly gave way to a clearing. Her eyes barely registered the thin wisps of smoke drifting throughout the area, or the bodies—human and *tabiranth* alike—scattered among the grass and rocks. But she knew they were there.

She had come to avenge them.

Her trigger fingers mashed down their studs, and the *Griffin* obliged immediately. A bolt of cerulean lightning shrieked forth from her particle cannon, stabbing into her enemy's left flank. At the same time, twin beams of crimson light flashed out, each aimed for the same spot. Superheated armor panels burst open, exploding away from the spindly-looking machine and exposing equally ravaged chassis supports beneath.

Its own weapons, arm-mounted lasers triggered a heartbeat after Brooke's salvo, found their aim spoiled as the wounded 'Mech twisted under the *Griffin*'s punishing fire. One—the right—managed to hit, burning a thin trench across the bigger 'Mech's left thigh, but the other shot harmlessly skyward as the arm it came from suddenly broke free of its mount.

With its balance completely lost, the BattleMech designated "*NXS-Quang*" crashed down onto its side even before Brooke had managed to close the distance. But she still wasn't done with it; growling, she slammed the left foot pedal hard. Once again, her captured *Griffin* complied with incredible ease, swinging a broad-based foot forward and into the enemy's "abdomen" with enough force to nearly fold the flimsy-looking thing in half. The Manei Domini 'Mech flipped over and onto its back, sparks and smoke pouring from a tangle of ruined armor and engine shielding.

Despite the stench, and the surge of heat now finding its way into her cockpit, Brooke almost managed to smile. In all the times she ever found herself using the firepower of a 'Mech—any 'Mech—in anger, she had never enjoyed a victory as swift or decisive as this one.

But where vid games, serial dramas, and even actual wartime holo footage agreed that an enemy would stay down after an assault like that, the NXS defied them all. With twists and turns that seemed almost organic in nature, the one-armed machine rolled itself over, tucked its feet in, and levered itself back up.

"No goddamned way!" Brooke hissed.

As BattleMechs go, the NXS already looked like the image of warmed-over Death to her. Half its body was gone, and the smoke flowing from its core was already giving way to open flames. And yet it stood up, faced her Griffin, and stabbed its right arm gun muzzles forward—both now caked in grassy hunks of soft earth. The lasers pulsed, instantly vaporizing the debris, and sent scarlet darts of energy into her chassis. The Griffin's damage readout registered no hits to critical systems, but the armor wireframe went from green to yellow.

Meanwhile, her sensors tracked two more "friendly" 'Mechs incoming.

The Griffin's PPC had not finished its recharge cycle yet, but her lasers were ready—as was the missile launcher (though she knew that thing would be useless at this range). Wincing in anticipation of the heat, she ground her teeth together and fired.

This time, only one beam found its mark, but it was enough. Lancing into the machine's burning heart, the laser finished off whatever high-tech components allowed the NXS to hang on as long as it had. Its support structures collapsed, and its head fell into the gap, vanishing amid a thick plume of smoke and flames as the rest of the chassis swayed awkwardly. Then the right arm fell limp, and the rest of the 'Mech soon followed suit.

As she drew in a lungful of hot, near-toxic air, waiting desperately for her *Griffin*'s heat sinks to do something about it, Brooke spared the wreckage one final glance before turning her attention toward the new contacts.

"And *stay* down this time, *Saftsack*!"

CHAPTER 3

"Even the "social generals" of the LAAF would tell you that fighting a force three times your number (or more) is a losing proposition. Hell, that magic number may be why the Clans tend to run their Trials of Position with three opponents per trainee, for surely, only the best warriors could even prevail in the face of such "impossible" odds.

And yet, how many battles in history have shown us that overwhelming numbers alone don't always determine the victor? Marathon, in 490 BC; Agincourt, in 1415; Samar Island, 1944; Longewala, 1971; or the Vale of Tears, in 1973—battles from Terran antiquity that easily match far more recent examples, like the Wolf's Dragoons on Crossing in 3028, or Kai Allard-Liao at Twycross' Great Gash in 3050. These rare instances stand as proof that numbers alone don't win the battle. Even an "underdog" may triumph even when massively outnumbered or outclassed.

In the end, it's guile that can make all the difference. With enough guile, a clever warrior can change the victory equation, even the odds, and defeat any enemy who might otherwise be too overwhelming, too overpowering, and too overconfident to understand the value of subtlety.

It also helps, of course, to be lucky, cat-shit crazy, or best of all: both!"

—TIBOR MITTERNACHT
AS QUOTED IN *"CHANGING THE OBJECTIVES"*
(WARRIOR DIGITAL PRODUCTIONS, SOLARIS VII, MAY 3061)

TRIBE ENCAMPMENT
FOREST OF SHROUDS
JARDINE (HERAKLEION)
FREE WORLDS LEAGUE
2 NOVEMBER 3067

Poltergeist Precentor Sigma Damien Lucille could not remember a time when he had been filled with so much rage as he was now—and he'd been among the blessed warriors who had fought, bled, and sacrificed so much against the traitorous heretics of Focht's ComStar! The rumbles of a 'Mech battle above shook the earthen walls around him, threatening to entomb him and the rest of his squad even as they rallied back toward his position in what may once have been the office of the tribal leader. Numerous fiber-optic light channels abruptly darkened, their surface connections somehow severed in the chaos, and at least one of the chamber's supporting beams tore loose, spilling boulders and large clumps of hard-packed soil as it fell.

As he had feared when Adept Quang first alerted him to the return of a MechWarrior they'd all presumed lost, the *Griffin* that closed in was not piloted by Adept Moakay. And there were no Jardinians Lucille ever heard of who had been trained in BattleMech combat and counted themselves among the Wayward.

That meant that whoever just charged Quang's *Nexus* was one of the two Lost ones he'd been slaughtering some of his own misguided people to capture! At the very moment that realization hit home, Quang's IFF and comm channel suddenly vanished from the heads-up display on Lucille's Achileus battle armor.

And *that* was what now had him seeing nothing but red.

"All units," he shouted into the tactical channel, "abandon pursuit! The Lost are here! Converge on primary site at once! Our target has commandeered Adept Moakay's *Griffin*! Repeat, the enemy has captured—!"

A new voice—feminine, with an unmistakably Lyran accent, and filled with nearly as much seething hatred as Lucille's own—suddenly cut into the channel.

"Verdammte Missgeburt!" it spat. "Call for all the help you like! I'll see all of your kind *burn*!"

"*Defiler!*" Lucille hissed back at her. "Identify yourself!"

The channel went dead before he even finished his demand. In its place came a horrific shriek of incoherent static that overwhelmed Lucille's helmet speakers and drilled into his very skull through his true hearing.

For a brief moment, Brooke felt rather proud of herself. Until that Word of Blake Guardian—or *whatever* the hell they called themselves—started spouting off orders in her speakers, it never even occurred to her that her new ride would be tuned to the same receiving frequency. It made perfect sense, though, and it also reminded her of the fancy communications and targeting suite she had at her command.

The same one they were *all* probably using, right this minute, to coordinate with!

After sparing a few seconds to indulge her need to verbally spit in that monster's face, she reached over to the *Griffin*'s fancy comm panel and dialed its transceiver to a specific frequency she knew by heart. After tuning the secondary dials to the same frequency, she then snapped the toggles controlling her Guardian ECM suite.

Star League-era push-button technology did the rest.

But the sense of accomplishment she got from all of that melted as her sensors noted not only the two 'Mechs approaching from the west, but now a *third* coming in from the north. And then the woods in front of her exploded as a short, blocky machine surged out, and unleashed a quartet of missiles at her as she threw the *Griffin* into a reverse walk.

Oh, this might hurt a little!

Explosions shook her BattleMech, but not enough for her to miss the stuttering bursts of scarlet laser darts and machine-gun fire that followed when the newcomer continued to bear down on her. The *Griffin*'s wireframe damage display showed its right arm was now a cautionary yellow, along with the 'Mech's "heart" zone. Its armor was holding, but starting to thin.

On Brooke's HUD, the targeting brackets now only gave her the enemy's range and a simple model designator *"OW1."*

Her crosshairs never flashed gold—the universal standard for a solid weapons track—but she couldn't imagine why against an enemy running slow close to her.

Instead, she simply fired another volley from her particle cannon and lasers.

And spat a curse as only a single laser found its mark.

The *"OW1"* didn't even flinch from the hit. It simply pivoted on one foot, tearing up the battle-scarred earth beneath its foot as it changed course to maneuver behind her, its machine guns still rattling away. Brooke tried to turn with it, but the smaller 'Mech was moving too fast.

And that's when the other one of the damnable machines showed up to add its own missiles to the melee.

"*Verdammt!*" she spat as the *Griffin* rocked under the new assault. The damage wireframe now put her left flank in the yellow.

Her mind raced, even as she rotated her 'Mech's torso around enough to confirm that the new attacker...looked just like the last one. On the sensor display, attacker number three was still coming.

Outnumbered and *outmaneuvered! Damn it!*

"*Scheiß drauf!*" she hissed, and slammed the throttle forward again.

The *Griffin* responded instantly, its next step propelling it forward just as the new *OW1* tried to skirt past. Brooke heard a crunch of metal on metal that accompanied the collision that was so satisfying she hardly minded the sudden struggle to keep her 'Mech upright. The smaller machine, probably unbalanced more by the surprise than the actual hit, careened away, slipped on some ground clutter, and crashed to the forest floor in an ungraceful heap.

Brooke almost wished that she had meant to do that.

Adding a spin of her own to the maneuver, she aimed her 'Mech southward, and twisted its torso far to the left—enough to catch the first *OW1* in her sights again. With only her lasers and missiles ready to fire, she triggered the lasers. Armor flashed away as one beam struck, but the boxy little thing kept moving as though nothing had happened.

Instead, the 'Mech unleashed another quartet of missiles from the sideways turrets it had in place of arms. Brooke felt each blast as they hit, tearing away more of her *Griffin*'s armor.

The damage wireframe now painted her entire rear torso in yellow.

Bracing herself, Brooke pushed her 'Mech into a full run, charging toward the southern end of the clearing. Behind her, the two *OW1*s appeared to hesitate. But not nearly long enough as two more missiles slammed into the backside of the *Griffin*'s right shoulder.

Her mind continued to race, rummaging through years of scattered, on-the-job training for any more pointers Tibor and other career MechWarriors had given her. 'Mechs could theoretically handle just about any terrain one could have any reason to fight in, but woods, she knew, cut the range and mobility options down a lot.

To deal with that, some 'Mechs had jump jets—integral thrusters powerful enough to launch their mass into the air and rocket it forward dozens—even hundreds—of meters at a clip. In her recollections, Brooke knew most *Griffin*s had jump jets...including this one, according to those pre-fight diagnostics she'd ran.

Okay, she mused, *so how do I make this damn thing jump?*

Even with his battlesuit's communications system shut down, Lucille's audio implants could hear the continuous screech of incoherent noise blasting from the intruder's stolen 'Mech. Although it was a simple matter of will to switch his hearing modes and shut out the electronic countermeasures, he could already sense the static was clearing. The enemy was moving away.

The burning rage that overtook him moments ago was gone, contained by a renewed focus on regrouping his team amid all this chaos. To that end, he welcomed the off-world woman's decision to flee the scene, and held onto the confidence that the MechWarriors piloting his faster-moving machines would be able to maintain contact and run her down.

In the meantime, he continued to dig at the hard-packed dirt, rocks, roots, and other debris that currently blocked his passage out.

The tunnel collapse had happened just as he and two of his fellow troopers rounded the last bend. Triggered, no doubt, by the fighting above, the last meter or so of the passage gave out as its wooden beams buckled. What little sunlight passed through the foliage above died as a sheet of earthen debris cascaded down to block the entryway. Only the faint glow from fiber-optic light channels in a few of the chambers behind him remained.

To be sure, this latest obstacle was nothing the enhanced muscles and armored gauntlets of Lucille's Achileus battle armor could not handle. Between himself and Adepts Rumiko and Assad, they would clear it in less than a minute.

But a lot could happen in a minute!

"Precentor!" a voice abruptly called into his true ears, breaking through the static with a welcome chirp. It was Adept Halua, the MechWarrior piloting his group's 50-ton *Raijin*.

"Halua," he responded without pause. "Report!"

"The target is presently moving south-southwest," Halua told him. "Adepts Evans and Laori are pursuing. I have no reading on Adept Quang or his BattleMech. My 'Mech has suffered minor actuator damage from a Wayward mine, but I am still able to pursue. Do you require assistance?"

Pride nearly compelled Lucille to refuse. Even as he listened to Halua, he could feel the last of the earth crumble away against the force of his armored gauntlets. But he thought better of it.

"We may," Lucille said. "Bring your 'Mech into the main camp clearing and stand by."

Switching his suit's communicator back on with a click of his tongue, Lucille felt a twinge of relief that the ECM screech was now completely gone. "Able and Baker squads," he called out, "sound off!"

A flurry of radio clicks and acknowledgments followed. Lucille tallied them up and frowned. Of the two six-man squads of battle armored Domini he had led to this Blake-forsaken camp, he only had seven troopers remaining—counting himself. Meanwhile, he had also lost three good MechWarriors, and a Frail off-worlder somehow managed to steal one of the Chosen's own BattleMechs.

There will be time enough for shame later, he reminded himself before dialing back to his command channel.

Dragging its narrow, backward-canted right leg just a little bit, Halua's red and black *Raijin* thumped to a stop just as Lucille led Adepts Assad and Rumiko back into the clearing. On the battlesuit's proximity sensors, he could see the other troopers either gathering ahead of them or just coming around from other tunnel entrances.

Looking at the nearest troopers, Lucille did a quick appraisal of their armor, and singled out two who looked the worst for wear.

"Adepts Rumiko and Warren," he snapped, "you two stay here. Secure this site and get me an accurate casualty count. All remaining troopers form up on me. Adept Halua...?"

The *Raijin*'s body twisted slightly, until its canopy faced him. "...prepare to be boarded."

FOREST OF SHROUDS
JARDINE (HERAKLEION)
FREE WORLDS LEAGUE

It was hard for Tibor Mitternacht to believe it when the call came buzzing into his ear implant, but less than twenty minutes had passed since Brooke hauled off in that captured *Griffin* of hers.

Dealing with Alahni's mood swings had made the time seem more like an eternity by now. In the relative silence that followed the BattleMech's departure, the reality of her situation—*their* situation—continued to sink in; the realization that her home, her family, everything and every*one* she ever knew or loved, were gone. Worse, they had been killed by those she had been raised to see as their guardians and protectors. Rage, aimed alternately at her "Guardians" and at the "Lost," seasoned with the pain and tears of immeasurable loss, all washed over the poor girl as Tibor stood by, helpless to soothe her. She'd screamed at him, cried on his shoulder, and even struck him once or twice—and in all of that, the best he could do was to just be there to endure it.

Be there and, of course, make sure they stayed out of sight in case any of those Manei Domini cyborgs came back.

The agitations had finally waned only a minute or two ago, as Alahni withered from the emotional exhaustion. Her head now rested on his shoulder, her face invisible beneath her long and disheveled hair, while he leaned against a tree and kept watch. His eyes kept drifting westward, toward the battle he could only hear in the form of thunderous rumbles that felt as if they were receding further into the distance.

In the comparative silence, the faint *chirp* inside his own skull, followed by the weak and scratchy sound of Brooke's voice, calling his name, nearly made Tibor jump. As it was, his body tensed enough to rouse Alahni, who pulled away from him and brushed her hair back, revealing eyes that were puffy and red, but still alert.

Tibor caught her attention and held a finger to his lips before answering. "Brooke?"

"Trouble," Brooke came back, the distracted tension in her voice still detectable, despite the weakness of the transmission. "So, I got their attention..."

Tibor blinked. "Um, was that something you *wanted*?"

"Yes, believe it or not. Bast, this thing is an *oven*!"

"Well, you *did* leave the cooling suit behind," he deadpanned, then shuddered at the thought. "So, what's the plan?"

"Gah!" Brooke yelped, for reasons Tibor could only guess at. "How do I...? Okay. Listen, I looked over the maps in this thing, and I think I've got my bearings. You guys keep heading east—the way we were going before we stumbled on the 'Mech. When you find the river, head south. And keep your eye peeled."

"My *eye*?"

"You'll know what you're looking for when you find it..."

Tibor turned back toward to Alahni, catching the look of confusion on her face. With a silent "Oh!" he pointed at his ear, then mimicked the act of holding a device against it. Whether or not the girl fully understood, he could not tell.

"East, then south along the river, then," he said, which only made Alahni's eyes widen. She opened her mouth to speak, but Tibor held up a hand first.

"Yes," Brooke said in his ear, her voice nearly vanishing in a momentary burst of static. "Hopefully, I'll catch up to you before long. If not…"

Tibor felt the tension in his own jaw, and saw Alahni's reaction in the form of an urgent tilt to her head.

"Understood," he said. "Luck!"

"Thanks!" Brooke said. With another *chirp* in his skull, the line went dead.

Alahni was still staring at him.

"She wants us to get to the river, then follow it south."

"South?" Alahni repeated. "But Hope is *north* along the river."

Tibor blinked. "Then why—? Oh! *Of course!*"

"What?"

"C'mon," he told her. "I'll explain on the way…"

When the damage monitor began to paint her aft torso armor red to the staccato rhythm of sustained machine-gun fire, Brooke realized the *Owl*s (the name she'd settled on for the "OW1s" now chasing her, anyway) still had her at a distinct disadvantage in a leg race. They hadn't overtaken her yet, but machine guns had a notoriously short range of effectiveness against modern heavy armor—which meant that, by now, they were probably close enough behind her to count any surface rivets on the *Griffin*'s rearward hull.

Knowing *that*, she finally felt bold enough to bet they didn't have jump jets, or she'd have trouble coming at her from both sides.

"Oh, I hope I got this right," she muttered as she slammed her feet down on both foot pedals at once.

Her 'Mech's computers instantly translated the command to its entire 55-ton frame. Its speed dropped for a second. Its legs braced, then bent a little. Its arms pulled inward, as the upper body leaned forward a little. Finally, an almost deafening hiss blasted in from the cockpit's still-open air panels. Brooke felt herself pressed deeper into her sweat-slickened command seat as the five half-ton thrusters in the *Griffin*'s legs and back fired in unison to blast a machine twenty-two times their own mass into the sky.

She suddenly felt very sick.

The *Griffin* vaulted high enough to clear the forest canopy, affording her a brief—but breathtaking—view of the woods around her. She squinted a little against the dazzling yellow sunlight, but not enough to miss what looked like a sea of greenery rolling off toward a hilly horizon. She glimpsed a few breaks here and there, but the biggest of these was far off to the left, where she could almost make out a single, coherent line snaking its way through the foliage.

The river!

At the apex of its jump, the *Griffin* abruptly cut its jets and realigned its posture, its complex computer systems preparing the 'Mech to brake its jump and land upright. From a technical aspect, thanks to years of working with gearheads and explorers alike, Brooke understood this was an effect of its limited stores of self-replenishing reaction mass. BattleMechs simply weren't built for sustained flight, and so few of them could leap farther than thirty meters or so (per properly-sized thruster) at a time. She also understood that most jump-capable 'Mechs incorporated the software to handle the entire process from beginning to end—freeing the pilot for other functions, like shooting.

Still, there were so many variables that could affect a 'Mech's jump, ranging from terrain and weather, to battle damage and the sheer lack of aerodynamics one can only expect from multi-ton machines built in a blocky parody of the human form. For those reasons, good MechWarriors preferred to take a more direct hand in navigating their jumps—lest their entire triumph of brute force and technology over physics end in a landing that could be equal parts embarrassing and deadly.

All of these things went through Brooke's mind at once as her *Griffin* crashed through the treetops nearly a hundred and fifty meters away from where it used to be.

The jets gave one last, momentary blast to cushion the landing, but even so, Brooke felt the shock through her spine.

Her top teeth bit deep into the flesh behind her lower lip, leaving her in eye-watering pain. The coppery taste of blood filled her mouth. She saw stars before her eyes, and imagined a tiny, sarcastic voice somewhere in the back of her head reminding her *why* she'd forgotten how to jump.

Almost instantly, she felt her 'Mech pitching forward, losing its footing on whatever uneven ground its feet had struck. For a few panicked heartbeats, she struggled with the controls and angled her head, hoping the *Griffin*'s computers could make sense of those efforts to restore its balance.

Then, as suddenly as it all began, it was over. The 'Mech and its warrior remained alive and upright. On one of the secondary boards, indicators for the jump jets flashed yellow as the fusion reactor and jet intakes began the process of rapidly processing the ambient atmosphere for reaction mass...

Meanwhile, the *Owl*s continued to rush toward them from behind.

"Bast help me," Brooke mumbled as she once more slammed the throttle forward. "There's no way I can keep this up!"

AEROSPACE HANGAR 104
CITY OF HOPE
JARDINE (HERAKLEION)
FREE WORLDS LEAGUE

From the air, the City of Hope's spaceport looked about the way one would expect of a centuries-old ruin. Trees and vines overgrew the decrepit hulls of rusted hangar buildings, wild grasses covered the rubble of fallen towers, and massive, ferrocrete blast barriers formed well-weathered rings around landing pads that were now little more than crack-filled craters in the ancient tarmac. Here and there, one could even spot the remains of ancient, forgotten vehicles and LoaderMechs— rusted and disintegrating hulks that now decayed in mute testament to what had once been a central hub of interplanetary commerce.

Of course, it was all just an illusion—a balanced mixture of pure artistry, Star League-era engineering, and meticulous

landscaping. Had anyone managed to land amid the spaceport—
or simply traveled there on the ground—they would soon see
through the ruse. The hangar buildings stood very much intact,
their rooftops covered in a masterful camouflage that was
equal parts clever paintwork and carefully cultivated foliage.
The fallen buildings were actually quite stable and upright, their
rooftops merely painted and cluttered with enough irregular
masonry and overgrowth to appear ruined. Even their actual
windows and doorways were deliberately skewed, arranged
to appear properly aligned with their "collapsed" orientation.

The tarmacs were smooth, level, and largely unblemished,
save for elaborate paint work that perfectly mimicked the few
actual cracks and clumps of wild grass that existed in only
the most infrequently used areas. Within the rings of blast
panels, even, the "craters" were actually the surface lids of
ultra-massive DropShip-sized elevators, artfully disguised to
blend in with the surrounding ferrocrete surface. Beneath them
lay cavernous bays large enough to contain most spheroid
DropShips, accessible through a multitude of reinforced tunnels.

In fact, the only authentic things in the entire affair were
the wrecked vehicles and WorkMechs. Keeping a few of
them around, strategically placed throughout the spaceport
hundreds of years before, and simply letting them decay was
an easy enough thing to do—providing excellent places to
hide the sensors and traps rigged to detect and discourage
any unwelcome intruders.

Inside one of the not-truly-wrecked hangars, within a space
large enough to stow a pair of *Leopard*-class DropShips end to
end, stood Specter Precentor Omicron Apollyon.

Impassively, he watched the technical crews as they busied
themselves with dozens of tasks about the floor. On the far end
of the hangar, maintenance teams were conducting installing
weapon pods into six of the division's newest aerospace
fighters—85-ton, ultra-sleek SHV-O *Shiva* OmniFighters.
Though freshly built from Free Worlds League factories on
distant Lopez, these six specimens already bore the distinctive,
red-to-black colors of the Fifty-Second Shadow Division. Four
were even further modified from factory specs; their cockpit

and control systems upgraded to accommodate their assigned pilots' direct-neural implants.

Closer to where Apollyon stood, a dozen suits of battle armor were the subject of similar maintenance and armament work. Like the fighters, half of these suits—Longinus models, which looked for all the universe like thick-bodied, over-teched versions of ancient knights—bore the colors and insignia of the Fifty-Second. The other six, set up ten meters away, lacked these colors—but that was only because the digital mimetics of the sleeker Purifier adaptive suits required no painting. With their mimetics deactivated, they stood in simple, gunmetal gray, their chest plates open as the tech crews worked on their interior interfaces.

Finally, and closest to the most powerful man on Jardine, there stood a K-1 class DropShuttle—a humble, lightly armed, 200-ton, civilian spacecraft. Bearing no distinct markings or livery to differentiate it from thousands of identical craft across the Inner Sphere, its only real "colors" were bare metal and the permanent scorching that blackened the entire lower half of its squashed-egg form, the inevitable result of repeated launches and landings over its decades-long lifespan.

It was this DropShuttle that held the Precentor's attention now, as well as the young, dark-skinned brunette, clad in plain light-gray overalls, who approached him with a noteputer in hand. Technical Adept Kaulana Tin showed little of the awe or fear many of her fellow civilians did when in the presence of the Manei Domini—a trait Apollyon found refreshing. Though he himself was born of this world, raised as a citizen of Hope, and as a follower of the Blessed Blake, his transformation in the years after Tukayyid, and his Ascension to the leadership of the Master's Hands had rattled many of his kindred. But Tin— all of seven years old when the first Domini Ascended—saw nothing to fear in the Guardians' new forms.

A true child of Jardine, this one!

"Precentor, sir," she said as she stopped before him, just far enough away to avoid any undue neck strain when she looked up to meet his eyes. "The shuttle is fueled and stocked as you requested. And the suits are undergoing final systems checks for vacuum ops, as you can see. We will be able to load as soon as you're ready and the DropShip is on the platform."

"Excellent, Adept Tin," Apollyon said with a sincere nod. "And the transponder codes?"

"Already set, sir," she said without hesitation. "I verified them myself."

"Your dedication honors us, Adept."

Without switching his true sight to thermal vision, Apollyon could not be certain, but he imagined from the way the young woman beamed at him that she was blushing. Her brilliant teeth flashed as she handed over her noteputer.

"The honor is to serve the Blessed Blake's Promise."

Apollyon accepted the device, quickly scanned its contents, and signed his name, using the index finger of his true hand instead of the stylus. With a short bow, he handed the 'puter back to Tin. "Blessed be those who walk the Sainted Blake's path, Adept."

"Blessed be, Precentor," she replied, her composure already reclaimed.

She had moved no more than two steps away when Apollyon's true hearing received a familiar chime. Turning away from the technicians, he opened the channel, and spoke without waiting for the voice on the other end. "How fares your hunt, Precentor Lucille?"

"Precentor," Lucille replied, tersely, "the target camp has been located and destroyed. I have a present estimate of thirty-two kills made on site—all Wayward. A few stragglers may have slipped away through the tunnels, but given the level of resistance we faced, I posit that any such survivors are would-be non-combatants of negligible consequence..."

Apollyon closed his frail eye and sighed. *Such loss!*

"Unfortunately, we have suffered casualties of our own. Wayward mines have disabled or destroyed two of our 'Mechs and damaged a third. We have also lost five troopers to mines and weapons fire. A chance encounter with a hunting party, several kilometers from the main objective, undoubtedly alerted them."

Apollyon resisted the impulse to grimace as the part of him that mourned the loss of Wayward lives warred with admiration for their ability to still cause damage to the Master's Hands. "And the invaders?"

Lucille's voice took on a much more guarded tone. "One is currently engaging us."

"Currently *engaging* you?"

"The female Lost we were told of somehow managed to salvage and reactivate Adept Moakay's *Griffin*. She attacked us at the campsite while most of my remaining units were otherwise occupied, and managed to destroy Adept Quang's BattleMech before the others could support him. She is now headed south. We're pursuing."

"Precentor, you are telling me that you have lost half of your force against a lightly armed platoon of our self-exiled kin, and a *single* Frail using one of your own BattleMechs."

It wasn't a question.

"As you say, Precentor," Lucille came back after the briefest of hesitations. "I accept full responsibility; once again, I underestimated the resourcefulness of our Wayward cousins."

"Your responsibility is noted," Apollyon said darkly. In his mind, he envisioned the regional map, and considered the only landmarks south of Hope that might hold any potential value to an invader at this point.

"Continue your pursuit, Precentor," he commanded. "But remember: I want these intruders *alive*. If this Frail is moving south, she may be trying to return to her shuttle for some reason. I will dispatch another team to that location; between them and your group, she should have nowhere else of consequence to run."

"Understood, sir. Lucille out."

As the line went dead, Apollyon finally opened his frail eye and took in his surroundings once more. Adept Tin and her techs were beginning to load the Longinus battlesuits onto the DropShuttle, aided by powered dollies specially built for the task. Nobody else stood close by the Precentor; nobody was even paying any attention to his presence.

Without a word, he strode out of the hangar.

On the plus side, Brooke thought as she reached up to dab the sweat from her eyebrows, *I hardly even notice the stink anymore!*

Despite executing a series of jumps, draining the *Griffin*'s reaction mass as quickly as the BattleMech could replenish it, the *Owl*s continued to pace her every move, plowing through forest and underbrush as quickly as their tiny, blocky forms could manage. Too far now to reliably cause any real damage with their machine guns, they both were forced to rely on their SRM launchers, their missiles tearing away more and more armor with each concussive blast.

In an increasingly frustrating effort to slow them down, Brooke had been zig-zagging her jumps, and twisting her 'Mech's torso side to side in a desperate effort to send at least some firepower back at them. Between her jumps and the occasional blast from her particle cannon, the cockpit had quickly become a sauna. She now regretted—in spite of herself—not taking the time to pour the *Griffin*'s last pilot out of his cooling suit before she started this foolish charge.

For that matter, a snarky voice from one corner of her mind reminded her, *you could have avoided this entire mess by never taking on these cyborgs in the first place!*

Right now, Brooke wished that part of her brain would just shut up already.

Slamming the pedals down once again, she sent the *Griffin* into yet another jump, sailing over a particularly thick group of trees she could not imagine driving a jeep through, much less a BattleMech. The leap carried her forward over a hundred meters, but not before one of her pursuers managed to pump two more missiles into the *Griffin*'s rear armor panels.

Sparks and fire flashed out from the large canister perched on the 'Mech's right shoulder. The small explosion startled her for a moment, but an internal alarm and the winking out of one of her weapon status lights quickly identified the extent of the damage.

A relieved sigh escaped her lips.

Not dead yet.

"You can have that launcher," she muttered to no one in particular. "I wasn't using it anyway."

Despite the damage, the *Griffin* managed another (relatively) smooth landing—in so much as it kept to its feet with only a little extra coaxing. Brooke rotated the 'Mech's torso left, and extended its arm to snap-fire a laser into the general vicinity of one of the *Owl*s. The shot flashed into the trees dead-center of the brackets her HUD placed around her target, but whether or not she actually hit the thing was beyond her.

Sweat stung her eyes, but she dared not blink. Instead, she pushed the *Griffin* back into a run, shifting course yet again, but continuing to keep it vaguely southward.

On the sensor board, Brooke noticed once more that the third 'Mech remained off the scope. Only the two *Owl*s appeared to be within sensor range. But years of experience had long since taught her better than to trust what *appeared* to be, especially when gunplay was involved. ComStar and the Word of Blake were known for having the best tech outside of Clan space, and that included Star League-quality ECM and stealth gear most folks only saw in holovid action thrillers. Hell, even something as mundane as ground clutter could be preventing her radar from picking up the third 'Mech's electromagnetic signature.

That happened in some environments, right?

A furtive glance at the map display put her close to five kilometers south of the Waywards' camp, now. The wireframe now colored both arms, her forward left flank, and one leg yellow, while the rear armor and other leg glowed red. Only her machine's head and the rest of its forward torso armor showed green. And her unfired LRM launcher was now dead.

Not that it had a prayer of hitting these bastards anyway, she mused.

The time to end this play was coming up fast, and suddenly she knew just how to do it.

Glancing up, she sought another thick cluster of trees in the forest, about a hundred meters ahead and to the right. The branches there spread out so thick that their leaves seemed to blot the sun out almost entirely.

Perfect!

With a hard jerk on the steering controls, Brooke swung the *Griffin* toward that dark grove. As she did, a keening wail from her sensor board gave her a second's warning about the pair of missiles one of the *Owl*s just lobbed at her. Both warheads struck the 'Mech's exaggerated right shoulder pauldron; already, her shadows were closing the gap.

Another double blast shook her a heartbeat later. A new alarm screamed for attention, but the new wave of heat that seemed to come from the floor beneath her told her all she needed to know: reactor damage.

Now or never!

The *Griffin*'s run continued, shattering branches and undergrowth with each step as it neared her objective. With only one hand on the steering controls, Brooke scanned her weapons panels. It took a few seconds to find what she wanted.

"Here goes nothing," she warned herself.

Releasing the controls, she allowed the *Griffin* to plod onward at full throttle, while she reached for the straps that kept her neurohelmet in place. Cringing in anticipation, she then reached out to the weapon panel, opened the black and yellow plastic cover marked "dump", and pushed the button beneath.

The grinding noise that followed sounded horrifically loud in Brooke's ears as she tore off the helmet and pitched it behind her seat. Bereft of balancing input from her temples, the *Griffin*'s gait became a drunken stumble on the uneven ground. The 'Mech slammed into one tree after another, each threatening to topple it while Brooke flailed to reach the ejection handles over her head.

The explosion she'd expected came just as she finally managed to grab one of them. Squeezing her eyes shut and yelling into the cockpit, she quickly grasped the other and yanked both handles down hard.

Between the ammunition explosion, the *Griffin*'s wild bucking, and the ejection itself, Brooke felt almost like she was being torn in several directions at once. Her eyes remained closed, and every muscle in her body stiffened. Wind and leaves whipped past her as the pilot's seat blasted clear of its dying host with a deafening roar. She felt herself soaring skyward, and bent her head downward while her hands clutched at the straps of her five-point harness for dear life.

She felt her ascent slow as gravity began to take over, and her seat shuddered a little to the sound of its parachute deploying. Only then did she open her eyes again, looking up to make sure the damned thing opened properly.

What struck her most about the first few moments of freefall was the cool and wonderful smell and feel of fresh, Jardinian forest air. Her arms and legs crawled with gooseflesh. Compared to the rancid hothouse the *Griffin*'s cockpit had become, she was now in heaven, even as she cast her gaze downward in time to see the 'Mech's fiery death.

Momentum, combined with the forward pitch the *Griffin*'s head had been at when she pulled the ejection handles, had launched her dozens of meters forward and slightly left of where the 'Mech died. As the chair began its lazy decent, she watched for the telltale shaking of trees to see where the *Owls* were moving, and used that to recover her bearings.

Only then, as she watched the forest canopy rising to meet her, did she draw in a breath, mentally declare herself insane, slap the release on her seat harness, and kick herself into the sky.

The next few moments were a whirl of green leaves and shadow, a symphony of snapping branches and pain-wracked grunts, and a desperate fight between blind panic and intense concentration. Falling was almost as familiar to Brooke as running, but in most of her previous jobs, falls tended to happen when she had the gear and protection to better weather the bumps along the way, and when she could be reasonably sure that certain death wasn't waiting for her below.

Dropping into an uncharted jungle-turned-war zone while practically naked and unarmed was another experience entirely!

The branch that finally stopped her fall was almost as thick as her body and stretched out over a clump of leafy underbrush some eight meters below. Dazed, but thankfully conscious, Brooke clung to the rough branch for several seconds, taking stock of her condition. A lot of places hurt, but miraculously, nothing felt broken. Still, she felt a bit woozy, and a part of her wanted to stay in this tree and rest a while.

The part that told her to keep moving, on the other hand, recognized that the burning wreck of her 'Mech and her empty ejection seat wouldn't keep the cyborgs distracted nearly long enough for a shock-induced nap.

Shimmying down the tree punished her mostly bare flesh, adding scrapes to the bruises she'd surely find all over her body when this was all over. When she reached the forest floor, she was glad she'd at least had the presence of mind to keep her boots; the underbrush was far rougher than it looked.

East and north, she reminded herself as she half-crawled, half-ran through the underbrush, doing her best to keep to the heavier undergrowth while putting the thickest trees between her and the flickering light of the burning *Griffin*.

East and north!

Oh, Tibor better *have my clothes ready when I get there!*

Scarcely five minutes had passed since Adept Laori reported the downing of Moakay's stolen *Griffin* to Precentor Lucille. In that time, he could do little more than wait tensely and refresh his grip on the large muzzle of the ER PPC that currently served as his saddle on Adept Halua's *Raijin*. The regular lurching motions of the 50-ton 'Mech, and the random blows of passing branches hardly fazed him. But the fact that this machine was not properly built or balanced to carry an extra eight to ten percent of its weight in battlesuits meant the only effective handholds were those a swarming infantry squad would normally be trying to destroy.

Halua was also complaining that the squad's presence made him itchy. While that initially amused Lucille, the occasionally violent hitch in the *Raijin*'s stride and the awkward, random swings of its turret-like arms betrayed the MechWarrior's efforts to scratch at the psychosomatic feeling his neural implants clearly kept feeding him. The result was an annoyingly unpredictable ride in which Lucille and his squad mates had nearly been thrown off several times.

Lucille grunted as another such lurch took the form of a torso spasm, and he once again focused on the mission. The Frail had fallen a little over five kilometers south of the Wayward camp, apparently while trying to move for thicker cover. In her flight, she inflicted only minimal damage to the pursuing *Owens*es; the worst damage reported was the destruction of

Adept Evans' TAG system. When Laori reported the kill, Lucille instructed Evans to secure the wreck, and tasked Laori with searching for any ejector seat beacons.

"Contain the Frail," he'd ordered, "but do *not* kill her when found; Apollyon wants this one alive."

That was five minutes ago, and since then, there had been silence. On the drop-down map in his armor's HUD, he could see he and his group were still a half-kilometer away; the two OmniMechs were fully resolved on the sensor display, and both read as active units.

Lucille's impatience finally got the better of him. "Report, Adept Laori!"

"Sir!" Laori replied instantly. "I have located the pilot's beacon and 'chute, approximately fifty meters from the crash site. The chair appears empty, but I am seeing a great deal of blood. The seat looks drenched in it. The Frail could be mortally wounded; I have been sweeping for a body."

A body?

"Did either of you score any headshots on the target during the pursuit?"

"Uncertain, Precentor," Laori replied. "Visual contact was spotty throughout the engagement, and the ejection left little of the head module to go by. It *is* possible."

"Anything on thermals?"

"Included in my sweep, sir, but ambient heat from Moakay's *Griffin* and resident wildlife has been generating false positives."

Lucille grunted again. "Continue your sweeps, Adept. Evans, assist her, but both of you maintain your proximity to the wreckage. My team will be there shortly to assist."

Even as he closed the line, Lucille realized there were only two possibilities now. The intruder was either dead, or she was alive. If dead, her corpse was probably hidden by some foliage on the forest floor, or hanging from a tree, and growing too cold for sensors to differentiate from the ambient environment. If alive, she was somehow stealthy enough to have eluded the Master's Hands in broad daylight.

Lucille now knew better than to underestimate this Frail again.

And with that decision came the sobering certainty that his team would find nothing there when they finally arrived.

After more than an hour of walking through the crowded forest, Tibor and Alahni finally found the river and began their trek southward, keeping well inside the tree line just to be on the safe side. Tibor struggled to keep his mind focused on searching for what he knew Brooke wanted him to find, but it wasn't easy. Between Alahni's ongoing shock that her people were being ruthlessly gunned down by their "Guardians," and the realization he'd simply *allowed* Brooke to take an unfamiliar 'Mech back there specifically to avenge them, his own dismay grew with each passing minute.

Now here he was; trapped on a world whose masters were so determined to hide it that no amount of murder was clearly beyond them; rummaging around a forest filled with God-knew-how-many natural hazards. His partner was effectively missing in action, and he had a native tagging along who now had no obligation to help him whatsoever—and *every* right to blame his very presence for the loss of her friends and family!

"This is *way* worse than Bob ever was…"

"What?" Alahni asked, her nervous voice coming from several steps behind.

The question surprised Tibor. He glanced back at her, and offered a sheepish smile. "Sorry," he said. "Didn't know I said that out loud."

The Jardinian tale-keeper made a noncommittal sound and lapsed back into silence for several seconds. Tibor was retreating back into his own thoughts when she suddenly spoke again. "Why do you do this?"

"Wh—?"

"Traveling to forgotten places," she added. "Is it just for money? Or did some House Lord send you?"

Her tone was hard to read. Behind her words, Tibor felt both genuine curiosity and scornful accusation in equal measure. He didn't dare glance back at her this time, preferring instead to keep moving, his gaze continuing to sweep the nearby foliage.

She wants to know why her people had to die, he warned himself.

"Sometimes," he admitted with a sigh. "Sometimes both. But that's never all of it."

"What do you mean?"

"How can I explain this?" he muttered. "I mean, the money can be nice, but only because it pays our bills, keeps us fed, helps us maintain our lifestyle. Basically all the reasons most folk in the Inner Sphere get jobs, you know? Yeah, sometimes the job offers come from a House or some other government, but a lot of times it doesn't."

"That sounds rather mundane for a 'job' that entails trespassing on worlds that may not wish to be found."

Tibor grunted at that. "I suppose that's one way of seeing it," he told her. "But most of the places we've seen didn't exactly hide on their own terms, if you follow me. Remember that planet Brooke and I talked about before? Bob?"

"The one that changed its name?" Alahni asked, her tone softening just a little.

"*Ja*. That one. Well, as funny as the story about *why* it changed its name was, the results of that choice were tragic."

"How so?"

"From what we could work out," Tibor began, "the people chose to make that name change at the very worst possible moment in history. The Star League had just collapsed, and their realm—the Draconis Combine—was in the middle of a full-scale invasion of the Federated Suns. 'Bob,' meanwhile, was a low-resource world way out near the Periphery. The name change, from...*Dunkelwalden*-something? *Dunkel...schatten...*? Well, believe me; it was a very *long* word, put together by some colony founder with a shaky grasp of the German language at best.

"Anyway, the local leaders chose to make the whole name change as a way to take their people's minds off the war. It seemed like a great idea at the time, especially for a world that looks gloomy all year round, and has a biosphere that's generally hostile to human life. So it was supposed to be a big morale booster. They took votes from kids as young as twelve years old, held big parties, ran silly advertisements on their local networks, and just had fun with the whole affair..."

Tibor trailed off for a moment as he found himself climbing over an old, fallen tree trunk. As he did so, his eyes caught sight of the length of bark that appeared to have been dug out of it by something with claws as big as his head.

Tabiranth claws? he wondered.

"So, what happened?" Alahni asked. The accusatory edge in her voice was gone now, at least for the moment.

Tibor shook himself out of his distraction. He turned back toward the young woman, prepared to offer his hand to help her over the trunk, but she waved him off. Her eyes, like his, seemed to fixate on the shredded bark for a moment, but if those gouges concerned her much at all, she didn't show it. Instead, she simply hopped over the fallen tree and threw him an inquisitive look.

"Well," he continued with a shrug, "when the votes were tallied, and the new name was all picked out, they sent word to the local district ministers, who evidently got as far as reporting the name change to the right people to get it recorded on some of the local star maps. But they apparently missed a few key people in the bureaucratic chain. Whole shipments of food, equipment, and other vital necessities sat in Combine warehouses light-years away, because they were earmarked for a planet that *wasn't* named Bob."

"Truly?" Alahni asked, bewildered. "Didn't anyone think to check up on them? Didn't the people of Bob think to send a message when the shipments didn't show?"

Tibor frowned. "The First Succession War, as you seem to know, was really bad. The strategy at the time, for pretty much every side, was to capture or destroy factories and shipping wherever and whenever possible. This extended even to civilian ships, which could always be used to carry troops in a pinch.

"And the Combine was moving a *lot* of troops into Davion space at that point. As more of their ships got lost in action, or were otherwise tied up on their front lines, the Kuritans started pressing more and more merchants into military service. Worlds that were considered lower priority—including pretty much anything near the Periphery—were generally stripped of their support first..."

"So there just weren't any ships to send to Bob? House Kurita simply abandoned them?"

"Yes," Tibor answered slowly, "and no. The war left the Combine with fewer ships to cover the local transit routes, but they still had enough for periodic supply runs. But between the planet's name change, and the confusion caused when the wrong people were left out of the loop, House Kurita was stockpiling supplies for that world under Bob's old name. So, they didn't really abandon the planet, so much as they effectively just *misplaced* it."

"Surely the people of Bob would have noticed the lack of supplies soon enough, though, right? Couldn't they call for help?"

Tibor winced. "ComStar was still repairing the hyperpulse network at that point," he said after a moment's hesitation, wary of her reaction. "And even Jerome Blake had to prioritize which worlds to get back online first as his organization spread outward from Terra. Bob's HPG had apparently gone down some time during the Amaris years—"

"Wait," Alahni interrupted, just as Tibor feared she would. "The Blessed Blake was still restoring HPGs in the Inner Sphere? I thought the House Lords rejected him in their rush to destroy one another."

Tibor drew in a breath before finally turning around to meet the woman's gaze. "Not exactly..."

Alahni's voice regained its edge, and her eyes narrowed. "What's *that* supposed to mean?"

Tibor felt his jaw go slack. *Oh, this is going to be fun,* he told himself.

"Um," he stumbled. "Alahni, I can see that Blake means a lot to your people, but it's becoming clear to me that not all of the history you've been told matches what really happened out in the Inner Sphere."

Alahni's expression darkened, and her hands twitched. For a real moment there, Tibor expected her to strike him, and he found himself unsure whether he should try to block it or simply take the hit.

To his surprise, she blinked instead, and suddenly seemed to reclaim some manner of control. Though her eyes still bored angry holes into his own, he could practically feel her reflexive rage subsiding.

"I'm sorry," he lamely offered. "Brooke's always so much better with stuff like this; I thought she would have told you some of this when you two were talking the other day..."

Mentioning Brooke's name appeared to help soften Alahni just a bit more. The young woman blinked again, and tension bled out of her posture.

"She mentioned ComStar," Alahni admitted, "and the division that followed its temporary victory against the Clans... something she called a 'schism'. She mentioned how bad the first two Succession Wars were as well, but nothing about ComStar being active among the Lost in that time."

"Well, that was when they came to this world in the first place, wasn't it?"

Alahni now seemed less certain of herself. "Yes," she began slowly, "but that was to save us from oblivion, after the Steiners bombed us..."

Tibor grimaced at that one, but decided to barrel through it. There was no point in making apologies for the inexcusable. "Didn't it ever seem odd to you that they would only pick your world to save at that time?"

"The Order was new back then," she said. "We were told they could only save a few..."

"That's likely true. Jerome Blake's primary mission, though— at least, the one given to him by the House Lords just before the Star League's collapse—was to rebuild the hyperpulse network across the entire Inner Sphere. After taking Terra, and convincing the various Houses to honor ComStar's neutrality, he *did* just that..."

"Then, he *did* try to save the Inner Sphere?"

Tibor offered a shrug. "I suppose you could see it that, way, yes."

"But we were taught that the Inner Sphere rejected him," Alahni countered, "that they'd all but destroyed themselves in less than two generations."

"You could say that, too, I guess," Tibor admitted with a sigh. "By the end of the First War, a lot of worlds began to die off, like Bob did. Like we all believed *this* world did. You told Brooke that there were five worlds like Jardine, didn't you?"

"The Five, yes."

"Well, maybe that was all Blake could save at the time, at least after taking over Terra."

Alahni stood mute for several moments, her expression almost blank. Tibor decided to continue. "What I guess I'm saying is that your knowledge of history beyond your world has a few gaps. Either that, or—for whatever reason—Jerome Blake exaggerated when he told your people the Inner Sphere had completely collapsed, and that he'd been rejected by all."

Anger flashed again in the young woman's eyes. "Are you suggesting the Blessed Blake *lied* to us?"

"*If* he did," Tibor said cautiously, feeling for all the world like a man trapped in a minefield, "it was most likely for your own protection. By convincing your people that the Inner Sphere at large was ruined, he would have discouraged anyone who wanted to leave Jardine at that time."

Alahni scoffed. "And now you make it sound like he wanted to imprison us! That's too f—!"

"Alahni! Please understand me; I'm not *trying* to offend you here! You see Blake as your savior and protector. I get that. But Brooke and I have come upon several worlds where the local leaders used deception on their own people to keep them complacent and allowed future generations to live on in blissful—" *Don't say "ignorance", Tibor!*"—um, un-awareness. Most of the time, it's less about control and more a part of the bigger plan to keep those people safe and hidden from pirates and other enemies.

"Think about it: Jerome Blake wants to save your world from the war. His Order changes the maps, fudges some data, and passes it around throughout the hyperpulse network as a free navigational update to all parties interested in avoiding planets that have been destroyed or infected during the most horrifying war since before the Star League. But what happens if someone from one of these now-hidden worlds just shows up one day because he realizes the neighbors are fine and he decides to open trade with them?"

Alahni continued to glower at Tibor. For a long time, she said nothing, but he could practically hear the gears turning in her mind. He found himself half-surprised she was even willing to entertain the idea; in most of their past encounters with isolated peoples, he and Brooke had found the locals so entrenched in their own dogma they couldn't accept any other truth at all.

"Is this why you and Doctor Stevens do this, then?" she asked at last, a slight catch in her tone. "To shatter the illusions of people who did you no harm?"

"Oh, for Christ's sake!" Tibor spat. "No! We do it to *learn*! We do it to find all that was lost since the Star League fell! We do it because we can practically *feel* what humanity has lost every time we set foot on an abandoned world, or find some city, or some priceless artifact, that was once part of our collective history! We do it for probably the same reasons you and your people left your Guardians' city, maybe even the same reasons that *you*, personally, chose to become the story-keeper you are! At least, I *assume* it was a choice!"

At that, Alahni flinched as if he'd just struck her. Suddenly realizing he'd begun shouting, Tibor clamped up, and instinctively glanced around as he remembered where they were.

Finally, he sighed, turned away from her, and continued on into the woods, resuming the search for what he knew Brooke expected them to find. But one more thought slipped into his mind, begging for release.

"Like I said," he grumbled, "it's not really about money, or fame, or any of that. And it's not about the Houses—Lord knows I did my bit for one of *those* long enough in my day! And it sure as *hell* isn't about spite! Brooke and I, we do this because it gives our lives some kind of meaning beyond mere existence."

Although Alahni remained silent, Tibor could hear her footsteps behind him. He didn't know if anything he'd just said made any sense to her, or if it did anything to help her cope with what had happened in the last few hours.

Hell, he wasn't even sure it did anything to make *him* feel any better about the situation as it now stood. After all of that, the doubt still nagged at him.

That was, until, barely five minutes later, he heard the woman freeze in her tracks and suck in her breath with an audible hiss.

Tibor spun around to check on her. Alahni's eyes, wide but not panicked, were locked onto something else. She gestured toward it with her chin, directing his gaze further to their right.

Instantly on his guard, Tibor turned slowly that way, until he suddenly spotted the graceful, feline form of a gray and brown-striped *tabiranth*, lurking among the brush barely fifteen meters away. At his movement, the animal's green eyes, originally focused on Alahni, flashed around to meet his own.

A low growl rumbled from somewhere within the beast's throat, but instead of baring teeth, it hunched down and stepped backward.

"Lower your hands," Alahni whispered, "hold your eye contact, but blink—*slowly*—at him."

Tibor wasn't about to ask how she knew the thing was a male. He forced his hands, which he'd automatically raised to chest level in anticipation of an attack, to ease their way back down. The giant felinoid took another step back, but kept its gaze locked onto his.

Exhaling through his nostrils as quietly as possible, Tibor closed his eyes slowly, like a young child fighting sleep. When he opened them again a moment later, the animal appeared to have taken yet another step back. He could see the tip of its tail twitching nervously behind it, and its gaze remained fixed on him, but it was now rising back to its full height.

"No sudden moves," Alahni whispered, her voice now recapturing the beast's attention. "Let it move away first..."

The *tabiranth* blinked at Alahni, raised its chin, and sniffed the air a few times. With a sound somewhere between a snort and a sneeze, it abruptly shook its head and whipped its tail. Without another noise, it turned away from them both, and strode off, meandering deeper into the woods.

Alahni let out a relieved sigh.

"Good," she whispered. "Wild tabis are not normally aggressive toward humans, but the males tend to interpret direct eye contact as a dominance challenge, and they panic easily at sudden moves."

Tibor felt like he needed to unlock his jaw before he could respond. "Thanks," he mumbled, his gaze still hovering over the brush.

And that was when he saw it, about twenty meters past where the *tabiranth* had stood just seconds before. Shaded behind a thick cluster of tree trunks and broad-leaved bushes, it was almost invisible at a glance.

"*Unglaublich!*" he blurted.

Alahni started to speak, but stopped short as she followed his line of sight and spotted it as well.

There, on the forest floor—sprawled on its side, with its broad, dull-green back jutting up above the lower foliage— lay the abandoned remains of a dull-green *Rock Possum* ProspectorMech.

CHAPTER 4

"Brothers and Sisters of the Master's Hand, hearken to these words!

"The day of the Promise fast approaches; the hour of the Third Transfer looms ever nearer. Soon, it will fall to us to strike from our Shadows at the enemies of all of Terra's Blessed Children!

"To the last, all of us have given ourselves to the Blessed Blake's cause! With no thought of reward, no promise of compensation, no expectation of survival, we have sacrificed our own blood, flesh, and bone. And, in becoming the Master's Hands, we have given our very souls to this cause!

"We have become the instruments of history, the greatest hope for Humanity's survival. When we fulfill our part of the Master's Promise, we will commit horrors that will damn us for Eternity! Future generations will see us as the monsters we became, as any rational being should...

"But, thanks to us—the Manei Domini—there will be future generations left alive to judge us!"

—Precentor Manei Domini Apollyon
Jardine, 3067

THE SANCTORUM
CITY OF HOPE
JARDINE (HERAKLEION)
FREE WORLDS LEAGUE
3 NOVEMBER 3067

"Don't you think this plan of yours is needlessly...overcomplicated?"

Those were the first words to tumble from the mouth of Precentor Damien Lucille since providing Apollyon with his report on yesterday's operation in the Forest of Shrouds.

The sun had barely risen over the horizon when he, his team, and the extra squad sent to the intruders' crash site, finally received their orders to return to Hope for further instruction. As soon as he had shucked his damaged Longinus battlesuit in the recovery bays of the city's southern staging grounds, Lucille donned his robes and headed for the tunnels leading to the Sanctorum entrance.

Through the window behind Precentor Apollyon's seat, Lucille could see the early morning mists were already dispersing over the western forests, their evaporation surrendering the endless greens to the golden glory of Jardine's day star. Having spent the better part of the last twenty hours in those woods, rummaging through the thick foliage and shadows for any sign of his prey, Lucille felt strangely impressed at how they still seemed so untouched from afar.

Assuming his customary descent to one knee, Lucille had recited the full report to his commander as bidden. The Shrouded Forest Wayward Tribe's camp was destroyed. Thirty-five Wayward men, women, and children had been killed during the main assault. Another six Waywards were encountered and dispatched during the mop-op, mostly by the two warriors Lucille left behind to secure the site. An additional ten to twelve survivors—all presumed to be non-combatants—were believed to have escaped, and may still be in flight at this time, with signs they were proceeding further westward, away from the city.

Of the twelve battle-armored troops and six BattleMechs taken for the operation, Lucille's force lost a total of six troopers, along with three 'Mechs and two of their MechWarriors. Adept Moakay's *Griffin* was recovered and could be restored (barely!), as was Adept Basset's EMP-shocked *Nexus*, but Adept Quang's *Nexus* had been a complete loss. And while all of the remaining units in Lucille's force remained functional, each one had suffered varying degrees of damage by the time they'd returned to base.

Worst of all, of course, was the fact that the two known interlopers—who he now knew to be one Doctor Brooklyn Stevens and one Tibor Mitternacht—had escaped. As Lucille had feared, the blood soaking the *Griffin*'s recovered ejection seat turned out to be Moakay's after all, debunking the initial theories of Stevens' demise. Thanks to the heat and electromagnetic clutter created by the 'Mech's collapse and the thick forest, the clever Frail had managed to slip past his warriors' sensors before Lucille's battle armor could reach the scene and begin their search.

Lucille found only miniscule relief in the fact that Apollyon's own presumptions about the woman going for her wrecked DropShuttle also proved to be false. Wherever the intruder was headed, it was either toward an objective they knew nothing about, like a heretofore undiscovered Wayward camp somewhere past the Open Plains...or it was a feint, in which case, Blake only knew where they might be right now.

Either way, it meant she had outmaneuvered *both* of them for the time being.

Naturally, Precentor Apollyon decided to apply some lateral thinking to the matter. Wherever Stevens and Mitternacht went, the only way to truly escape Jardine was to get to their JumpShip—something that was supremely difficult, given the fact that all of the planet's functional spacecraft were currently stored in the hangar bays beneath Hope's thoroughly secured spaceport. Combined with the orbiting sensors and drone launchers, Stevens would need divine intervention if she and her companion were to leave Jardine's atmosphere alive, let alone undetected.

And even then, Apollyon noted, she'd need a JumpShip to leave the system entirely. Given the broadcast Stevens had made when she crashed, the leader of the Master's Hands knew said JumpShip was somewhere in the system, but it was clearly running silent and likely positioned far enough away to be missed by passive sensors.

Capturing or destroying that ship before it could leap out-system was the best way to guarantee Jardine's secrecy remained intact and ensure that Stevens could neither escape nor receive any outside help. The biggest problem there was the certainty that Stevens' JumpShip had already been tipped off to a hostile presence in the system, and so would almost certainly bolt or relocate if Jardine's elaborate, system-wide sensor network suddenly pinged them after switching from passive to active detection mode.

And so the plan was hatched—and initiated—while Lucille was still in the field. After taking in the junior Precentor's report, Apollyon bade him to rise and presented the basics to him. Using a DropShuttle of the same mundane make and colors, with IFF codes copied from those found in Stevens' wreck, Lucille and a boarding team would "escape" Jardine and call for help from Stevens' JumpShip. Voice-modification software, expertly configured by Ghost Precentor Lamashti, would allow Lucille to communicate with the intruders' vessel, and answer any questions necessary to bring their Trojan Horse into striking range.

That much of the plan was basic.

The complexities that now concerned Lucille were in the extra details Apollyon had added to make the whole mission "more convincing."

Apollyon stood behind his desk, peering over the translucent pane upon which a schematic map of Jardine's solar system had been projected in a clever mimicry of three-dimensional space. His hood was back, leaving the brown flesh of his scalp exposed. The mechanical orb of his true eye was dimmed, while the brow above his frail, natural eye arched with interest. His arms were crossed, but uncharacteristically exposed; he'd pushed the broad sleeves of his red and gold robe back to the elbows. Lucille could thus plainly see the contrast between the unnaturally bulky flesh of Apollyon's left forearm and the noticeably sleeker collection of metal, plastic, and myomer that comprised his right.

"In this day and age," Apollyon said, "there's no longer a guarantee of what resources the frail heathens of the Inner Sphere might have. A charged and ready lithium-fusion battery could nix this entire operation before our people even get into firing range."

"But doesn't having my shuttle barreling in—with a hostile DropShip hot on its tail—risk overplaying the hand? They could see through the ruse, perhaps even open fire upon my shuttle before we draw near enough, and then jump out before the bigger guns can reach them."

Apollyon's frail eye narrowed slightly. "Do I detect a hint of *fear*, Precentor?"

Lucille felt as though he'd just been slapped. Fear was the very first conquest all Domini made before beginning their path toward Ascension; those who yielded to fear could never make the first sacrifice of the flesh—the one that came without promise of reward! To fear was to value personal well-being over the greater good. It was selfishness in its most primal form.

Fear was the *ultimate* Frailty!

Lucille absorbed the insult without allowing its sting to pierce his soul.

As it was, Apollyon held up a hand to forestall any possible retort. "The pursuit ship will add to the immediacy of the threat and help reduce the chances of the target suspecting your ruse. The intruders' JumpShip is aware that Stevens crashed while under fire, and Ghost Precentor Lamashti has already set the stage for you to explain any oddities in your flight path and communications as lingering damage. That would, naturally, include why you will be 'unable' to transmit video or send and reply using laser tight-beam methods.

"Meanwhile, your voice masker will even send intermittent bursts of static to maintain consistency with the earlier transmissions. If they try to get you to reveal any pertinent information on this system and our presence here, you will, of course, refuse this, because there is a hostile craft close enough to eavesdrop. This will encourage them to stay put at least long enough to collect you, as the alternative is fleeing this system completely empty handed. This gives your 'pursuit' ship an incentive to spend as little time as possible debating the options, while their colleagues' lives are on the line."

Lucille's gaze returned to the projected map again, and he studied the flight plans. Based on the sensor contact data of the intruders' original arrival, he noticed his shuttle's "return trip" was plotted to begin by moving back along that same general heading from a lift-off point near the original crash zone. That was a sensible enough choice, which would likely raise no red flags among the target's crew, should they be able to perceive it somehow. "Stevens" would then radio to her unseen cohorts for current telemetry as soon as she clears the planet's ionosphere. This will be the first such transmission in which "she" requests a response, while continuing along her initial course (roughly along Jardine's main orbital plane, heading outward) until corrective data comes in. The timing of the response would help narrow down just how far out the target JumpShip lay, which would naturally be fed back to Hope along a secure frequency to aid in triangulation and any potential avenues for alternate interceptions.

The pursuit DropShip—a *Union*-class—would then launch roughly one hour or so later, burning hot. This chaser would be running with active sensors and a Free Worlds League IFF, which should make perfect sense to a JumpShip lurking in League space. With both Lucille's shuttle and its pursuer roughly matched for acceleration, they could pace themselves and manage their separation naturally enough to be convincing. Since the shuttle should be damaged and low on fuel, this would easily excuse the DropShip's gradual gain as they flee across the system, adding to the "incentive" Apollyon talked about... maybe even enough to convince the outworlders to make an in-system jump in an effort to close the gap and rescue "Stevens" sooner.

It was those details, Lucille realized, that would all need to be played by ear, since so much relied on the JumpShip's reactions.

"My concern, Precentor," he finally said, "is not for myself, but for the mission."

Apollyon nodded slightly, but said nothing.

"The success of this operation relies entirely on the reactions of people who have already managed to surprise us several times," Lucille continued. "Should they do so again..."

"Then you improvise," Apollyon said gravely. "These people must *not* be allowed to reveal our existence before the Third Transfer. The lives of everyone left on this world—and perhaps all of the Inner Sphere—depend on it."

FOREST OF SHROUDS
JARDINE (HERAKLEION)
FREE WORLDS LEAGUE
3 NOVEMBER 3067

"*Digger One*" was the name stenciled just below the lowermost transplas panel of the *Rock Possum*'s cockpit. The canopy window itself was largely missing, with only a few shards in the corners to indicate it ever existed at all. Indeed, of the seven distinct openings reserved for the control module's polarized windowpanes, only three of the smallest remained intact; the rest were shattered, exposing the seats and controls within to the elements.

When Tibor Mitternacht led Alahni back to the wreck, he explained to the young Jardinian woman that it was what Brooke meant for them to find. Having driven the machine to this point only days ago—before falling to a combination of Manei Domini cyborgs and a Wayward EMP mine—she would have been most familiar with its route and general position relative to the surrounding terrain features. By her estimates, Tibor realized, the fallen WorkMech would make a decent "midpoint" between wherever she was driving her stolen BattleMech, and where she'd originally left Tibor and Alahni to wait for her.

Although part of Tibor silently hoped to find something worth salvaging at the wreck site, he told Alahni that Brooke was using it as a rendezvous point.

What struck him first when they arrived was how thoroughly "cleaned up" the site was. He could easily make out several tracks in the area. Most were made by human footwear, but there was no shortage of *tabiranth* paw prints either; telltales from the Wanderer hunting party that had saved—then captured—him and Brooke. But gone were any Manei Domini bodies he half expected to find there.

"Our hunters would take any weapons, electronics, and other technological equipment they could carry," Alahni explained, "but a whole 'Mech would be rather conspicuous."

"Would they have taken the cyborgs' bodies?" Tibor asked, incredulously.

"No," she answered after a few moments' thought. "Some of their modifications can be useful, but the Guardians always recover their own."

"Yet they left Digger One..."

"Your WorkMech?"

"Yes."

"They likely felt it was useless. The Guardians have left many old machines out to decay, most in open areas, like Sentinel Valley and the Open Plains..."

"The Word of Blake *abandoning* tech?" Tibor chewed on that thought for a few moments, ignoring the scowl that flashed across Alahni's face.

"*Useless* tech," she stressed. "Like your 'Digger One'. They have far superior equipment in Hope, and in storehouses elsewhere, both here and among the others of The Five."

"Makes sense enough, I suppose," Tibor conceded as he gave the 'Mech another cursory examination. "Leave the junk out to rust in the open, and any curious prospectors who get close enough will naturally see it as forgotten wreckage. Exactly the kind of stuff you'd expect to see on a world that was bombed to death in the First War..."

With that, he began to climb up into the *Rock Possum*'s cockpit. But no sooner had he reached out to grab part of the bent canopy supports and started to hoist himself up a step, when a high-pitched chittering pierced the air, and he suddenly found himself swarmed by a flock of tiny, winged creatures. The storm of blue and green alien feathers passed quickly, but not before he'd lost his grip and fallen back-first onto the forest floor.

He was halfway into a curse when he heard something he genuinely did not expect:

Alahni's laughter...

EXPLORER-CLASS JUMPSHIP *SACAJAWEA*
PIRATE JUMP POINT
JARDINE (HERAKLEION) SYSTEM
FREE WORLDS LEAGUE

"*DropShuttle* Magellan *to* Sacajawea... *Guys, it's Brook... We're still here... Trying to repair the ship... We think we'll be able to... When we're ready, we'll try to sig... But fuel is limited... We'll need telem... Not send anyone else! I repeat: do not... Still unsafe...*"

The message ended with a *chirp* just as Lawrence Pohl, captain of the independent JumpShip *Sacajawea*, heard the bridge hatch close behind him. He half-turned away from the communications station to see its normal occupant, Gretchen Morden, floating toward him. In her left hand was a squeeze thermos undoubtedly filled with almost as much dissolved sugar and cream as hot coffee.

Gretchen's cool brown eyes met the older man's ice-blue gaze, and she gave him a short nod. Lawrence was already pushing himself out of her way, allowing her to reclaim what had become her favorite chair over all these years. Still, he hung onto one of the crash rails along the console's right side, anchoring himself to the station for the time being.

"How long have you been reviewing that same message now?" Gretchen asked while she reached for the chair. As she settled herself in, she locked her thermos into its usual cradle—a worn (and somewhat stained) adjustable cup-holder along the console's left side.

"A while," Lawrence admitted. "It's just nagging at me."

"Yeah, me too. But I don't think listening to it again and again is really going to help get that out of your head."

"Maybe," Lawrence agreed. "Just wish I could put my finger on whatever it is that makes the message sound so odd."

"Well," Gretchen began. "There's the fact that she broadcasted that in the clear after saying she was attacked by hostile aerospace..."

"Which could just be a calculated risk."

"Or the fact she named our JumpShip on the same open frequency…"

"Hmmm…"

"Or that she added 'Guys, it's Brooke,' like we could somehow *not* know that…"

"You've been thinking about this a lot, haven't you?"

Gretchen shrugged. "That was really all I had. But it's not like these are things we'd *never* seen her do if she was rattled."

"And getting shot down over a supposedly dead world *is* a bit rattling," Lawrence conceded.

"I almost wonder what would happen if we answered her, really."

"You mean, apart from possibly giving our position away to whoever else might be listening—besides Hara, that is?"

"Sure," Gretchen said as a sly, knowing grin suddenly spread across her face, "if we broadcast on open channels."

Without breaking eye contact with her contact, she leaned back in her chair, grabbed her thermos, and squirted a shot of coffee into her mouth.

"We're a good fifteen Units out from the primary here, Gretch," he told her. "There's no way we can laser-beam at this range."

Gretchen's smile faded into a look of disappointment. "Of course not! But, we can send messages on channels *other* than those approved by the merchants' playbook and IE, you know."

Lawrence stared at her for a moment more before the final pieces locked into place in his mind. It was *still* risky, especially if the bad guys really *were* the folks that everyone now suspected them to be.

But it was *something*.

"Alright," Lawrence said, finally. "That gets a message to *them*, presuming nothing's happened to Trouble. But that comm implant of his just isn't strong enough to get a signal this far."

"True," Gretchen said with a nod, "*but* it's not too weak for us to not detect that he's sending a signal."

"How so? You mean, like a 'ping'?"

Gretchen nodded again. "Just about everything in this system aside from those ancient buoys seems to be running under EMCON conditions, so any spike on Tibor's channel—

however small—should show up if we're focused enough to hear it. We'll need to rig up a better detector for the job, though. If this tug of ours hadn't been modified by someone's grand-folks, we'd have a radio telescope or three handy and ready to go, but I think we can whip something up using some parts and gear we have around the ship. There's some reflective parachutes and tarps in storage, which can be used to make a receiver dish. And a few of those portable radar sensors we have could be put together as a focal point. With a little liquid helium drawn from the core—"

"You really *have* been thinking this through!"

"It's either this or rely on prayer that they have reliable access to a radio. But since we're *both* uneasy with the message we already got that way, that's a bridge too far for my tastes."

Lawrence let out a heavy sigh. It was a long shot, but it was better than just...waiting.

"Okay," he said at last. "Let's do this. How long do you think it'll take to set up?"

"I'll grab some of the others to help out. Figure we should have something together in...maybe an hour or so?"

"Alright, then. If nothing else, it gives us something to do."

"Think *positive*, Cap!" Gretchen chided, offering a thin smile.

"Didn't you just say you weren't prepared to rely on prayer?"

"That's why I'm relying on myself," she answered with a wink and another swig from her thermos. "But I do have one more question for you: Do you think we should tell our shadows about any of this?"

Lawrence looked up and stared into the space beyond one of the armored viewports ringing the *Sacajawea*'s bridge module. Somewhere out there—eight standard astronomical units away—lurked the JumpShip and DropShip that carried Anton Hara and the liaison Interstellar Expeditions had assigned to watch over him. Hara was the blustering type, who rubbed everyone the wrong way from the moment he and his ship inserted themselves into this mission.

But Hara's fighter jocks *had* helped cover the escape from Shasta, at no small risk to themselves. And, of course, were it not for the information Brooke managed to get from his IE liaison, they wouldn't have been able to get this far to begin with. Lawrence harbored little doubt that Hara and his crew had picked up the same signal that was now giving him and Gretchen such pause, but he was absolutely *positive* they were having none of the same gut reactions.

It would be common courtesy to let Hara's team know the *Sacajawea* was now working on a plan to try and verify the call's legitimacy...

And yet, Lawrence could not bring himself to fully trust them.

His decision made, Lawrence looked back to Gretchen and shook his head.

Gretchen smirked. "Yeah," she said. "I didn't think so, either."

FOREST OF SHROUDS
JARDINE (HERAKLEION) SYSTEM
FREE WORLDS LEAGUE

Digger One was most definitely dead.

As the sun moved across the Jardinian sky, casting beams that lazily swept across the forest floor through gaps in the canopy above, Tibor had focused most of his attention on the fallen *Rock Possum*. Although its structure was completely intact, and much of the military-grade armor remained in place, its left leg actuators appeared to have been almost completely fused. Partially melted strands of myomer peeked out from blown joint housings, and sprung tension governors jammed themselves awkwardly into the gaps, locking the knee, ankle, and hip joints in place. Tibor recognized a replacements-only job when he saw one; even if the ProspectorMech could have been restarted, it would be so terribly hobbled that foot travel would be far safer.

Of course, the leg damage was just one of many issues that had killed Digger One. After quickly realizing Alahni also had some degree of technical knowledge—she'd found the hip joint failure before he even noticed it—Tibor had her check several other systems while he tried to diagnose the fuel cell engine. Given the lack of proper tools to open the maintenance housings, it took some doing, but he eventually managed to get a good enough look to see that the main hydrogen cells had ruptured. If the power plant had any juice left at all, it was stored in the engine's limited back-up capacitors—which would only be good enough to turn on its searchlight (were it not already shattered), or run the cockpit life-support systems for half an hour (at best).

Meanwhile, Alahni had nudged aside the bird nest Tibor accidentally disturbed in the cockpit so that she could get a look at the control panels. (She refused to toss the nest out entirely as he'd suggested, saying that there were several unhatched "turqueet" eggs in it, and she didn't want to see them abandoned by their "flock litter.") She confirmed that several panels were completely dead or fried, including the sensor board and the all-important DI monitor.

"The comm panel looks good!" she exclaimed at one point, while the two of them were resting in the hulk's shadow.

"Great," Tibor responded sarcastically. "No engine, minimal control systems, and a busted leg...but there ain't nothin' wrong with the radio."

"Perhaps you could call your friends in space?" she asked. "That's where you're trying to go, isn't it?"

Tibor shook his head. There were so many things wrong with that suggestion, but he decided on humoring rather than humiliating her; he didn't want to risk upsetting her all over again.

"They're so far out-system it would be hours before they heard it," he said, "if they heard it at all. Then, it'd take about two weeks for a shuttle to reach us if they sent one. At which point your Guardians would undoubtedly shoot them down just like they did us. That'd, of course, be long after they also detected our outgoing signal and came for us here."

"Then what was *your* plan to leave this place?"

Tibor sighed. There weren't many *good* options, under the circumstances. "Well," he began, "the long and the short of it is basically sneaking aboard one of the Guardians' outbound DropShips. The stowaway approach."

Alahni seemed intrigued. "And hope you don't get caught? How would that take you where you need to go?"

"That's always risky. See, out in the Inner Sphere, where merchant traffic is common, and a lot of JumpShips pull double-duty as military and civilian transport, a stowaway can potentially climb aboard an outbound ship and stay hidden for the ride in some cargo bay or maintenance area—give or take some rather bumpy moments and enough food, drink, and erm, waste disposal to pull it all off undetected. Then, when the DropShip links up with a Jumper, they slip through the dock whenever they can, and either ride that JumpShip to its next destination, or get to another DropShip that's headed toward a safe port.

"A lot of refugees and outlaws do it. Many get caught, especially when boarding military ships, but you'd be surprised how many don't."

"That sounds...*incredibly* dangerous!"

"It is," Tibor conceded. "But when the alternative is staying on a world where you're marked for death, with no ride of your own that can run an armed blockade, it's about the best anyone can do. The alternative is to live out one's days in the wilderness."

Alahni's voice became sad again. "Like my people did..."

Tibor looked at her and frowned. He put a hand on her shoulder in as reassuring a way as he could, but steeled himself for another grief-stricken outburst. "Alahni," he said softly, "to your people, Jardine was—*is* home. You clearly love this world. You didn't seek to escape it..."

"No," she agreed sadly. "We just sought a life outside of the city."

Tibor found nothing he could say that he already hadn't repeated several times before. He gave her shoulder a squeeze and then let go, turning away for her to stare off into the darkening woods. How long had they been there now? It felt like the better half of a day had passed, with still no sign of Brooke.

And he really didn't like that.

Tibor closed his eyes and inhaled deeply, drawing in a mix of natural, earthy air, and the lingering scent of spilled coolant and burned electronics. At the sound of a flutter, he looked up to find one of those "*turqueets*" returning to the broken cockpit. The strange bird, which seemed to have two sets of tail feathers almost as large as its wings, was a striking shade of blue-green that he imagined lent to its native name, but its eyes—or perhaps just the flesh and feathers immediately around its eyes—looked bright red. The tiny creature perched on the cockpit frame, and blinked at him repeatedly as it continuously tilted its head from side to side.

He released a soft sigh, trying not to startle the bird. After a few moments, the animal evidently decided the two humans below were no threat and hopped into the cockpit, disappearing from sight.

"What will *you* do now?" he asked, softly.

The question seemed to snap Alahni out of whatever deep thoughts had gripped her. She refused to meet his gaze, or even look in his direction. Instead, she stared out into the forest. "I don't know..."

"Would the city be safe for you?"

Alahni shook her head.

"Are there any more Wayward settlements around here?"

"Maybe..."

Tibor paused. Not sure if he wanted to suggest what now came to his mind.

"I don't know," Alahni weakly repeated.

"Do you want to..." Tibor began, but trailed off. Leaves were rustling somewhere nearby. He looked around quickly, closing his real eye and focusing his attention on what the implant saw. A blurry image of reality, painted mostly in dark greens and blues, appeared against a mostly-black backdrop. Heat sources—most of them tiny—appeared among the trees, and some small forms appeared to be crawling among the brush in the distance.

But nothing that appeared to be human. Not from where Tibor was sitting anyway.

"Want to what?" Alahni asked, her voice still weak.

"Um," he answered uncertainly. "I mean, have you considered, maybe, leaving *with* us?"

Alahni blinked. Suddenly, she was looking back at him, her expression confused. "Wha—?" she began.

But then they both heard it: the snap of a dry tree branch, from somewhere behind the dead 'Mech's outstretched leg...

...Accompanied by a curse, muttered by a female voice. In German.

Tibor bolted to his feet. Alahni rose quickly behind him. The turqueet inside the cockpit bolted into the sky with a high-pitched twittering.

"Brooke...?" Tibor called out in a low voice.

Limping into view from around Digger One's foot, her athletic figure covered in scratches and smears of dirt, her long, auburn hair a tangled mess, Brooklyn Stevens came into view. Her underwear, stained a deep red with blood Tibor hoped came from someone else, covered her modesty, and her hiking boots were intact, but her arms crossed over her chest, holding in place what seemed to be the tattered remnants of her sports bra.

She looked up at both of them and offered a weak smile, before finally fixing her gaze on Tibor. "*Please* tell me you still have my clothes..."

BENEATH LAUNCH PLATFORM A7
CITY OF HOPE
JARDINE (HERAKLEION)
FREE WORLDS LEAGUE

The reinforced chambers beneath the City of Hope's spaceport were designed and built using the same techniques Star League engineers had used to construct their infamous Castles Brian. As such, they were—at least theoretically—immune to the detonation of all but the heaviest strategic nuclear weapons widely available in their day. This was a particularly wise choice, given the fact that Hope was established perilously close to an immense, but largely dormant, super-volcano.

The subterranean magma chamber closest to the surface was identified early in the planet's colonial period, but was initially classified as stable. Stable, that was, until a low-grade earthquake in the area spontaneously transformed a 3,000-square kilometer expanse of forest into a desolate geyser field a mere fifty years later.

Rather than relocate the settlements already established in the area, the colonists opted to harness the hotspot, and built the planet's first large-scale geothermal power plant. The centuries since saw many of the earlier enclaves damaged by periodic earthquakes, until—by the mid-2600s—the locals ultimately undertook a massive project to consolidate most of the regional towns and cities into the high-tech metropolis now known as Hope. Benefiting from the latest in Star League mega-engineering techniques, every building, road, and bridge in Hope was safe, clean, and tremor-resistant.

The now abandoned cities, located mostly to the north and east of Hope, eventually vanished as the forest rapidly reclaimed the land. This not only left Hope free to harness virtually all output from the nearby geothermal power plants, but also established the city as the *only* major population center within a hundred kilometers of the sleeping caldera.

These factors made the city a natural focus for ComStar's eventual stewardship over Jardine after the Star League's demise. Built with the integrity of a fortress, powered by non-nuclear means so close to a natural heat source, with an ample water supply amid fertile lands, surrounded by other ruins, and isolated from the more densely populated areas that always became targets on so many worlds in their day—it was contained, defensible, and easily overlooked.

And so, when Jardine itself was excised from the maps of history, the city that would become Hope rose as the only settlement on the planet worth saving. As the First Succession War raged, secret teams of engineers, scientists, and troops—all sent by the Sainted Jerome Blake himself!—built on the work started generations before, adding hidden facilities, defensive bunkers, and even an entire subterranean spaceport.

It was in the vast underground chambers of this spaceport that Poltergeist Precentor Sigma Damien Lucille now stood, surveying the final preparations for his latest mission.

The hood of his white robe was drawn back, exposing his face and black-stubbled scalp. The subcutaneous filaments of his direct neural interface implants etched symmetrical rows that mimicked the furrows of a freshly planted cornfield, sketching an almost stylized mimicry of a hairline that began in a neat line from his forehead to his temples, then streaked backward, over his ears, before uniting at a circular metal nexus at the back of his skull. To an untrained eye, they looked almost like faded tattoos, but in fact they were the very latest in vehicular control implants, the likes of which the Clans dabbled in, and which the Federated Suns had once tried—and failed—to develop fully.

Also exposed, by virtue of his pulled-back sleeves, were the metal and plastic prosthetics that replaced his original, frail arms. These too were state of the art, even though they eschewed the cosmetic modeling and synthflesh that could make them pass for the real thing. Built for the battlefield, Lucille's true hands each featured retractable claws that could rend flesh and scale the armored skin of a BattleMech with equal efficiency, while his true forearms each concealed extending vibroblades—for what he occasionally liked to call "extra emphasis."

Blake willing, he would be able to *use* them soon enough.

As Lucille watched in silence, the launch bay techs and acolytes guided a high-capacity lifting hoist to the K-1 DropShuttle that would soon be his ride into space unknown. The small craft had already been loaded with two complete six-man sets of battlesuits—one for each of the boarding teams he was to command in this operation. To conserve its limited fuel, it was now being placed on board the *Union*-class DropShip *Hera's Shield*, a 3,600-ton assault vessel that looked like a stubby, iron-skinned, age-worn techno-mushroom. He and his team would launch the shuttle from the *Shield*'s bay as soon as they cleared the atmosphere, after which the DropShip would make a few "frantic" orbits around Jardine before rushing off to "pursue" them. This little modification to the original plan would give his shuttle more of a "realistic" head start, he felt.

His gaze drifted to the distance beyond the large underground bay, where shadows enveloped the gigantic cubicles reserved for other large DropShips. From his vantage point so close to *Hera's Shield*, where banks of bright, wall-mounted spotlights bathed him, the work crews, and the ship in a blue-white glow, the rest of the underground complex was all but invisible. Yet he could still make out the ovoid hulls of at least three more *Union*-class DropShips, each stowed in its own open-framed hangar of reinforced ferrocrete pylons and heavy, multi-level gantries. Beyond those, however, he noticed that one more bay was lit; another DropShip—this one a newer *Merlin*—was being serviced or prepped for launch.

He was distracted from his thoughts by the approach of a young, dark-skinned brunette in plain light-gray overalls. Technical Adept Tin carried her noteputer as if it was some kind of prize, but presented it to Lucille with a curt—almost banal—remark: "Your final inventory, Precentor."

Lucille took the device and tapped the side to light its screen. His eyes scanned the display without expression, taking in the manifest. Most of it was mundane; field rations, fuel cell-powered recharger units, emergency back-up batteries, tool kits, med kits, and so forth—all the basics for operating a twelve-man team in the field for up to three weeks. Then, of course, were the battlesuits: all twelve certified for vacuum operations, including optional equipment that could swap out the Longinus suits' short-range missiles for extra maneuvering fuel.

But Lucille's jet-black eyes narrowed on the last line item, one he simply did not expect to see here at all: *"Type 1-Alpha 0.5 Kt Infantry-Portable Tactical Device – Qty: 6"*

Allowing himself no further reaction, Lucille took the notepad's stylus and signed on the indicated line, recognizing the payload that would now be his to command. He managed to maintain his stoic façade just long enough to thank Adept Tin, send her on her way, and make sure nobody else was within earshot, an effort that only grew more maddening as the seconds ticked by.

Only when he was reasonably certain none were left to hear him did he finally key the communicator socketed over his left wrist...

...So he could ask Precentor Apollyon exactly *why* he needed to carry six nuclear warheads into this battle!

FOREST OF SHROUDS
JARDINE (HERAKLEION) SYSTEM
FREE WORLDS LEAGUE

While being fully clothed again was a relief in and of itself—one at least half as pleasant as finding Tibor and Alahni again—

Brooke now felt as though her skin was crawling. Dozens of scratches and bruises vied for her attention, but Tibor's quick inspection assured her that nothing was "too broken." Still, her run through the forest had done her no real favors. Her legs ached, and she felt as though her body was covered in an oily grunge that was a mix of sweat, dirt, and Bast-only-knew *what* else. Combined with the occasional twig, leaf, or unidentifiable bug that still tumbled from her hair—even after she'd finally managed to tame it into a simple ponytail—she found herself longing for a scalding hot shower.

Preferably delivered by a power washer.

The awkward looks she was getting from Alahni and Tibor, combined with their apparent determination to stay at least three meters away from her at all times, told her she undoubtedly looked—and *smelled*—just as bad as she felt.

They remained in the shadow of Digger One for the moment. Tibor had already explained the old WorkMech was dead. At best, he could maybe broadcast a signal from its radio, but that would accomplish little more than drawing the cyborgs' attention. They'd found no weapons among the wreckage, either. Brooke would have been lying to herself if she said she hadn't hoped for *something* more when she'd sent them here.

"So, what's the plan?" Tibor finally asked. "I know the city's our best—and maybe *only*—hope for a ride out of here, but I seriously doubt we can convince the locals to let us in by pretending to be a pizza delivery service."

Alahni threw him a quizzical look. "'Pizza' delivery?"

Tibor responded with an expression that was a mix of mild surprise and pity. "I mean," he said, "it's not like we can just stroll into town and not expect to be shot, right?"

"These Manei Domini don't seem the type to skimp on security," Brooke agreed with a sigh. "Alahni, do you have any ideas?"

Alahni frowned and looked away. Brooke caught the concerned glance from Tibor that swung first from the girl and then back her way. During his earlier poke-and-prod inspection for broken bones and other trauma, Tibor had explained what happened between them after Brooke decided to play "Immortal Warrior" (as he put it). She knew about his struggle to try and keep Alahni from a complete breakdown at the realization that her entire tribe was most likely dead, "thanks to us" (again, as he put it). Brooke understood all this, and sympathized with the poor girl. Her blood *still* boiled with rage toward those Bast-damned "Guardians" and their needless cruelty.

But, as much as it pained her to admit that the girl's people would *certainly* still be alive had she and Tibor not come along, Brooke couldn't escape the fact that Alahni now represented perhaps their only real hope of getting off this planet in one piece.

Or her relief that, after everything else so far, that she was still *here*.

Tibor might have his doubts about the young Jardinian's willingness to help them any further, but something inside Brooke told her the girl was—and remained—a friend.

"The water lines," Alahni said quietly.

Brooke arched an eyebrow.

"Hope relies on the river," she went on without prompting. "For drinking water, irrigation, sanitation. Blake's Guardians improved the system over the years, maximized the flow-through to work as clean and efficiently as possible with no surface pumps or obvious signs of active technology. Like everything else, they wanted to make the city self-sufficient, while still looking abandoned to outsiders."

Alahni turned toward Brooke, finally meeting her gaze with those brown eyes she found so alluring. "Those newer lines are well maintained and well secured by the Guardians. Lots of filters and gates, and passages too small for people. But there remain a few older lines that date back to the times before the coming of Blake. Many were collapsed or shut off during the reconstruction, but a few remain intact. Mostly."

"Mostly?" Tibor repeated.

"Through the years, we Waywards have used these lines to sneak out of the city…or back in. But they're not maintained like the active lines. Most have a lot of debris in them. They're still big enough for people to swim through, but it can be tricky, especially with no light down there."

"Swim through?" Brooke felt her stomach tighten a little at the thought.

Alahni nodded. "Water from the river still fills these passages. There are air pockets here and there, I think, but it's the only way in or out of the city that the Guardians don't really seem to care about."

Brooke frowned and looked to Tibor.

Tibor matched her expression and added a shrug.

"Beggars can't be choosers," he said. "Alahni, do any of these passages lead to the spaceport? Or maybe an armory?"

The story keeper shook her head. "The only one I truly know about leads to the Overseers' Quarter. It's the part of the city where the most privileged of our people reside. The ones who work closest with the Guardians."

"That sounds...less than ideal."

"The Overseers are highly entrusted by the Guardians," Alahni explained. "They work as administrators for most of the city functions, and lead work teams when needed. They have access keys and pass codes that can let them travel more freely among restricted sections—"

"But they also sound like the types who'd turn us over to your Guardians the moment we showed up."

"Trouble's got a good point there, Alahni," Brooke cut in. "It sounds too risky."

Alahni's voice took on a slight edge as she focused on Brooke again. "Try to remember, Doctor Stevens, that for years—*generations*—before you two came along, the Guardians tolerated the existence of Wayward communities. Many of us were allowed to simply walk openly into the forests, so long as we all lived as secretly as do the people of Hope. It was a humane policy; we were *never* slaves to the Guardians, but we couldn't leave the system for fear of revealing our kin to the Lost. So, they allowed those of us who chafed under the more restricted rules of the city to simply leave, and—as *you* put it, Mister Tibor—'let nature take its course.'"

Brooke saw Tibor open his mouth, but whatever retort he had in mind was silenced when Alahni quickly held a quieting hand up toward him.

"My *point*," she continued, "is that we of the Wayward tribes were never seen as enemies of our city-dwelling kin. Truly, it was actually the Overseers who helped us leave the city most of the time, getting us out with the least amount of disturbance, even giving directions to nearby camps. Some even trade with the tribes."

"All without their Guardians' knowledge?" Brooke asked.

Alahni shrugged. "If the Guardians know, they never did anything about it."

"Meaning this *could* be an 'open secret,'" Tibor muttered. "They could know and just allow it to happen as long as it doesn't pose an actual threat."

Alahni's impatient sigh oddly reminded Brooke of how Marie used to act whenever she and Tibor got into their periodic spats.

We could second guess ourselves about this forever!

"Unless you have a better plan, Trouble," she said. "Like you said, 'beggars...'"

Brooke suddenly noticed Tibor's head was tilting awkwardly, his real eye appearing as glazed as its artificial companion. He held a hand up toward her absently, then raised a finger to his lips. Picking up on the abrupt silence, Alahni's gaze alternated between the two off-worlders, her expression growing increasingly concerned by the second.

"Why, that clever little minx!" Tibor finally exclaimed.

"Who—?" Brooke started, but Tibor was still holding a hand up for silence, his expression still blank, listening to something she now suspected was in his own head.

But who could be signaling him on his implant frequency?

After a few more seconds, Tibor shook his head, blinked, and looked back at Brooke as if he'd just awakened from a particularly interesting dream. "You're not going to believe this," he said, "but I just got a call...from the *Sac!*"

CHAPTER 5

"When you get down to it, it's pretty much impossible to sneak around in space these days. Most DropShips, JumpShips, and even shuttles have the means to intercept and identify any type of radio signal and track it back to its source. And sensors can detect the plasma exhaust of your ship from hours—even days—away at best speeds. Sure, your chances are better if everyone's trying to run silent and you're coasting more than you're burning, but even then, you're still just gambling that nobody is paying attention when you do something.

At greater distances, it can get even more ridiculous. With so many cues to go on, your ship class and acceleration profiles can be pegged from so far away that some pretty simple math can guess where you're going, and when you'll get there long before you do. At that point, intercept strategies can be formed, reinforcements can be called to action, and what started as a stealth job can end up as a sorrowful note home to your next of kin (if you're lucky)!

All of this is why a lot of covert missions rely on indirect travel or long-range pre-ops. Sleepers can spend months, or even years, living among the populace of a planet that might never be targeted for spies, but just happens to lie along a routine trade route to someplace of more importance. When time's not on your side, stowing away on ships is another option, but comes with its own obvious risks. And sometimes, another is to basically toss something juicy at the enemy guards in the hope they'll *take the bait and be too busy looking another way when you do whatever it is you came to do.*

That last option in particular is a bit of a dick move, of course, especially if your "decoy" happens to be an innocent bystander—or worse, a friend."

—TIBOR MITTERNACHT
AS QUOTED IN *"CHANGING THE OBJECTIVES (PART 2)"*
(WARRIOR DIGITAL PRODUCTIONS, SOLARIS VII, JUNE 3061)

THE SANCTORUM
CITY OF HOPE
JARDINE (HERAKLEION)
FREE WORLDS LEAGUE
3 NOVEMBER 3067

The rumble of the DropShip's engines could be felt in the floor and walls of the Sanctorum, even though its launch platform was more than half a kilometer distant.

From his vantage point, by the north window, Precentor Apollyon could see the bone white *Union* rising majestically toward the heavens on a column of yellow-gold plasma. His eyes—true and frail alike—tracked the great vessel's skyward journey for close to a minute.

Enough time for him to utter a quick prayer.

"May the spirit of Blake smile upon those warriors, and may Fate favor them with victory in his name," he intoned. *For if they fail,* he mentally added, *our very home may pay the price.*

"Blessed be those who walk in Blake's Divine Light," came the solemn reply, spoken by the man behind him.

"Blessed be," Apollyon acknowledged.

Turning away from the window, he found Ogima Lunalla had not moved since his arrival. The chief administrator for the City of Hope was not one of the Master's Hands. He was not even a soldier. But, to Apollyon, he was still a brother, a fellow son of Jardine.

They stood in Ogima's office, rather than his own. Apollyon felt the news he had to convey was best delivered in person, and he was not going to add insult to their injury by making this innocent soul come to him. Compared to Apollyon's personal chamber, Ogima's was luxurious, with blackwood paneling covering its ferrocrete walls, a textured ceiling, and two tinted glass windows compared to Apollyon's one. Paintings, all produced by local artists, adorned three of its four walls—the largest, of course, being a rendition of the sainted Jerome Blake so reverent that the ComStar founder looked positively messianic. Native broadleaf ferns, kept in tall planters of polished marble, occupied the corners behind the administrator's handmade blackwood desk. Three black, synthleather chairs were present in the office, but all of them—including Ogima's own—stood unoccupied at present. Ogima's personal workstation was also disengaged at the moment, its flat-projection monitor blacked out, since the man had switched it off as he rose to greet his unexpected visitor.

Ogima wore a simple, light brown robe over a set of khaki coveralls, unadorned with any form of decoration or insignia. Here on Jardine, formal attire outside of the military was rare; the locals prided themselves more on their works than their appearance, and Ogima himself rose from among the ranks of the Technical Guild. He was no stranger to getting his hands dirty—just not in the same manner as those of the Guardians and the Manei Domini.

In his hand was a slate gray compad. Though the device's screen was lit brightly enough to cast a slight white glow across his face, Ogima's eyes appeared to have glazed over. The moment did not last; sensing somehow that Apollyon's attention had turned his way, the city administrator blinked and turned to meet his gaze, his posture stiffening at the same time.

Apollyon favored him with a slight nod.

"I feel as you do," he admitted, in tones as sympathetic as they were foreboding. "They were still kin to us, even if they *were* Wayward. It pained me greatly to order their destruction."

"But the Lost," Ogima said, sadly. "They escaped?"

"Precentor Lucille and his team were unable to locate the invaders. Presuming them killed in the fighting would be unforgivable in the absence of evidence. Reclamation teams will be sent into the woods shortly, to comb for stragglers; until then, our secret—and the Promise—remain in danger."

Ogima hesitated a few long moments before he finally placed the compad down and nodded. "I understand."

"Then you must also understand what I must say next," Apollyon told him. "These invaders have forced us to take extreme measures. We cannot risk allowing the Lost to taint our world, not even now, with the Third Transfer so near at hand. Not while the Clan corruption lies so close to their hearts.

"And so, while Lucille attempts to neutralize their compatriots in space, I must ask you to prepare for the cleansing of our own house..."

Ogima's eyes again seemed to glaze over again for a time, only to snap back into focus as the realization dawned on him. "The city?" he whispered. "You believe the Lost will come *here*?"

"Almost certainly. And it is imperative that they do not, or that they are captured and surrendered to my soldiers if they somehow manage to do so."

Ogima bowed his head solemnly. "I understand, my Precentor."

As the words hung in the air, Apollyon considered blinking his true eye into infrared mode without activating its usual crimson glow. That way, he could study Ogima's thermal reactions, gauge whatever emotional struggle the man might have as the implications set in.

But he held himself back. It was one thing to peek at the hidden emotions of a captured Wayward whose tribe had already broken the Promise. It was quite another to presume guilt from a child of the City of Hope.

"Do you, my friend?" he asked instead. "I am aware, as you are, that some of Hope's children sympathize with the Waywards. Like you, I was willing to overlook it; they are, after all, kin to both of us. But the Wayward have always been more susceptible to the influence of the Lost.

"Ogima, we stand now on the eve of the Third Transfer— the time of our Great Promise—and we have been infiltrated from without. At this critical juncture, I fear what decisions the Master might be forced to make, if word of our work here reaches the wrong ears."

Ogima's eyes rose to meet those of Jardine's most powerful resident, the first of those rebuilt in the Master's image, for a crusade meant to save mankind itself from madness by fighting its savagery with even greater savagery. In years gone by, he had felt perfectly at ease with this man, his brother and countryman. But now, he felt only an unresolved mixture of dread, sorrow, and desperate hope.

Shoving aside the sorrow, and driven by the dread, Ogima clung to that hope as he held Apollyon's gaze.

"I promise you, Great Guardian of Blake," he said firmly. "I promise you that I shall personally relay your orders to the people, and make them understand this grave danger. If the intruders come here, we will find them, and they will pay for the pain they have caused our world."

**BENEATH THE CITY OF HOPE
JARDINE (HERAKLEION)
FREE WORLDS LEAGUE**

The water was dark and cold, but the thermal sensor replacing Tibor Mitternacht's left eye kept him more or less glued to Brooke's tail. Well, that and the improvised lifeline made from former WorkMech power cables, which now tied the three fugitives together. Still, in the silence and shadows, he felt alone and isolated just enough to notice the accumulated pain from all the injuries and exertion he'd sustained over the last few days on Jardine. These combined aches tortured him with every move through the narrow confines of Hope's ancient water mains, adding painful difficulty to the already arduous task of avoiding the wreckage and false turns created by centuries of neglect and the incidental damage of later renovations.

Holding his breath against every impulse to cry out, of course, was just the final insult on top of it all. How Brooke was handling all this in her condition—while completely blind to boot—Tibor could only guess.

It had been a long swim, but fortunately one with enough breathing points to avoid drowning. Alahni seemed a little unsure of their course, reminding them at each pause that it had been some time since she had navigated these tunnels. Twice now, she had promised that they were "almost there," or that they had "one more to go," At the last pocket of air, though, she warned them: "This will be a long dive; get as much air as you can."

She was definitely right this time. By Tibor's estimate, they'd already been under for close to a minute.

It now felt like they were inside a broad sewage line, but one that was particularly compromised. In the inky blackness, Tibor's hands had struck large hunks of what felt like stone or collapsed masonry. But the real trouble began when his body brushed against something sharp.

Whatever it was, it raked him all along his left side, starting just below his shoulder blade, then tearing along his rib cage as he tried to twist away from it. The pain was intense, and he gasped through grinding teeth.

And that was when the choking began. Losing what little air was left in his lungs, Tibor struggled—and failed—to keep himself from coughing underwater. As panic and adrenaline took over, he began to thrash; there wasn't even time to think about what was happening.

Suddenly, a hand slashed down and seized him by the collar of his shirt, yanking him upward.

He broke the surface in a frenzy, desperately flailing in the darkness while trying to cough, inhale, and vomit water all at the same time. The rational part of his brain quickly recognized that he was out of danger, but his body still had a multitude of involuntary actions to work through as it caught up. Someone—Brooke—was talking to him, her voice low and intense, worried. He didn't get the words, but knew the intent.

Through all the coughing and gagging, he managed to croak out a reply. "—I'm okay."

Eventually regaining control, Tibor managed to take stock of the situation. Whatever had caught him underwater, it left little more than a deep scratch. He now found himself with the others in what seemed to be a narrow, horizontal tunnel of formed cement, its walls slick with mildew and God-knew-what-else. The air here was dank, reeking of stale, tainted water.

"It'll be a miracle if we don't catch something from all this, though," he grumbled.

He felt a gentle tug on his lifeline; Brooke, silently urging him to follow her as they started moving again.

"It's here someplace," Alahni whispered. "Hold on... There!"

Tibor saw Alahni's heat aura begin to rise, reaching up for something he could not make out on thermals. His line tugged again as Brooke moved to follow.

"Going up, Trouble," she muttered.

"Thank Christ!" he hissed. "Don't think my lungs can take much more of this!"

They were following a set of metal rungs that felt cold and rusty to Tibor's hands, ascending through a vertical shaft. Idly, he pondered its function; a sewer line would have a grate of some kind that would let fluids, small debris, and light through. But he saw no light above them. Just the thermal images of Brooke and Alahni—all legs and butts, covered in soaking wet clothes.

And that was the moment some embarrassingly primal part of Tibor's brain *really* wished there was some actual damned light in here.

Then he saw a small hand moving about in the distance; Alahni was searching again. He saw her fingers grasping, then heard the sound of metal grinding on metal. The Jardinian grunted, fighting the mechanism with as much strength as she could manage one-handed. More metal on metal. Flecks of something—corroded metals and bits of concrete, perhaps— dropped past, bouncing off his shoulders like a shower of pebbles.

And suddenly, there *was* light—precious little of it, but definitely light!—as Alahni won her battle with the hatch above and shoved it away. A shiver ran through Tibor that could have been caused as much by the chill of fresh air flowing past him as it could the elation of knowing their journey back to the surface was finally near its end.

Either way, he embraced it, and let that sensation power him on for the last few rungs of their climb.

They emerged in a cell-like chamber that stank of age, mildew, and rot—but at least it was relatively free from stagnant water. An ancient LED lamp in the ceiling, its diffuser painted a deep, brownish-yellow by stains likely older than the three of them put together, provided the weak source of light that made anything visible. Tibor saw two old metal hatches on opposite sides of the room.

"Where are we now?" Brooke asked in a low voice.

"Almost there," Alahni told her as she fumbled at the knots to her lifeline. She then reached out for Brooke's end of line and began tugging at its knots for a moment before Brooke seemed to figure out what was happening and began to work with her.

As he finally began to undo his own knots, Tibor felt the line go slack. Glancing up at Brooke, he cleared his throat loudly when he noticed she'd somehow forgotten to let go of the girl's hand.

If Alahni was at all embarrassed, she hid it well as her attention bounced between the room's two door hatches. Still, it took her a few moments to decide which one to open. After all the twists and turns of their swim through the ancient drainage lines, Tibor had given up trying to figure out which way was north, and he doubted their guide was any better off by this point.

The latch Alahni grabbed was ancient and heavily corroded. She grunted as she tried to force it, the muscles in her arms and back clearly straining through the drenched fabric of her top. Brooke took a step toward her, but Tibor moved more quickly. Together, they managed to break open the rusty seal, but it still took extra effort to force the door itself to open, its hinges loudly protesting as only decaying metal on decaying metal could.

Dim light streaked into the chamber beyond, partially illuminating what looked like a service access no wider than a child's closet. Scattered about the floor, Tibor could just make out bits of ancient, unidentifiable debris, and the decayed remains of what he could only presume were Jardinian vermin.

"Oh, this is promising," he muttered.

Alahni shrugged weakly as she stepped into the passage. Tibor followed, leaving Brooke to follow him for a change. He could almost feel her glare on the back of his head.

"I think this is an old service line," Alahni whispered as they walked into a narrow corridor of ancient pipes and power conduits, all badly corroded, bent by age, and covered in dead roots and other decay. "It runs parallel to the old city water mains, under what is now the Overseers' Quarter. Some of the lines here are still active, used for city communications, residential power and such, but the main power grid, the one the factories, administration centers, and hospital facilities use, is a completely separate network that's better maintained."

"Fusion?" Tibor asked.

"No," Alahni said. "Geothermal. Hope stands near the outskirts of a truly large volcanic zone. It's mostly stable, but a lot of the land north and east of the city is covered in active geysers and hot springs. The early settlers decided to draw power from the subterranean magma chambers, and it's been that way since. Hope was reinforced in the early days of the Star League, and was one of the few cities left in this valley area when the others were abandoned during the Fall. The rest were in the eastern side of the zone, where the Menehune now rule."

"The Menehune?" Brooke asked. "Another Wayward Tribe?"

"No," Alahni told her with only a glance backward. In the near-complete darkness of the corridor, Tibor noticed, she was carefully guiding herself forward by lightly dragging her fingertips along the corridor's walls. "The Menehune aren't people. Just truly smart creatures who live on this world. Tricky little monkey-cats, you might say."

"Sounds cute," Brooke said.

"Interesting that we never saw any of those around here," Tibor said.

"Not precisely," Alahni said. "Most see them as pests these days, especially in Hope. Even Wayward hunters usually shoot them on sight, so they've learned to stay far from humans."

Suddenly, Alahni stopped and let out a huge sigh. In the minuscule light, Tibor almost couldn't see why, even as he peeked over her shoulder. Then he noticed the jagged darkness that turned the entire path ahead into pitch black.

"What is it?" Brooke asked.

"Cave in," he told her.

"Have I mentioned lately that I haven't been here since I was fifteen?" Alahni muttered to no one in particular.

She then excused herself as she squeezed past Tibor and Brooke, so she could lead them back the other way...

LEOPARD-CLASS DROPSHIP _KAYLIN_
PIRATE JUMP POINT
JARDINE (HERAKLEION) SYSTEM
FREE WORLDS LEAGUE

Jacoby was once again the man at the sensor console when the signal came in. A veteran of countless missions with Anton Hara, he knew his job well, and flew through the verification procedures without any unnecessary prompting. So, when he finally did turn his attention back to the captain, there was no question of what his nod meant.

Brooklyn Stevens' shuttlecraft, the _Magellan_, had just boosted from the atmosphere of Herakleion.

_No_, Hara reminded himself. _Not "Herakleion." Jardine!_

With its emergence came a desperate, somewhat broken, audio-only transmission from Stevens herself, requesting telemetry for the return flight. It was everything they'd been hoping for—although it _was_ odd that the _Sacajawea_ remained silent.

Hara had asked Jacoby to double-check the back logs, just to be sure. After all, given the sheer distances involved, it was at least vaguely possible for the _Sac_'s reply to have reached them at the same instant they picked up Stevens' initial plea.

But there had been nothing Jacoby could detect on any of the frequencies IE or Stevens had been known to use.

Meanwhile, Hara knew Stevens' shuttle had only so much fuel capacity for its return trip, especially if things were as desperate as the good doctor sounded. So, she couldn't just idle in orbit and wait for her JumpShip to acknowledge. She'd have to have boosted for deeper space, starting with a best guess on her out-system course to start with—something to refine when the _Sac_ responded. For her jump skipper to maintain EMCON even now made little sense.

Could they have simply missed the call, or were they just _that_ paranoid?

In either case, Hara made his decision with a simple nod to Jacoby. With a single finger tap on the man's console, a pre-recorded signal went out in a condensed, electronic burst—one that, Hara hoped, would light up whatever receivers in the solar system were even casually turned their way, from the *Sacajawea* to Jardine itself.

Settling back in his seat, Hara steepled his fingers and stared into the emptiness of space for a few silent moments.

"Jump charge?" he requested at last.

Jacoby checked his instruments. "Twenty-four-point-three percent."

Hara closed his eyes and did the rough calculations, rounding for simplicity. When he opened them again, he turned to his exec.

Lenard Bryce, for his part, was leaned forward in his chair, assuming the classic "Thinker's pose," complete with one hand supporting his chin. With only the barest of turns, the dark-skinned officer met his captain's stare, and arched an eyebrow.

"I come up with about thirty-six hours," Hara told him. "Half, if we redline it."

Bryce nodded, confirming the estimates. "But do we really want to push the redline?"

"Knowing Bellamy, he'd want the jump skipper to go past even that, but it gives us a window."

"Alright," Bryce sighed at the mention of IE's liaison, and pushed back in his seat. "Jacoby, give us two clocks. Eighteen hundred and thirty-six hundred."

"Aye," Jacoby responded. Swiveling his chair back around, he turned his attention to one of the substations beside his main console. On its attendant screen, two digital stopwatches popped up and began counting down. The first, in glowing yellow, began its count at "36:00:00", while the second started at "18:00:00" in searing red.

The same readouts appeared on multiple displays through-out the *Kaylin*'s bridge, including the small flip-down monitor anchored above the navigation table near the chamber's heart. Moments later, a chime accompanied text alerts that flashed on both Hara's and Bryce's armchair displays.

Neither man needed to review the alerts. At this stage, acknowledgment from the skipper of their *Scout*-class JumpShip, *Broken Knee*, was little more than a formality.

"Speaking of Bellamy," Bryce said, "should we let him know yet?"

"He'll figure it out soon enough," Hara replied. "Either way, the decision's out of our hands right now."

"And what about the *Sac*?"

Hara stared blankly into the space beyond the *Kaylin's* thick, armored windows. Somewhere out there hung Stevens' JumpShip—due for a rude surprise in about twenty minutes or so. "Fortunately for them, that decision's even out of Bellamy's hands now. Shooting up Jumpers is bad business, anyway."

UNION-CLASS DROPSHIP HERA'S SHIELD
HIGH ORBIT
JARDINE (HERAKLEION)
FREE WORLDS LEAGUE

"Doctor Stevens, this is DropShip Kaylin. *We and Sacajawea have received your message and are sending telemetry now. We are on station and able to scramble for advance intercept at your request. Please advise."*

Poltergeist Precentor Sigma Damien Lucille was still fascinated, in spite of himself, as the playback concluded for a second time. Although he was still awaiting confirmation from passive listening buoys spread across the system's asteroid belts, the preliminary data and the telemetry included with the audio-datapack message looked authentic. The sender—this DropShip *Kaylin*—was apparently floating eighteen AUs out-system, and perhaps only ten to twelve degrees above the solar plane.

As pirate points go, it wasn't really the kind of choice for a quick raid or even a full-on assault mission, but the position and distance was sufficient for the incoming jump pulse to escape easy detection. In that respect, it was kind of clever. But it also meant the intruders who came here likely had to coast for more than two weeks on their inbound flight, as much to conserve fuel for a return trip as to keep up their stealthy approach.

Of course, that didn't exactly work out so well for them, did it?

But what truly amazed Lucille was that *Kaylin* identified as a *Drop*Ship. If Stevens had a DropShip at her disposal, why did she take the riskier option of a shuttle? The difference in ship sizes and thrust plumes would not have lowered their detection profile enough to offset the relative security of a vessel with greater armor, fuel stores, and onboard support. The intruders had been nearly obliterated by the drones on approach, for Blake's sake; a DropShip would have been able to either weather that storm and land or immediately burn away for the safety of its crew at a fraction of the risk.

Perhaps the DropShip was used as a midway point, giving her a boost in velocity before launch and acting as a rendezvous point or fast reaction option just in case? That was possible, Lucille admitted, but if so, what was it doing transmitting from eighteen Units away, rather than holding station much closer to the planet, to better support its landing teams? If anything went wrong in planetary orbit, a distance so far away would put any type of rescue over a week away at best.

And if the telemetry matched what Lucille was beginning to suspect, that meant…

Lucille turned to the *Hera's Shield*'s comm officer, a short, pale-skinned, black-haired Acolyte who had yet to earn his first augmentations. The crewman responded to Lucille's attention with an arched eyebrow.

"Acknowledge that signal with text only," Lucille told him. "And give me a direct line to Precentor Apollyon. Our targets have multiplied."

BENEATH THE CITY OF HOPE
JARDINE (HERAKLEION)
FREE WORLDS LEAGUE

Brooke sensed they had doubled back at least one more time before taking the route they now found themselves following.

Although there were dim lights working here and there—powered, she presumed, by some bit of long-forgotten wiring still somehow connected to the city grid—most of this time was spent in darkness so complete even Tibor's thermal vision was barely useful. And so, they had all banged into, tripped over, or brushed against more mysterious obstructions than she cared to count.

Because of all this, Brooke knew they had entered a new area at last when they found themselves in a passage where the walls and floors of jutting debris became suddenly, conspicuously clear. Her hands—stretched out cautiously to either side—quickly discovered smooth surfaces, which her fingers lightly explored further. She felt seams, and differences in material from cool metal to dull plastics. In her mind, she pictured storage crates, stacked neatly along the walls.

"Supplies?" she asked in a whisper.

Ahead, she felt Alahni pause for a moment, perhaps long enough to discover the stacks for herself. When the younger woman finally answered, it came after what sounded like a small sigh of relief.

"Yes," she said in a low voice. "A secret stash, you could probably say. Even before there were Waywards, our ancestors stored food, medicines, equipment, and even some weapons down here. Things the Guardians preferred to ration otherwise. Some of these were found, but others were used by Waywards. Entire tribes were born, or survived, thanks to these caches. But when the Guardians began building strength about ten years ago, it was said that they rooted out most of what remained."

"Looks like they missed one," Tibor quipped from the shadows behind Brooke.

"No," Alahni said. "This one's newer. This means we're close. Come along."

Blindly, they continued further, following the wall of crates mostly by touch. Until, with little more than a thump and a muffled grunt, Brooke heard Alahni come to a hard stop.

But before she could say anything to the girl, she heard the scrape of what sounded like a metal latch being worked. Moments later, a seam of feeble light appeared, widening to reveal a passageway that cast an eerie glow through what

Brooke could now see was a narrow corridor lined with floor-to-ceiling stacks of assorted containers. Ahead, Alahni's silhouette peeked through the opening, and something approaching a smile appeared on what little of her face reflected the light.

"This is it," the Jardinian whispered. "Keep silent."

They entered what appeared to be little more than a storage closet that smelled of dust and mildew. An ancient but clearly abandoned sink was anchored to one wall by rusting fixtures, its control knobs and faucet removed, leaving behind only a basin of stained enamel that was now good for nothing more than a place where old rags and other debris accumulated. Metal shelves, built along the wall opposite the door they'd come through, buckled with the weight of cleaning supplies and other random junk so faded and dust-covered that their purpose could only be guessed at on a quick glance. The light in the room came from an old, uncovered fixture in the center of a cracked and flaking ceiling.

Looking back at the door behind them, Brooke noticed it was set behind a break in the wall's normal contour, and was painted and stained to match the rest of the scenery when closed. Cracks she could make out along the surrounding wall suggested the secret passage had probably been made using crude tools, but the result was good enough, she imagined, to fool a quick inspection.

Alahni headed toward the other door in the room, a heavy metal hatch that looked dented and corroded, and lacked any obvious handle or features beyond a panel of blackened glass. The young woman hesitated for a few seconds, her head turned just enough for Brooke to see her closed eyes and pensive expression. Her lips moved silently for a moment, when suddenly, whatever it was she was trying to recall must have come through. Nodding once to herself, she glanced back at Brooke and Tibor with the shadow of a smile before finally confronting the hatch with her full attention.

It was easy enough for Brooke to guess that the strange, irregular rhythm Alahni used when she rapped on the age-worn metal was some kind of code knock. But if it came from any kind of song or cadence, it wasn't any she had learned or heard before. She glanced back at Tibor and was met with little more than a blank expression and a weary shrug.

In fact, under this light, the man looked gaunt and sickly. His clothes hung awkwardly on his frame, clinging in some places, and drooping in others. His short, dark hair looked equally soaked and disheveled. But it was the play of shadows on his wiry physique, combined with the pallor of his ever-pale skin, that made him look only slightly better than a reanimated corpse.

All the same, Brooke imagined she would probably say the same about her own appearance right now, had there been a mirror around to confirm it.

Alahni repeated her knock twice more over the next five minutes, and was midway into her third repetition when the blackened glass panel suddenly snapped open, and a pair of dark eyes flashed their intense gaze at her and the others.

"*E imi i ka malamalama*," Alahni said to the eyes.

"*Ka malamalama imi oe*," a gruff, masculine voice answered.

With those words, the panel snapped shut and a series of loud clanks sounded from the other side of the hatch. The door opened to another room shrouded in shadow—but not nearly so darkened that Brooke failed to notice the three rifle muzzles leveled in her direction.

Nor did she miss the broadsword insignia of the Word of Blake that caught the light from the tunic of one of the weapons' holders.

As Alahni did before her, Brooke raised her hands slowly. From behind, Tibor let out a low, frustrated groan.

"Who are you?" a deep voice growled from the darkness. "Why have you come here?"

"I am Alahni," Alahni said, with no trace of hesitation or fear, "of the Shrouded Forest. We've come for help."

"And *them*?"

"Friends. From far away."

"Step through the door," the man said as the three rifles moved back, deeper into the shadows. "Slowly."

Alahni never lowered her hands, but made a gesture with one for the others to follow her as she walked through the hatch and moved slightly to the left. As Brooke joined her, she noticed they were in another storage room of some kind, albeit one that currently stored very little beyond its current occupants. Like the last room, it smelled of dust and neglect, and felt as cool and damp as an abandoned basement.

As her eyes quickly adjusted to the weak lighting, Brooke took stock of the rifle-holders. Of the three who greeted them, two were young men whose complexion and facial structures, like Alahni's, suggested their descent from Terrans of the Pacific Islands. The third was a girl—younger even than Alahni—whose skin was lighter and whose features were more much more Asian. Another armed woman stood by the far door, her weapon also raised and ready. All four of them wore loose, open jackets over what seemed to be simple coveralls, but only one of them displayed any kind of insignia, in the form of the Word of Blake broadsword, set upon a green disc on the left side of his jacket front.

The man wearing that symbol stood nearest to Brooke right now, squinting as he studied them. "They look foreign."

"They are Lost," Alahni admitted.

"Tabi shit!" the other man snapped, hovering dangerously close to Tibor. "This one has a false eye! This has to be a Guardian trick!"

"Jerome Blake was Satan incarnate!" Tibor snarled before anyone else could answer.

In a flash, the second man swung his rifle around until the blackened carbon steel of its butt smashed across Tibor's face. The blow sent him tumbling back onto the hard, musty concrete with an agonized grunt. Instinctively, Brooke moved toward his attacker, only to find two guns in her face, their owners one twitch away from firing.

"*No!*" Alahni cried out.

Tibor's assailant stood over him now, his weapon trained on the fallen man's head as he hissed, "Filthy savage! Never take the name of the Blessed Blake in vain! *Never!*"

With one hand covering half of his battered face, Tibor fixed him with a defiant glare. "For a man who seemed worried about whether or not I'm a Guardian," he growled, "you certainly seem eager to do their dirty work for them."

The man sneered at him for just a few moments longer before the words registered. Within the blink of an eye, his tension bled away, and the faintest approximation of a smile appeared on his face. "Heh," he grunted. "You have a point there, little barbarian!"

Leaning back a bit, the man lowered his weapon, and twisted to offer Tibor his free hand. Tibor hesitated at first, but finally accepted the help in getting back to his feet. At the same time, Brooke noticed the other Jardinians were relaxing as well. The rifles in front of her moved back and away, and she saw the man with the Blakist insignia now wore a lopsided grin as he once again ran his gaze over her and Tibor both.

"So," he said at last. "You are the invaders Apollyon and his soldiers turned the woods upside down for, are you? You don't look like much to me."

"Thanks," Brooke muttered back as she slowly—and, to her annoyance, somewhat painfully—lowered her hands.

"I'm Uku," the man explained. "Tech Overseer Epsilon. I should probably tell you that coming to the city was foolish—" his eyes settled on Alahni, "—for *all* of you. Ogima has already sent out orders calling for any who see your like to report you to the Guardians immediately. You're fortunate my friends and I here put little stock in Ogima's demands these days."

"Well, thanks again," Tibor dryly said.

Uku's glare immediately speared him. "You can thank us by leaving, Housespawn!" he snapped. "Your being here is disruptive enough. Just because we chose not to end your lives doesn't mean we wish to risk ours to help you with whatever treachery you came to do."

"We're not spies or House agents," Brooke said. "We're just explorers. We didn't come here with treachery of any sort in mind. We just need to get aboard one of the Blakist DropShips, and—"

"Are you deaf?" the other Jardinian man snarled. "Uku just said we will *not* help you!"

"Please, Uku," Alahni said, her voice soft and pleading. "These people are not our enemies—"

"They are *Lost*," Uku reminded her. "Off-worlders. They and their kind have never been friends to us. Maybe they don't look as monstrous as those machine-men *things* the Guardians have made, but at least the Domini *protect* us."

Alahni stood her ground. "The Guardians 'saved' our world by keeping us prisoner upon it, Uku," she said. "And the Domini were made to keep it that way."

"That was the price for our salvation, little one. Even a Wayward should know this. Barbarians like these two destroyed the Inner Sphere in their lust for power. And now that the wretched Clans have come to finish them off, they look for the last havens we have left—!"

"The people you call barbarians have hardly destroyed the entire Inner Sphere," Brooke interrupted, resisting the impulse to flinch when Uku's eyes and rifle turned her way again. "Yes, there were wars, and yes, many worlds were lost in the process, much as we thought yours was, but hundreds of worlds still thrive, and the Houses still stand. They even restored the Star League to oppose the Clans, defeating them on their own home worlds. This Wayward knows this, so I'm certain you do, as well.

"In the meantime, your Guardians—the Word of Blake— contributed *nothing* to that effort. They've been keeping you from the universe, and making these cyborg monsters of theirs, for wars that are already over. Why do you imagine that is? What possible good can come from this?"

"Deceptions," hissed the other male.

"My companion and I are living proof," Brooke said without looking away from Uku. "We had wars, and some were pretty savage, but more worlds survived than died in them. And when the Word broke from ComStar, we soon learned that some of our troubles were sparked by the very people who faked your planet's death in the name of this 'protection' you now enjoy."

"The new Star League you talk about is a sham," Uku said. "Yes, we've heard of it. We know your Houses still stand, and of their desperate alliance to stop the Clans, led by House Lords terrified of Kerensky's vengeance. We also know it didn't end the fighting between them. But true peace, they say, is coming, with the Great Promise..."

"A 'Great Promise?'" Brooke echoed. "Can you hear yourself, Uku? A part of you—all of you—*knows* there's something wrong here, or you'd have shot us already, or turned us over to these Domini of yours. You know the Houses still live, and that they effectively united to defeat a common enemy, but you call it a sham and a lie when *we* say it. You talk about true peace coming with this 'Promise,' while your Guardians make an army of monster soldiers out of whom? Your own people? Where do you think such things fit in with this vision of true peace?"

"Meanwhile," Tibor added, briefly capturing Uku's attention, "they've starting using the Waywards for target practice."

In the corner of her eye, Brooke saw Alahni wince at those words. Uku turned to the young woman with questioning eyes.

Her nod was shaky, reluctant, and her voice dropped to a near whisper. "They sent Domini soldiers and BattleMechs into the woods," she said, "to kill us all. There was no call for surrender. No warning at all. They just started shooting..."

"They... They killed *everyone*?" Uku asked, his face growing pale.

Alahni was fighting tears, but she still met his gaze and nodded grimly. "As far as we know now," she said, "I'm all that's left of the Shrouded Forest."

"Just to get at these Lost...?" one of the Jardinian women asked, incredulously.

"They didn't say *anything* about the Lost," Alahni told her. "I heard no demand that we turn them over. I'm not sure they even knew whether or not we'd seen them. Likeke, our tribe leader, sent me out of the camp with these two before the Domini got close. He stayed behind. We saw dead hunters as we came this way..."

"There would have been children there... They even killed the children?"

Alahni looked helpless. Brooke reached out to put a comforting hand on her shoulder.

"I went back," she told Uku, but her gaze eventually settled on the poor young tale-keeper. "They left a 'Mech down in the field when it hit a mine, didn't even try to recover it on their way to the camp. I had some experience with 'Mechs, so I took it, and tried to stop them. I tried so hard... But there were too many, and I was too late... I saw no survivors. I'm so sorry, Alahni."

Alahni didn't—and, perhaps, *couldn't*—look at Brooke. With tears still pooling in her eyes, she spoke to Uku instead.

"They didn't do anything to us," she said. "All they want to do now is leave."

For a long time, Uku was silent, but Brooke could sense a tremble in his expression even in the dim lighting. He lowered his rifle entirely, allowing it to hang limp at his side, while his comrades turned uneasy glances his way. Brooke felt a fleeting, survivalist's urge to take advantage of the tactical situation and seize the man's weapon, but she held herself back.

Uku's gaze fell to the floor. "We knew the Guardians were clashing with the Waywards since they put down the Malu," he said. "But after that, Apollyon promised they would never make war on a tribe again. He swore to Ogima they would only fight if provoked..."

"Seems to me your Destroyer had a change of heart," Tibor grumbled, earning himself another savage glare from the man looming near him.

"If that's true, Uku," the other man said, "maybe we *should* take them to the Guardians?"

Uku put his hand on the other man's shoulder, and it looked to Brooke as if that act alone bled out all the tension left in the darkened room. "No," he said. "Stand down, Lani. Everyone, stand down."

Slowly, the other Jardinians—including the one named Lani—lowered their rifles. With a dismissive gesture, Uku ushered his people toward the far door. Only after they were out of earshot did he turn his focus fully toward Brooke.

"Understand this, Lost One," he said. "Your words would have meant nothing to me if this Wayward sister hadn't backed you up. We know the monsters the Guardians have made here. We have witnessed their creation, and the rise of their master, and we know why they have come. We know how and why we were hidden from your kind for generations. It was *your* ancestors— the Great Houses who destroyed the Star League—who made all of this necessary, and I feel no sympathy for you, even now."

"Oh, don't hold back," Tibor scoffed. "Tell us how you *really* feel."

"*Trouble!*" Brooke growled at him.

Uku's free hand clenched and relaxed as his eyes shot daggers at Tibor. "What I *really* feel," he hissed, "isn't your concern, Housespawn scum. But what I'm *not* feeling right now is any particular desire to kill for the Domini. So, if you want to commit your suicide on one of their DropShips, I'll oblige you. A *Merlin* is preparing for liftoff as we speak, taking on supplies in the underground bays for some kind of support mission or other. I can slip you on board in a crate if you do exactly as I say and keep your filthy mouths shut.

"But after that, you off-worlders are on your own."

Brooke nodded stoically. "Fair enough," she said. Sensing Alahni's gaze, she turned to the young Wayward and offered her a brief smile that she hoped was reassuring somehow. "I suppose this is it, Alahni. It only gets more dangerous from here. But, one way or the other, once Trouble and I hit space, we won't be coming back."

Alahni, her eyes strangely unreadable, stared at Brooke for a long, uncomfortable moment, and nodded.

CHAPTER 6

My Dearest Tyler,

I know we've had this discussion before. I know where you stand, and I know why you stand there. Truth be told, if our positions were reversed, I'd probably be every bit as upset with you as you get with me. The risks we take out here, no matter why we take them, can get pretty insane. So the fact that we do them for trinkets and historical footnotes the rest of mankind has forgotten about makes it all the more questionable. Perhaps as questionable as any other mercenary job, really.

But, of course, if I hadn't chosen this line of work, we'd probably never have met in the first place. You have to give me that, *at least!*

With that said, I think I must finally admit that there are limits, even for me. I've seen savage locals, noble intrigue, and beasts of all sizes scarier than the works of humanity's greatest horror writers. I've visited worlds and shipwrecks from the Axumite Providence to the Outworlds Wastes. I've been sued, shot, stabbed, assaulted, arrested, poisoned, plagued, and propositioned more times than I care to remember.

But after Jardine, I don't think I can do this anymore.

There's just a point where the thrill of discovery pales in comparison to its costs, and after what I saw here... Well, maybe it's just time I listened to you for a change.

Just promise me you won't gloat too much about it when I get home, alright?

—From the journals of Brooklyn Stevens

LEOPARD-CLASS DROPSHIP *KAYLIN*
PIRATE JUMP POINT
JARDINE (HERAKLEION) SYSTEM
FREE WORLDS LEAGUE
7 NOVEMBER 3067

Maybe it was the short distance, or the uncommon, mid-system destination they'd plotted, but something about this last jump felt even more disturbing than usual to Captain Anton Hara. He felt a strange vibration to the air, in his nerves, or both. Sounds and silence echoed and reverberated through his consciousness, and ghosts of the people around him blurred ahead of their every move. Even his mind felt like it was out of synch, processing past, present, and future at different and overlapping rates. It was both just like, and a distortion of, the sensation of déjà vu he normally experienced only in his dreams.

Though it felt much longer this time, the experience truly took only one or two seconds to subside.

As usual, Hara felt himself return to normal space with all his muscles locked up, and his jaw aching, but aside from the psychedelic strangeness of this leap, everything appeared normal when his eyes, ears, and other senses finally caught up. Slowly, he relaxed himself, slowing his breathing and reclaiming his faculties by sheer force of will. He briefly closed his eyes again while the soothing sounds of his ship's bridge systems filtered through the last of his jump-induced haze.

An unexpected gasp for breath snapped Hara out of this inward focus. Turning toward the source of the sound, he found his exec, Lenard Bryce, gripping his own console so tightly that his knuckles appeared stark white. Bryce's face was twisted in a way that suggested pain at first, but as he drew in another breath, Hara recognized it was more like shock. The black-haired, dark-skinned, and bespectacled officer wrestled with this state for only a few more seconds before he finally shook his head with purpose and reclaimed his normal, self-commanding composure.

Glancing suddenly to Hara, Bryce let out a heavy sigh filled with relief and his lips formed a thin, sheepish smile. Hara nodded reassuringly to him; the jump clearly affected them both in much the same way.

Bryce turned back to his displays. "Jump complete," he croaked. "Showing us seven-point-one-eight units further in-system, position-aligned with target's last-known trajectory."

"Good," Hara said with a crisp nod. "JumpShip status?"

"No report yet," Jacoby called out from the sensor station. His voice was calm and firm; if the jump had affected him any differently than usual, it certainly wasn't showing now. "But umbilical power and data feeds show green and stable."

"They're fine, then," Hara declared. "Their skipper knows we have a four-day window now. They're probably resetting the reactor feed to the drive."

"Assuming nothing blew out from the last quick-charge," Bryce cautioned.

"We'd know by now, I think," Hara told him. "I'm more worried about Stevens' crew pulling the same stunt, and why they didn't do it already after we gave away their position."

Bryce merely shrugged. For the last several hours leading up to their mid-system jump, he and Hara spent much of their time debating possible reasons for the *Sacajawea*'s apparent lack of any reaction at all to recent events. Even when *Kaylin* broadcast a message and telemetry to Stevens' shuttlecraft, revealing both of their JumpShips' presence together for anyone to hear, they picked up nothing from the rogue *Explorer*.

In Hara's mind, there was no way the *Sac* couldn't have built up a full jump charge by now, especially not after having a two-week head start over *Kaylin*'s JumpShip. Yet they just... sat there. It made no immediate sense to him, and Bryce had few ideas to offer. Perhaps their KF drive was damaged during the attack back at Shasta? If so, they requested no help when they saw the *Kaylin* and her JumpShip arrive. Well, they *did* have little reason to trust them, but at the risk of simply stranding themselves in hostile territory? And not even talking to their own mission leader? What could that have been about? Did they really think Stevens could make a fifteen-AU journey in a shuttlecraft with a hostile DropShip on her tail?

Whatever was going on with the *Sac*, though, it didn't seem to faze the liaison officer IE assigned to Hara. Nathan Bellamy insisted there was no point puzzling out the inscrutable, when the real prize was busy racing her way across the solar system.

Pointing out—and rightly so, much to Hara's eternal disgust—that any hope of rescue now hinged on them jumping ahead with painfully narrow transit and recharge windows, in hopes of catching the good doctor before her friends could try and do the same. And since there was little practicality in simply obliterating the *Sacajawea* to take them out of the equation (as Hara explained to him just before the jump), Bellamy decided that their open-channel broadcast was enough to give those ex-IE runaways pause while the *Kaylin* claimed the best intercept point first.

Thus began a race that, maddeningly enough, the *Sac* did not seem to even care about, and so Hara and Bryce alike were left on their bridge, trying to imagine what they might have missed.

Meanwhile, somewhere out there, on a course that should take her straight to them, was a shuttlecraft carrying one Doctor Brooklyn Stevens, and whatever evidence she had to prove that this system truly was home to the lost world of Jardine.

EXPLORER-CLASS JUMPSHIP *SACAJAWEA*
PIRATE JUMP POINT
JARDINE (HERAKLEION) SYSTEM
FREE WORLDS LEAGUE

"—And there they go," Gretchen Morden said as an indicator flashed on the sensor board before her. The electromagnetic pulse from the JumpShip carrying IE's other mercenaries washed over them just a few moments ago, but the infrared surge had been picked up a few seconds earlier—the telltale signs of a hyperspace jump.

"I thought they'd never leave," Lawrence Pohl dryly replied. Seated as he was at his regular command chair, he caught Gretchen's sidelong smirk only in profile before turning to the only other occupant in the *Sacajawea*'s command center at the moment.

Juan Lafferty was only half-seated at the jump station, dividing his attention between two displays filled with scrolling data. A few indicators on his panel flashed in lights of cool green.

But for all those distractions, the man immediately sensed his captain's attention and looked up.

"Well, Cap," Juan said with a crooked smile, "No pulse close by, so I guess you win this round."

"You're the one who picked the long odds," Lawrence told him. "Hara and his crew might have gone for Crazy Jane-ing us, and getting some digs in, but he's no jump skipper, and I doubt that blood limpet, Bellamy, would risk his own hide that way even if he was."

"Never bet against good old-fashioned IE spinelessness, eh?" Juan asked.

"Maybe they just ran, then," Gretchen suggested. Swiveling her chair enough to face them both, she favored Juan with a wink and a smile fueled by the knowledge that *her* bet was still in play. "What with all the radio chatter and other signs we've seen here, they have to know we've found their Atlantis by now—if not something just as juicy. They could just as easily toddle off to Croft and the others, claim mission accomplished, and write us off."

"Oh, sure," Lawrence agreed, "but I'm sticking with my theory. They moved in-system; they want Brooke."

"Wish I could see the look on Hara's face when he finds out it's not her," Juan said.

"After blurting our position to those guys on open channels, he deserves it," Gretchen said. "I just hope they were smart enough to give themselves some escape time."

"Which brings us back to us," Lawrence said. "Juan?"

Juan glanced at his panels again before returning his attention to Lawrence and nodding. "Calcs are done, and the window's open. It's close, though; we're not leaving ourselves a lot of time if they have ships that can pull more than three gees."

"I don't think we can afford to push the drive too hard with the quick charge this time," Lawrence said. "We still have some minor damage from that freak show that boarded us, after all. Five days is our best."

"Then, we're ready on this end, Cap."

"Gretch?"

"Nothing since Trouble's last ping," Gretchen said.

"Then pray for them and for us," Lawrence said as he pushed himself back in his chair and reached for its straps. "Juan, start jump procedures."

As his crew settled in and got busy, Lawrence closed his eyes and drew in a deep breath, wishing he was as confident about all of this as he tried to sound. There were at least a hundred ways he could think of that this could all end badly. He knew it, and so did they.

But sooner or later, everyone had to take a chance and just throw the damned dice...

MERLIN-CLASS DROPSHIP _AGRAVAIN_
HIGH ORBIT
JARDINE (HERAKLEION)
FREE WORLDS LEAGUE

"Captain on the bridge!"

Adept Petra Inagi, captain of the _Agravain_, had barely stepped onto the bridge when she heard an alarm sound from the sensor station. The crewman already seated there, Acolyte Ru Yuen, an olive-skinned Jardine native with black hair and eyes, immediately turned his fleeting attention away from Inagi to inspect the readings on his displays.

Inagi met her first officer's gaze and arched an eyebrow. Adept Jakab Lantos, a pale-faced, green-eyed man with short, brown hair and a goatee, stood at ease beside the captain's chair, and shrugged. Whatever was going on right now, it was also news to him.

"Jump pulse, Captain," Yuen said after a moment. "Three AUs out, by the look of it."

Inagi made it to her chair, but instead of claiming the seat, she took an extra step forward and engaged the small holotank that occupied the nearby tactical station.

Instantly, a map of the immediate vicinity flashed up, projecting Jardine—and the arc of its orbital path—in the center, with the _Agravain_'s position as a speck of white slowly circling the planet well beyond the exosphere. Dialing out the zoom, Inagi widened the view field, past the orbits of Jardine's two moons, until the path of the next-nearest celestial object came into frame. "Position?"

"Getting listening sat data now, sir," Yuen answered. A silent moment passed, when suddenly a series of red, concentric rings appeared on the tactical display, their focus shifting slightly and narrowing swiftly, until they settled on a position... "Approximately four degrees above the solar plane, retrograde of Jardine."

"No IFF signal," Lantos added, as he leaned over the unoccupied communications station. "But no random pirate could make a jump like that."

"Not unless they've been here all along," Inagi added, "quietly mapping the place."

"Precentor Lucille's second JumpShip?"

Inagi nodded and approached the comms station, gesturing for Lantos to take the helm. "I'll call this in," she said. "Take us off auto and get ready to plot a high-V intercept. We'll need to get to her before she can recharge."

Brooke Stevens awoke to the sensation of being carried upward by an elevator run amok. She heard the creaking of metal, the irregular thumping of something heavy, and a dull, but persistent, rumble that sounded like it came from everywhere. The darkness around her was total, and when she moved, she felt as though she was trapped in a web. Disoriented by her sudden rousing, a panic welled up in the pit of her stomach, and instinct drove her to convulse against her restraints.

Somewhere in the darkness to her side, a feminine voice groaned, then gasped.

"Easy," came a reassuring male voice from just a bit farther away. "We're okay."

"Trouble?" Brooke called into the darkness.

"Good morning, Sunshine," said Tibor Mitternacht. "And may I say again how wonderfully *quiet* you sleep when strapped to a wall?"

Brooke's mind was already clear enough to disperse her initial terror. For three days now, she guessed, they had made their home in an empty crawlspace between the outer and inner hulls of this Blakist ship.

After being smuggled into one of the cargo bays with the final batch of supplies—courtesy of the one or two citizens of Hope Alahni and Uku managed to persuade enough to help—they'd endured the initial burn into orbit within the confines of a single, slotted storage bin. Escaping the bin with the aid of a vibroblade dropped in with them, they pillaged additional survival supplies—mostly rations, weapons, and four bundles of cargo webbing—before Brooke and Tibor managed to find and pry open an access panel both secluded and innocuous enough to let them into the space between decks and hull supports.

It was a time-honored approach favored by smugglers and stowaways since the early days of spaceflight, but Brooke had to admit she'd never snuck into a hull gap nearly as clean and fresh as the one they'd found. Even the insulation pads appeared to be pristine, as they shoved them aside to build their makeshift nest.

"This ship's brand new," Tibor observed when they rigged up the harnesses that would serve as their safety beds during the long flight. For a day or so—long enough to be sure they weren't detected, they figured—the plan was to remain in silent hiding before deciding on their next steps. In the meantime, they'd eaten little, and spoke to one another only in low tones and whispers.

"We're under thrust," Brooke said now, even as she felt the netting tighten around her body. "Hard acceleration."

"They made a reorientation burn a few seconds ago," Tibor said. "A sharp turn, definitely not routine. There was a brief yellow alert sound at the time."

"Think they smell something?"

"If so, it's not us. They'd have us already. And this certainly doesn't feel like the kind of acceleration they'd use for reentry. It feels like maybe two gees. Probably an intercept."

This DropShip—"*Agravain*" according to the Jardinians who slipped them on board—was being deployed on an orbital patrol, a sweep the Blakist Guardians occasionally (if rarely) performed when there was concern of intruders lurking in the system. In addition to scanning the immediate space around

Jardine and checking on the various "ancient" satellites that served as the planet's normal, passive-defense network, it would also perform sensor sweeps over Jardine's two small moons, just in case.

While the ship was equipped and supplied with the means to service those satellites—including those that could deploy ancient drone fighters, like the ones that had attacked Brooke and Tibor's shuttlecraft—its primary mission was simple reconnaissance. For that reason, the locals claimed, the crew should be pretty light, perhaps barely more than half dozen men and women in all. Admitting the hull design was new to him, Tibor could neither confirm nor deny that advice, but most military DropShips could be flown by only a handful of souls these days, so it seemed a good enough estimate. The crew would be necessarily spread out to various sections, so the main worry would be less about numbers and more about how competent (and how deadly) such crewmen could be in the inevitable close-quarters combat that was sure to come.

After all, it was one thing to stowaway on a ship one knew was already leaving the system; but sneaking aboard a ship one knew was just going to return a few days or so later necessitated a far more *proactive* strategy.

"Intercepting what, though?" Brooke asked. "I thought they already sent a ship for the *Sac*?"

"Or for Hara," Tibor hastily reminded her.

"Right," Brooke said, recalling the message Tibor received through whatever sorcery Gretchen and Lawrence had rigged up to call him. IE's other mercs apparently managed to find their way to the system well after the *Sacajawea*'s arrival, but maintained radio silence ever since. That was, until *someone* claiming to be Brooke had called out into the void for return telemetry. Then, not only did Hara respond, betraying his own presence to the Blakists, but he also fed them telemetry that led straight back to the *Sac* herself.

Foolish, opportunistic bastard! Brooke thought when she heard the news, but she couldn't be sure if she was thinking of Captain Hara or Nathan Bellamy, the IE liaison who had probably put him up to such a stunt.

Regardless, Tibor received another of Gretchen's "secret messages" at about the same time, asking if Brooke really was asking for telemetry. For whatever reason, it seemed, neither she nor Lawrence believed it entirely. With a "ping" he managed to somehow send back, Tibor confirmed their suspicions, so at least the *Sacajawea* knew the message was false.

But that still left them in the path of the DropShip the Word of Blake already launched—a DropShip that, if the locals could be trusted, possibly included a team of those Manei Domini cyborgs specifically equipped for boarding and capturing operations. Tibor's math assured Brooke there was no way the *Sacajawea* could be in any immediate danger from such a mission. Not yet, anyway—especially since they now had a full drive charge and complete awareness of the Blakist ruse. The *Sac* would be safe, but they were now waiting on a "ping" from Tibor to tell them when they could move to pick up their actual crewmates.

A "ping" Tibor had been sending at semi-regular intervals as best as he could, while hoping the *Agravain*'s hull didn't completely mute him. At this stage, there simply was no way to know one way or the other.

But there was one last concern still lingering on Brooke's mind as she once more tumbled the thoughts of how and when they should move through her head...

Beside her, Alahni moaned again. "Ooooh," she said, groggily, "I think I'm going to be sick again."

Brooke looked in the girl's direction. Even at less than half a meter's distance, she still couldn't make out any of her features in the blackness. Whatever had possessed Alahni to come along, Brooke couldn't be certain, but the part of her that feared for the young Jardinian's safety was glad she came anyway.

In theory, Alahni *could* have stayed behind, *could* have melted into Hope's native populace, or perhaps even sought out another Wayward settlement, where she *might* have been safe from reprisals. But the loss of her tribe—to the very Guardians they'd admired, even as they hid from them—had severed all her connections to the world below. She'd insisted on boarding the DropShip with them, even though it was clear she didn't know a thing about what it would be like to fly into space. Nor did she seem to even consider that they would all need to seize the ship by force if they were to secure any real hope of escape. It occurred to Brooke that Alahni might have learned to use small arms and such to protect herself or hunt with her tribemates in the wilds of Jardine's forests, but could she possibly be ready to fire upon another human being, especially one she'd been raised to see as one of her people's saviors?

"Breathe," Tibor told Alahni. "Don't think about your stomach. Just breathe deep."

"This air still smells like metal," she complained. "And I feel so heavy."

"Yes," Tibor said. "The ship's speeding up."

"Is it always like this?"

"Well, not *always*. But it's common enough."

"Only this time," Brooke added, "we think they may have spotted something, which could be our friends."

"Your JumpShip?" Alahni asked.

"The *Sacajawea*, yes," Brooke said. "I think we're going to have to get out of here and get to work."

"You won't hear me complain," Tibor said. "If this ship's on an intercept alert, they're probably not watching the cargo bays right now. We can slip out, get our bearings. I think I saw a crate marked 'Boarding Ordnance' during our last gear search..."

"*Boarding* ordnance," Brooke repeated. "Probably nothing too destructive."

"Right. I'm imagining smoke bombs, flash-bangs, maybe tear gas. Whatever it is, should make our work a bit easier... maybe."

"What should I do?" Alahna asked, nervously.

"Keep your head down," Tibor told her before Brooke could. "From here, things can turn ugly really fast."

LEOPARD-CLASS DROPSHIP *KAYLIN*
PIRATE JUMP POINT
JARDINE (HERAKLEION) SYSTEM
FREE WORLDS LEAGUE

"Jump pulse confirmed," Bryce reported from the navigation console. "Looks like a pirate point on the solar plane, five days or so trailing the primary."

Hara sat in his command chair and processed this news. In his mind, there was no doubt whatsoever that the pulse came from any ship other than the *Sacajawea*. After spending days just floating out there, seemingly oblivious to the signals shooting back and forth between the outbound shuttlecraft and the *Kaylin*, IE's rogue *Explorer* must have decided to make its move less than an hour after they last saw her.

He felt no surprise that the *Sac*'s crew had merely waited him out, but their destination concerned him. It was nowhere *near* close enough to intercept Stevens' shuttlecraft; in fact, it was entirely in the opposite direction.

What was he missing?

"Have they contacted her yet?" He asked, directing his attention to Jacoby at the communications station.

"I'm not seeing anything," Jacoby said.

"The shuttle's course hasn't changed," Bryce volunteered, "so, my guess is no. That, or she has no choice."

Hara nodded absently, though he remained unconvinced. Whatever modifications Stevens and her people might have made, her shuttle was still based on a standard, old-model, K-1 class craft. That meant it burned at least two tons of reaction mass for every day spent under thrust, and probably couldn't carry much more than thirty tons of fuel in all. Of that reserve, the craft heading toward *Kaylin* had already spend about eight to ten tons that Hara could be sure of. Turning about and accelerating to the *Sac*'s new position would force the shuttle to use up almost all its remaining fuel, even on a full tank.

Meanwhile, there was apparently a heavily armed *Union* DropShip lagging behind—a combat vessel, with a much greater operational range. Though slower than the shuttle in a short race, it would still eventually run Stevens down even if she held her course. Turning back would only end the chase faster once the DropShip adapted to the course change. And even if they couldn't match the shuttle's new speed for long in passing, a *Union* boasted more than enough firepower to take out a K-1 in a single volley.

These immutable factors gave Stevens few options, if she hoped to survive.

But something about it all was still off, and Hara sensed it the moment *Sacajawea*'s jump had registered on their sensors. Could Stevens' crew have truly miscalculated *that* badly? Or was this perhaps an attempt at some kind of diversion, hoping to distract whoever wanted to keep this planet hidden long enough for *Kaylin* to make the pickup? Were they desperate—or merely naïve—enough to entrust their commander's fate to *him*?

...Or did they know something he didn't?

Hara frowned as that thought finally hit him, and his eyes narrowed at the space beyond the *Kaylin*'s forward viewports. "Something's wrong," he said. "Call the launch deck, Len. Tell the techs I want our planes loaded and ready to fly ASAP."

"We lost two during that shootout under Shasta," Bryce cautioned.

"That's why *we're* going with them," Hara said, turning to meet Bryce's gaze.

**K-1-CLASS DROPSHUTTLE *STILETTO*-7
OUTWARD INTERCEPT COURSE
JARDINE (HERAKLEION)
FREE WORLDS LEAGUE**

"Flash from *Shield*: Target is separating from its Jumper."

Precentor Damien Lucille nodded gravely to the square-jawed woman seated beside him. Adept Talia Rumiko wore her raven hair in a queue that sprang from the top center of her head and split just above the circular interface jack mounted at the lower backside of her skull. From there, twin braids curved forward, over her taut shoulders, and ended just below her collarbone. The rest of her tanned scalp was shaved bare, exposing the thin scars along her temples that hinted at the procedures used to enhance her hearing and vision.

Her all-black eyes, set in almond-shaped lids that never blinked, met Lucille's for just a moment before returning to their instruments. Lucille did the same, noting the data now scrolling onto his navigational displays.

"About time," he said. "Coming to 'rescue' us before we run out of fuel. We'll give it a few more hours before 'Doctor Stevens' asks for a sitrep. For now, let's push the engines a bit."

"Understood. Any idea what that other Jumper's doing?"

Lucille scowled. The news of the JumpShip arrival closer to Jardine had come in hours before. It was an unwelcome confirmation of his suspicion about just how many ships now lurked in-system, but there was no way to go back now; their course was locked. And it didn't really change his mission all that much, anyway. *All* invaders to this system would need to be dealt with, no matter who they were and what games they were playing.

But what truly bothered Lucille now was the dark certainty that he'd never get the chance to kill that Stevens Frail personally. Once again, the universe seemed to deny him his chance for redemption.

That this DropShip ahead of him, *Kaylin*, was now moving to speed up their rendezvous could have something to do with the other JumpShip, or it couldn't. Either way, it was now his primary target, and its JumpShip was the immediate secondary. Like the second vessel, it also had just executed an in-system jump deeper from wherever it had lurked, which meant its crew was now desperately recharging its drives directly from its fusion plants—if they were smart. That gave Lucille's team perhaps four days, at best, to splash both of the ships ahead of them to the uncaring void.

That *other* JumpShip—probably Stevens' *Sacajawea*—had effectively become someone else's problem.

"Whatever that's about," he finally told Rumiko, "Precentor Apollyon will see to *them*. Our targets lie ahead of us."

Rumiko nodded, this time acknowledging his words without glancing away from her boards. Her hand reached out for the thrust controls and paused there. Lucille switched open the tactical intercom that linked both his shuttle crew and that of the *Hera's Shield*, behind them.

"*Manei Domini*!" he declared. "The enemies of the Promise lie ahead, and our time grows short! But the legacy of Blessed Blake is with us, and we shall not allow them to escape! Brace for acceleration!"

MERLIN-CLASS DROPSHIP *AGRAVAIN*
RETROGRADE INTERCEPT COURSE
JARDINE (HERAKLEION) SYSTEM
FREE WORLDS LEAGUE

Agravain's main engineering chamber was so factory-fresh, one could still smell the paint, polish, and metalwork. Brightly lit, and efficiently laid out, its main deck encircled the bulkheads that protected the ship's fusion reactor housing. The deck grating was finer than the old Succession Wars standards, designed for comfortable travel whether one was wearing magnetic engineer's boots or simple slippers. The computer panels and keyboards were clean and shone with equal intensity. Fire suppression kits and tool lockers—all with crisp, new paint—lined the outer bulkheads, fully stocked and well secured. All of it was a marvel of engineering and ergonomics, brought to life by the fine folks at Brigadier Corporation of Gibson.

Three crewmen, in spotless, light-gray coveralls, were on duty at the moment, strapped into their station seats and monitoring their systems while idly chatting with each other in soft voices. Even with the DropShip pouring out a constant acceleration slightly past one-gee, the chamber was oddly serene. The sound baffles that lined the under-floor kept the roar of the engines to a dull hum that practically harmonized with the soft buzz the reactor constantly gave off, if only to remind the crew that, yes, it was still active.

And so it was, in that well-lit, library-calm chamber—until a side hatch, reserved for outer structure maintenance purposes only—suddenly unlatched and swung inward, startling all three of its occupants. Slapping their restraint releases, two of them were nearly out of their seats when a pair of small, green, cylindrical canisters clanged onto the floor nearby, and exploded.

In seconds, the clouds of noxious vapor and smoke engulfed them, racing to fill the entire chamber.

The two standing engineers gasped and choked on the gas, struggling to keep their feet, while the third one fell into a coughing fit and turned his wild eyes to the panels in front of him. In their distraction, none saw the two filter-masked figures poking their heads and arms out from the hatch with weapons in hand.

Firing first at the Blakist standing to her left, Brooke caught him in chest once, and sent another slug his way for good measure. Tibor also put two rounds in his target, with one slamming into the woman's abdomen, and the second to her neck. Blood sprayed across computer panels and bulkheads as both crewmen dropped in the haze, and the chamber rang with the echoes of gunfire and short, alarmed cries.

Ducking back in unison, they waited a few tense seconds for explosions that never came. Instead, they heard the loud, whirring hum of the chamber's air filtration system ramping up to overdrive, sucking away the gases and clearing the haze that crept after them.

Then came the alert klaxons, blaring over the din with shocking power. It was only then that they peeked around again and saw the third crewman.

"*Scheiße!*" Brooke spat as she fired her pistol again. The blast caught the remaining Blakist in the head just as his mouth opened to say something. Once again, no explosion followed.

Tibor raced through the opening, toward the third man's panel. He arrived just in time to make out an angry voice coming through the speakers.

"Engineering!" a male voice shouted. "What in Blake's name is going on down there?"

Tibor blinked and swept his eyes across the blood-splashed panel, but didn't find the mic until he dared to look back at the operator's corpse. Snatching it from the ghastly remains of the engineer's head, he brought the device toward his lips while trying to ignore just how warm and slick it was.

"Ah, sorry, sir," he stammered. Finding the panic switch the engineer struck, he slapped it again. Mercifully, the alarms stopped, but his ears still rang painfully. "We've had a slight...

coolant breach down here, but we've managed to lock it down. Everything's fine now, sorry."

Brooke was at his side now, her focus divided between watching the other ingress hatches around them and scanning the controls for anything useful. Tibor's spidery fingers were already working at them, poking and fumbling across buttons and switches half-obscured by her handiwork.

"Who is this?" the voice from the console demanded.

"Crap, crap, *crap!*" Tibor hissed as he tossed the mic away. His hands moved faster, slapping overrides and throwing switches. The monitor above his panels flashed up a schematic of the DropShip, with various decks and sectors blinking from green to red, but only for a moment. Finally, the engine room lights flickered, and Brooke could hear a brief change in the reactor's buzz, a momentary hum that reminded her of several times when the *Sac*'s suffered a power surge.

It all passed in a heartbeat, and the alarms began anew.

"Trouble?" Brooke asked.

"They didn't buy it, obviously!" he snapped back. "I tried to kill life support on the bridge, but of course they've already cut me out."

"*Scheiße!*"

Tibor studied the displays one last time before glancing back at the dead engineers. A grim, uneasy smile appeared on his face as he bent down to snatch a set of small, colored cards from the belt loop of the corpse at his feet.

"It's not all bad," he said. "Well, okay. They slaved control through the bridge directly, and their effort to stop me from voiding everything else above us has locked the ship into anti-breach mode. Emergency bulkheads are down all over the place; should slow down anyone left between here and the bridge. There's two fighters of some kind in a bay above the cargo hold. And these engineering keys should allow us to override the locks at will, though a portable E-console would be better, if we can find one. If we move fast enough, we may have a clear path to either place."

Brooke stared at the screens for a moment, tracing the routes in her mind.

"Alright," she said. "Try to find a console, in case they remote-kill those keys. I'll get Alahni."

Petra Inagi pounded a fist on the edge of the tactical station holotank. The state-of-the-art device barely flickered at the disturbance, which only magnified her frustration.

"What do you mean, we have intruders on board?" she demanded as her eyes speared those of her first officer.

Adept Jakab Lantos was still leaning over the communications station, holding one half of a headset to his ear. Though his pale cheeks flushed in the face of his captain's rage, he nevertheless met and held her gaze. "Someone in engineering tried to void the bridge," he said quickly. "Half the airlocks in the gunnery stations, crew quarters, engineering, and flight decks have blown. We've locked them out and initiated breach control, but I can't raise anyone down there now."

"How the hell—?"

"Must've triggered an emergency containm—!"

"I know *that*!" Inagi snapped. "Override engineering control and repressurize the main decks. Sound ship-wide alert and get someone down there. I don't care if you have to go yourself; I want these bastards *found*!"

"On it!" Lantos said.

"And get me a direct line to the Sanctorum; Precentor Apollyon must be informed!"

CHAPTER 7

Forgive me, Master, for I have sinned.

With all my heart, flesh, and soul, I have embraced the wisdom of the Blessed Blake, and your Promise for the days ahead. Though I freely admit I gave in to despair in the wake of the traitor Focht's heresy, and the failures of our fallen Saints Waterly and Aziz, it was by your grace and that of your Thrice-Blessed that I was saved. It is through your inspired will and the glories of the Great Architect that I was made whole again, that I was reborn in your image. That I became one of your Hands.

Your faith in me, in my devotion, was as a gift from the Heavenly Father himself! I could not have asked for a greater honor than becoming one of Apollyon's Chosen, even without my final Ascension!

Yet, in my zeal to prove myself worthy of your gifts, I have found myself tempted by the sins of Pride, of Arrogance, of Ambition. It is for this, I seek your forgiveness and redemption!

Apollyon, my Pater, *I can see his disappointment in my frailty of late, and I am shamed. It is not for the Hands to defy the Will. Flesh, blood, and steel must do as they are told, without question, without hesitation, without desire for glory. Yet, for moments—mere moments!—I have weakened to these petty impulses, these frailties of the mind.*

And so I venture to the void, incomplete, to save my home, my people, and my soul, knowing that my life is forfeit without redemption.

> Mea maxima culpa, *Master! Forgive me, for I
> have sinned.*
>
> —FROM THE JOURNAL OF DAMIEN LUCILLE (FINAL ENTRY), 3067

**THE SANCTORUM
CITY OF HOPE
JARDINE (HERAKLEION)
FREE WORLDS LEAGUE
7 NOVEMBER 3067**

Had she been flesh and blood, rather than a mere projection on a flatscreen monitor, the *Agravain*'s captain would've died under Apollyon's metal shod fist. But this fact offered the Precentor Domini no comfort. As he stared at the shattered glass and circuit boards, his first impulse was instant regret. Such blind rage was a frailty, not an expression befitting one of the Master's Hands—let alone the Master's personal champion! As the last wisps of smoke from the broken screen dissipated, he closed his eyes—both true and frail—and chastised himself for this moment of petty weakness.

Inwardly, Apollyon sought the cause of this lapse. Was it the disappointing failures of his *own* chosen to catch these two frail mercenaries? Was Lucille's disappointing tendency toward immaturity and hubris soaking into his own psyche after all these years? Could it be his own sense of ego at the heart of this, for that matter? That part of him which was enraged that the possibility of Jardine's three-hundred-year bliss now stood just days away from being ruined on *his* watch?

Or could it be the frailest and most primal of all human emotions driving him: *fear*? Fear of the contingencies the Master Himself would ask of him, should news of this world reach the Inner Sphere at large?

Apollyon opened his eyes again and turned them solemnly to the windows of his nearly featureless office. Beyond the boundaries of Hope's faux ruins, the lush, thriving jungles spread across the hilly landscape as far as he could see, so beautifully green beneath the clear, azure skies of his homeworld.

Protecting this splendor had already claimed so many lives, and more sacrifice would be necessary if it was to continue.

Already, his orders had gone out to the hangars. Every vessel possible was preparing for launch, the usual concealment protocols suspended for expediency. But these invaders had half a day's head start on one of the fastest ships in his fleet, itself racing to kill their JumpShip. Though he knew Adept Inagi would heed a self-destruct command from him to ensure Doctor Stevens' death, it would also buy Stevens' compatriots more time to fast-charge their drives before any other ship from Jardine could reach them.

And so now, all Apollyon could do was pray.

Pray, and prepare for the worst.

MERLIN-CLASS DROPSHIP *AGRAVAIN*
RETROGRADE INTERCEPT COURSE
JARDINE (HERAKLEION) SYSTEM
FREE WORLDS LEAGUE

"I *knew* we should've taken the bridge first!" Brooke groused as she climbed up the maintenance ladder. Behind her by a few rungs was Tibor, followed by Alahni, both of whom were already gasping and grunting for breath.

The shaft they were in ran alongside the DropShip's main starboard personnel lift, and was roomy enough for techs to traverse, even while burdened with oxygen tanks and tool satchels. There were ample handholds and overhead rails for climbing in either normal gravity, or the complete absence thereof. But the fact that the ship was still pouring out enough thrust for something past two gees of acceleration—by Brooke's estimate, anyway—made what should have been a "quick and easy" ascent a test of herculean endurance.

Now her limbs ached at every joint, with even her fingers and toes screaming in agony at every step. She'd tried to distract herself by counting the steps, but every time she'd glanced up along the shaft, her goal just looked that much farther away. Already, they'd had to pause to take quick breathers, resting their limbs by sitting on the thick ridges that both reinforced the shaft and marked the passage of each deck level.

"If they'd not been so damned fast," Tibor grunted, "we would've taken it with no problem, I tell you!"

"And I'm sure firing off that escape pod to distract them *really* helped," Brooke said between gasps.

"It *might* have..."

"The Guardians," Alahni breathed from behind him, "are hardly fools."

"Well," Tibor grumbled, "*we* clearly are, trying to storm the bridge when we know it's going to be a fortress—"

"Trouble," Brooke snapped, "shut up, will you? We broke orbit all of four hours ago. There's maybe a four-*day* trip ahead of us at a constant burn. Whatever fighters they have in the launch bays, they can't make a haul like that, and you know it."

"*Ja, ja...*" Tibor said, "Still—"

With a loud hiss and a metallic *clang* that nearly deafened her, metal plates inside the ridge just above Brooke's head suddenly emerged and slammed together, blocking the shaft. Behind her, she heard Tibor's yelp of alarm as another set closed beneath them, right under him and Alahni.

"*Scheiße!*" Brooke spat.

"They're onto us!" Tibor growled. "Swing across! Let me at that side hatch next to you; Maybe I can—"

It was at that moment the hatch Tibor was talking about slid open on its own. Instantly, Brooke found herself face-to-face with a pale-faced, goateed man wearing crisp black coveralls under an open red jacket. The Word of Blake logo appeared prominently on his shoulders, and a rank insignia she didn't recognize was pinned to his collar. In his right hand, already leveled at her, was a nasty-looking flechette pistol.

Brooke reacted almost purely by instinct. Reaching out with her right hand while anchoring her left arm to its current rung by the elbow, she seized the man's jacket and pulled him forward with all her might, deliberately twisting her arm back and away from her. The Blakist yelped and fired his pistol, but all she heard was a hail-like rattle of plastic on metal in the tube behind her.

Suddenly unbalanced and teetering into the shaft, the man clutched at the hatchway and might have been able to right himself under normal conditions. But with the ship pulling more than two gees, his efforts amounted to little more than flailing against physics. Losing his footing, he tumbled head-first into the shaft, and slammed against the pressure bulkhead three meters below with a sickening *crunch*.

"*He aha lā!?*" another voice shouted from further beyond the open doorway.

Brooke looked up and her eyes widened at the sight of a second Blakist in the hall. Though he was dressed just like the man she'd tossed, this one looked far more imposing, with dark skin, stubble-short blond hair, and glowing red, metal-rimmed eyes set beneath a hairless brow.

Lunging forward, he reached out with a leather-gloved hand and grabbed her forearm. As he ripped her off the ladder and flung her into the hall like a ragdoll, a sharp new agony radiated out from Brooke's left elbow and shoulder. But before she could even cry out about it, the back of her head banged heavily against the metal bulkheads of the inner corridor. Stars swam before her as her vision dimmed.

"Kaha to Bridge," a deep voice said from somewhere in the haze. "I have them."

Brooke was only partly aware of her surroundings as the large Blakist tore the pistol from her belt and tossed it away. But everything came clear again in a flash, as the monster seized her by the throat and dragged her up against the wall. Over the conflicting noise of her ears ringing and the faint rumble of the ship's thrust, Brooke could hear a sickly popping in her neck, and her vision began to swim and waver once more. She tasted blood and felt her lungs spasming in vain for even a single gasp of breath.

"Frail, feeble, ungrateful *wretch*!" The Blakist roared in her face. "You—*Rah*!"

Brooke suddenly found herself back on the deck, half-upright against the bulkhead, as the brute swung around. A flash of reflected light drew her eyes to the aluminum accents of the otherwise carbon-black metal knife hilt, jutting out from the man's back. It took another moment before she recognized it as that of a vibroblade Tibor must have claimed from the corpse of a ship's engineer. Tibor himself now stood in the hallway before the Blakist, just inside and to one side of the still-open shaft.

Despite the presence of a humming, twenty-centimeter blade jammed into his back somewhere near where a lung should be, the cyborg moved as though unfazed. If anything, Tibor's attack only angered him further. With two steps forward and a vicious backhand, he swatted Tibor across the face, smashing him against the wall with a sickly *thump*. Tibor sagged and dropped to the floor.

"Savages, all of you!" the Blakist seethed as he twisted a hand back and ripped the blade out as casually as one might scratch an itch. The deep red blood that spurted from the wound spattered along the corridor wall behind him, but didn't even slow his rant. "You profane our worlds like you would your own!"

Looking away, Brooke found her pistol down the curved hallway, just a few meters away. Though her left arm screamed in a chorus of agony and her entire body shook as though electrified, she forced herself to tumble forward and crawl toward it. But before she could reach the weapon, she felt a large hand grip her leg, and—once again—she was airborne, clanging against another bulkhead.

This time, she didn't strike the walls head-first, but instead managed to twist her body just enough to let her back absorb most of the impact. The impact left her momentarily breathless, but nowhere near as dazed as before. As quickly as she could manage, she began to tuck her feet in, struggling to rise again.

"And, to *think*," the red-eyed monster went on as he stepped closer, the blood-slicked vibroblade now buzzing menacingly in his hand, "we did all of this for the likes of *you!*"

With one more, purposeful step, the Blakist towered over her, and raised the blade. Automatically, Brooke raised both arms to intercept it, crying out in defiance of the pain that shot through her tortured joints. But before the man's arm came down, she heard a deafening *bang* from somewhere behind her, and felt a warm spray wash over her arms and scalp.

Even with no eyebrows and crimson camera lenses for eyes, the Manei Domini's expression registered a look of complete and utter shock. Blinking away pain-induced haze and tears, Brooke stared in wonder at the gunshot wound that now appeared right where the man's heart should be. He stumbled back one step, then two, before dropping to his knees. The vibroblade clattered to the floor.

The Blakist's head came up, just enough for Brooke to realize that he was looking *past* her, when a second shot rang out. This one smashed through the man's left eye, sending fragments of bone, flesh, and electronics exploding through the air.

Only then did Brooke finally find the desperate strength to surge forward, plowing headlong into the man's chest. Knocked back by her bull rush, the dying cyborg tumbled past Tibor's insensate form, and into the service shaft. One fast heartbeat later, his suicide implants went off with an air-sundering *boom*.

Even then, it was not until Brooke felt someone tugging gently on her arm, and looked up into Alahni's worried face, that she realized the danger was over—if only for now.

Even without the sudden wail of warning alarms from several of the monitor stations around them, the three officers within the *Agravain*'s forward command center could tell something—somewhere belowdecks—had gone terribly wrong. Mere minutes before, Adept Kaha had confidently radioed in, reporting he'd found the intruders who had somehow stowed aboard their ship. But whatever relief that news promised was shattered by an explosion in one of the service shafts just two decks down, aft of the bridge. The blast tripped more of *Agravain*'s automated damage control alerts, adding to those already sounded by multiple deck decompressions (and the seemingly random launch of the aft escape pod).

Pressed into her command chair, Adept-Captain Petra Inagi turned a fierce look to the comms station. Adept Lantos, wearing his headset askew to keep one ear free, was already on the case, calling Kaha's name into the microphone. He didn't look up from his screens, but the flush on his face assured Inagi that he knew she was watching.

"Kaha," he repeated, louder now. "What is your situation? *Respond!*"

Inagi turned to the sensor station, catching Adept Yuen's attention. With a twitch of her neck, she directed the sensor tech to man the damage control station. "Kill those damned alarms," she snapped.

Yuen nodded curtly and forced himself to rise.

Inagi's eyes were back on Lantos a moment later, only to find him staring back at her. "Tell me," she commanded.

"I can't raise Adept Kaha or Acolyte Senne!" Lantos shouted, his last words echoing as the wailing sirens abruptly fell silent.

Inagi stared at him for a moment, her mind reeling. After first learning the fate of her engineering crew, she recognized the stowaways for the threat they were. So, naturally, within minutes of their failed attempts to vent the ship's atmosphere and Lantos' ship-wide lockdown, she'd asked Adept Modesto Kaha—the sole Guardian on board—to hunt them down personally.

Confident that two "frails" would be easier to defeat within the confined spaces of a DropShip, Kaha took only one other crewman with him, junior tech Acolyte Ellick Senne. But Inagi was far from reassured. According to Precentor Apollyon, these invaders had not only proved crafty enough to penetrate Jardine's centuries-old veil of secrecy, they had somehow managed to elude some of the Master's finest warriors, and were responsible for the death of an *entire* Wayward tribe.

"Captain," Yuen called out from his new station, "that last explosion came from Support Shaft Charlie, on Hab Deck One!"

Inagi's heart sank. That was right where Kaha and Senne were headed when Kaha radioed in and said he had them.

...Just one deck below the bridge.

"Damn it!" she spat.

Between the original Engineering crew, the unfortunate loss of Acolyte Olanu to one of the blown airlocks, and whatever Lost One trickery just took the lives of Kaha and Senne, half of *Agravain*'s complement was now dead. Instantly, Inagi's mind raced to tally who was left. Aside from her three-man bridge team, there were only three other crew left on board, two of whom—Adepts Monro and Sykes—she'd sent down to reclaim Engineering. The third—Adept Lorne—was posted to the launch bay, in case the intruders went there to capture an escape craft. Prior to the intruders' discovery, all three had been strapped into their bunks, having come off-shift less than half an hour before. Positioned as they were now, none of them could possibly move forward in time to be of any help.

Inagi's eyes went to the main hatch at the back of the bridge. Even under lockdown, she knew, it would be only a matter of time before the enemy would breach it. Her own technical expertise could think of at least a half dozen ways to circumvent a locked hatch (unless they actually welded it shut)—and she could only assume these invaders also knew them, if they already made it *this* far.

She turned back to find Lantos and Yuen staring at her, their expressions grim.

"Vac suits and sidearms," she snapped at last, pointing at the storage lockers tucked between the stations ringing the bridge's operations center. "They're not taking *this* ship without a fight!"

Before he even reached out to grab the latch, Tibor knew it wasn't going to move for him. To leave their bridge doors unlocked while known stowaways were running about the DropShip, these Blakists would have to be stupid on levels beyond even the comically bad field agents of the Clan Watch he'd encountered a lifetime ago. Still, he reckoned, he had to try.

Across the door from him, leaning against the door-side bulkhead with a captured pistol at the ready, Brooke smirked for half a second and shrugged slightly. Tibor returned the gesture and stowed his own pistol, freeing his hands to grab the small utility computer hooked on his belt. The device was already lit up and ready for use, but Tibor still needed to fumble along the wall to find the right access panel he needed to pry open and plug into.

Portable engineering consoles were a staple of spacecraft technology since long before the first JumpShips launched mankind into the void beyond the Terran solar system. Part diagnostic tool, part emergency rescue system, they could be used to bypass severed control conduits and open doors auto-locked during a catastrophic hull breach. Like most high technology, they became scarce during the Succession Wars, but even then, it wasn't uncommon for local recharge stations and system patrol craft to carry at least a few for the express purpose of boarding damaged or crippled ships in search of survivors. But while many holovids through the years made them out to be magical ship-hacking devices—capable of overriding everything from the doors and lights to a DropShip's engines and weapon systems—the fact was one could only do such things when the proper conduits and ports were available to patch into, and those things simply didn't exist everywhere.

Tibor had a little more than passing knowledge of such things, but only because of the many times he and Brooke had boarded derelicts in their days with (and after) Interstellar Expeditions. Even then, he didn't consider himself an expert in hacking a DropShip, *especially* on a ship class he'd never seen before. So finding a vital system's control port to patch into was scratched off his list of priorities since before he grabbed his factory-fresh console back in Engineering. Plus, as long as a bridge crew remained active on the ship, it probably wouldn't have done much good anyway.

But doors were another matter. For the same emergency rescue reasons PECs existed to begin with, doors were easy to override. If one had the time.

The door's access panel, barely larger than his palm, was higher on the wall than he anticipated, but its sheet metal cover popped open readily enough under the pressure of his vibroblade. Inside, it took a little bit of blindly feeling about to locate a connection port to plug the console into, and when he found it, it proved remarkably difficult to plug into, thanks to its odd placement and the PEC's short interface cord. These little inconveniences were deliberate, he imagined—just enough to slow someone down who was perhaps not *supposed* to be doing this.

Someone like him.

As he began to work the console, Tibor glanced over to Alahni. Like Brooke, the girl was holding a captured pistol at the ready. Any nervousness he might have felt about allowing her to handle a weapon ended when she had shot one of her world's vaunted "Guardians" to save them. He felt a little guilty about doubting her—and, for that matter, Brooke's judgment in letting her come along on this suicidal escape plan—but he couldn't deny that the expectation of a double-cross had lurked in his mind since the moment he'd met her.

It certainly wouldn't have been his first betrayal, after all.

He was nearly finished inputting the hatch's emergency override sequence when the console suddenly flashed a pressure warning.

"Oh, *Scheiße*!" he spat.

"What?" Brooke said.

"The bastards in there just purged the bridge!"

"Bast *damn* it!" Brooke hissed.

"What does that mean?" Alahni asked.

"It means they shunted the airflow systems to space," Tibor said. "We'll be walking into vacuum if we open this door now. If this was an older ship or had an aerodyne setup, we'd probably find ourselves spacediving to boot."

"We're a few meters from outer hull, though," Brooke said quickly, her tone softened just enough to reassure the girl. "So, we're safe from getting shot into space."

"But there's still air out here," Alahni said. "Won't it just push in with us?"

"For a few seconds," Tibor said. "But not much longer while the bridge vents stay open. Depending how good the venting is, the pressure shift could even blast us into the chamber the second this hatch pops, leaving us gasping for breath the whole way like fish out of water. Hell, if they just waited another second—or opened the door themselves—that's exactly what *would* have happened—"

"Then we got lucky they didn't open up for us," Brooke cut in.

"I guarantee you that means they're already suited up and waiting for us behind any cover they can find in there."

Brooke looked around quickly. "Plenty of handholds by the door here," she said, pointing out one for Alahni on the far side of the hatch. Wide-eyed, the Jardinian reached for it and pressed her body against the wall. "And you still have the filter masks."

"*We* do," Tibor agreed as Alahni took the hint and pulled hers into place. "But yours was broken by that cyber-brute back there."

"Then we'll need to work fast, won't we?"

"Wait," Alahni started. "What are you—?"

"Tear gas won't do anything to them if they're suited," Brooke explained while Tibor settled his own mask in place, "but the smoke they create will give us a brief bit of cover. We'll just need to deploy it creatively."

"Flash-bangs and spike-bombs would be better," Tibor said through his filters. "Especially if we also had needlers."

"We'll make do," Brooke said, "but maybe we can add a little more chaos to the mix..." Her eyes darted quickly about, before settling on a large, scarlet, metal box anchored to the wall just across the corridor from them.

Tibor followed her gaze and snorted out half a chuckle. "Well, thank the gods of the interstellar safety code."

As Brooke stepped across the deck to crack the seal on the firebox, Tibor tucked his console under one arm and reached into his hip pouch with the other. His hand came up with a pair of green-striped mini-grenades, the last of the ordnance they'd used to take Engineering. He passed them both to Alahni.

"Keep your mask on, grab hold of something, and stay close," he told her as he made a show of hooking his arm through one of the handholds by the doorway. "And get ready to pop those when I say. Brooke and I will handle the rest..."

A subtle change in the deck's vibration warned Adept-Captain Inagi that the main hatch was cycling open seconds before it did so. Buttoned up in a light-duty vac suit that fit easily over her duty uniform, she half-crouched behind the far side of the sensor station, pointing her Sunbeam laser pistol at the opening. Flanking the doorway, Adepts Lantos and Yuen pressed themselves against the cover of gee-chairs, likewise covering the command center's sole access with lasers of their own.

The bridge was nearly black. Every monitor within was shut off and every console light had been deactivated or covered up by whatever spare suits and duty robes they could find in the emergency lockers. In the dark, airless chamber, Inagi quickly found the sound of her and her crewmates' breathing deeply disturbing, but she resisted the urge to switch off the comm channel they shared out of tactical necessity. Blake willing, she prayed, the maddening wait for their enemy would end before she went completely out of her mind.

The defense plan was simple enough: the moment that hatch opened, all three of them would fire at any form that darkened the doorway—and keep shooting until all that remained were light and corpses. Voiding the bridge would force the intruders to fight their way through a windstorm, only to risk a final death from asphyxiation if they weren't prepared for it.

Of course, Inagi wasn't about to put all her Eagles on that strategy alone. There were any number of ways these Housespawn scum could acquire vac suits or breathing masks on this ship. Hell, every crew deck had to have at least three lockers stocked with emergency-grade safety gear, just in case of a hull breach or coolant leak. None of that would be combat-grade, but she'd insisted on lasers over needlers anyway. If the results were hits guaranteed to breach an enemy space suit, she could accept the risk of a missed shot or two popping open whatever utility lines they might hit along the corridor bulkheads.

The hatch opened with a gentle rumble Inagi felt, but could barely hear. As the door slid into its bulkhead, a blast of smoke rushed inward—smoke that was tinged green and black in the light that spilled in with it. Inagi felt a strange sense of wonder that these intruders would truly expect *tear gas* to work in a vacuum.

Lantos and Yuen started firing wildly, their lasers flashing blindly into the green smoke storm to add an irregular, reddish strobing effect to the surreal scene. Inagi fired a heartbeat later, but the buffeting force of smoky air spoiled her stability; her first shot actually struck the ceiling just above the hatch.

Only then did she make out the strange shadow that sprang up in the doorway, for just a moment. Bigger than a grenade, but much smaller than a human, it spun in a wild arc on what looked like a jet of white steam. Careening off one of the command center's arresting columns, the black canister whirled right toward Inagi. Instinct sent her diving for cover again. The console shuddered against the jarring impact.

"The hel—!" Lantos spat into the channel, followed by a strangled "Ack!"

Something fast, small, and hard struck the deck less than twenty centimeters in front of Inagi and ricocheted with a muted, metallic clank. She flinched back.

"Shit!" Yuen yelled. "Captain, I'm h—aoo!"

Inagi's eyes went wide. The silence that followed was even stranger and more nerve-wracking than the breathing that threatened to drive her crazy mere seconds ago. Instantly, she realized she was alone, coiled into a near ball in the shadows behind a bridge console. Hazy puffs of whitish smoke stretched and scattered about her only to vanish into the air vents just as quickly as they came; the extinguisher thrown at her, sputtering out the last of its foam.

Over the ever-present thrum of the ship's engines, Inagi felt footsteps thumping on the deck. The intruders were coming in! Shaking off her surprise, she quickly keyed her comm to another channel.

"Engineering, Inagi!" she hissed urgently. "The bridge is lost. I say again, the bridge is lost! Set Condition O—!"

A tall, wiry man in crew coveralls stepped around the console right in front of her and froze there, a slugthrower in one hand. Despite the dim lighting, Inagi could see enough of the face behind his filter mask to know he wasn't one of hers. Instantly, she raised her weapon and pulled the trigger—

Her life ended in a blinding flash before she ever knew if her shot found its mark.

THE SANCTORUM
CITY OF HOPE
JARDINE (HERAKLEION)
FREE WORLDS LEAGUE
8 NOVEMBER 3067

Specter Precentor Omicron Apollyon, commander of the Master's Hands and de facto governor of the thrice-blessed world of Jardine, stared out the northern window of his office with infinite regret. Before him stretched the false ruins of Hope, its streets concealed beneath camo nets and a canopy of trees and vines arrayed just randomly enough to look natural from the air. Beyond its boundaries, the semi-tropical forests covered most of the landscape, stretching out toward the distant mountains and cut sharply only by the line of the Providence River. To the northeast and east, Apollyon could see the gray-white fog rising from the nearby geyser fields, and idly noted how easily their mist blended into the gray skies above. Already this morning, a drizzling rain was falling across the valley—as if the world itself shared in his sadness.

The smell of ozone lingered in the air, and his true arm still tingled even as he flexed and relaxed the fingers of his true hand. Glancing down, he noticed the blackened stripes crossing his palm, and used his frail hand to rub at them experimentally. A little of the carbon scoring came off, but the heat-scars from his now-retracted grapple cable remained clearly visible. Closing his eyes—both true and frail—he inhaled deeply, holding his breath an extra second or two before trusting himself to speak.

"The cancer has touched our very heart, my old friend," he finally, quietly said. "Or, perhaps, it has been here all along, silently growing while we ignored it."

The man he could still feel standing behind him said nothing.

"I have prayed," Apollyon went on. "In all my years, I have prayed that this day would never come."

When silence again was the only reply, Apollyon turned slowly.

Administrator Ogima Lunalla's face was white as bone, his eyes glued to the still-smoking shell of lifeless flesh now draped across Apollyon's desk. The body was cooling rapidly, its twitching finally ceased. Through his true sight, Apollyon knew the man—Uku—had died almost instantly. The jolt, delivered to his heart by the equipment stowed within Apollyon's true arm, carried more than enough current to get the job done. But it took the traitor's brain and nervous system a full ten seconds or so to catch up with his expired heart.

Ogima, standing less than half a meter from the man when the attack came, felt some of the shock himself, and stepped back, but not before a thousand strands of his short hair shot up in all directions. Still charged, they remained that way even now. Hope's civilian administrator hadn't moved a muscle since Uku's execution, but through his true vision, Apollyon could see that he was unharmed.

"Ogima," Apollyon said. His voice, soft yet commanding, caused the other man to flinch, but that was all.

"*Ogima!*" he repeated, much more forcefully. "Are you listening to me?"

Like a cadet struck by his superior officer, Ogima instantly snapped to attention, his gaze finally tearing away from Uku's corpse. "Y-yes, Guardian Master!" he croaked. "I hear you!"

Apollyon briefly glanced at Uku before turning his sympathetic eyes back to Ogima. "I know your pain, my friend," he said. "This is a terrible loss to our community, but we will move on. We *must* move on!"

"Yes, sir!" Ogima answered, his voice still shaky. "We shall!"

"Then purge your doubts, Administrator," Apollyon snapped. "Let none hear it in your voice, nor see it in your eyes—lest we suffer more like *him*! Our time is near, Ogima, and we need you to help see it through. The Promise is upon us, and all we have done here has been for our people—for *all* people."

At that, Ogima finally managed to look up and meet Apollyon's gaze head-on. Fear remained deeply etched on the administrator's face, but the signs of recovering self-control came through in his stance, and his voice. "What, then, are your orders, my Precentor?"

Apollyon nodded gratefully, but his expression remained grim. "Our home has been compromised, my friend," he said. "And I fear that this time, with so many of our brethren called to station, we may not be able to staunch this wound to our most cherished of havens in time."

"The Lost will find us," Ogima said. It wasn't a question.

Apollyon stepped around his desk, Uku's remains already forgotten, and placed a fatherly—frail—hand on Ogima's shoulder. "I shall contact the Master," he said, "beseech him for guidance, and for mercy. But I fear the Protocols of Karpov are clear enough..."

Ogima's eyes narrowed and fell as Apollyon's voice trailed off into uncertainty. "May all the gods, in all the heavens, have mercy on us," he whispered.

Apollyon said nothing, but the hand on Ogima's shoulder gave a gentle, momentary squeeze before falling away.

CHAPTER 8

"Now, stowing away, pulling the old bait-and-switch, and the good old frontal assault are all nice ways to score a ship, sure. Pirates and House militaries use these tricks all the time to subvert a transport for whatever strategic goal they have in mind. But most folk in these cases prefer to take such care in situations like these that a cool-headed captain has a good chance of countering them. The presumption is that your attackers want to capture your ship and use it when all is said and done, so even if you're outgunned, simply running and/or jumping away will do the trick.

But what happens when your attacker doesn't really care what they might break while trying to capture your ship? For many covert missions, even the mutual destruction of both sides can be considered an operational victory."

—TIBOR MITTERNACHT
AS QUOTED IN *"CHANGING THE OBJECTIVES (PART 2)"*
(WARRIOR DIGITAL PRODUCTIONS, SOLARIS VII, JUNE 3061)

K-1-CLASS DROPSHUTTLE *STILETTO-7*
JARDINE (HERAKLEION)
FREE WORLDS LEAGUE
9 NOVEMBER 3067

On the aftward viewscreen, the *Leopard CV* appeared as little more than a dense collection of blinding suns, looming ever larger as the DropShip's tail engines continued to burn for deceleration. From the angle of camera, *Stiletto-7*'s own drive flare—minute in comparison—was visible as little more than a glare that stretched across the image's lower-right quadrant. Assuming their pilots were competent enough, the two ships, still separated by hundreds of kilometers of void, would reach each other in just ten minutes or so, at or near a relative velocity of zero.

To this point, Precentor Damien Lucille and his crew maintained the charade they committed to six days ago. Through the voice modulator Lamashti had programmed, Adept Rumiko sent to and answered hails from the *Kaylin* as if she were Doctor Brooklyn Stevens herself. When the *Kaylin*'s commander—a cocky man named Anton Hara—failed to mention the second JumpShip himself, Lucille had Rumiko fish for some information on it. Hara's response was coy, teasing "Stevens" about losing track of her own people, and feigning ignorance of their whereabouts as well.

The news was like a dagger in Lucille's heart, proof positive that the real Stevens had indeed managed to elude capture, and that her crewmates were hard at work on an effort to rescue her. In the first moment of solitude he could find after that discovery, Lucille prayed to God, Blake, and Apollyon himself for the universe to find a way and bring those defilers the swift and bitter end they so richly deserved.

In the meantime, his journey continued toward the unknown factor of this second group of House-spawned violators—and the orders remained unchanged. As the hours and days continued to crawl by, Lucille focused on that, hardening his resolve and planning the assault.

Now merely minutes from the moment of truth, he knelt behind the shuttle's copilot station, the bulk of his Purifier battle armor—lacking only its helmet and forearm modules—taking up the space where ordinarily there would be a standard gee-seat. At the pilot seat beside him, similarly clad, was Adept Rumiko, controlling the craft's final approach with the deft touch of her haptic-gloved hands.

To Lucille, these final maneuvers felt disturbingly quiet. Although communications between the two ships' pilots remained open, it sounded to his true ears as though their instruments did all the talking for the past few hours, whispering data through the void in the elegant language of machines. Rumiko's last voice transmission from "Stevens" was met with the barest of acknowledgment; Hara's usual snide banter was entirely absent. Even with all the EMCON protocols under which Jardine's space crews operated, Lucille found this lack of chatter particularly conspicuous.

That was, until an alert sounded on his console.

Lucille spotted the flash of smaller lights for only a fraction of a second on his rear-view display, breaking away from the massive flares of the Kaylin's engine. Glancing down at her radar screen, Rumiko blinked her oily black eyes in the closest expression she had to surprise since the destruction of that Wayward camp back home.

"Fighter launch," she said. "Two craft. *Lightning*s."

"As escort?" Lucille wondered aloud. "At *this* stage?"

"Could just be clearing space for us," Rumiko suggested.

"*Two* spaces? For a shuttle that can't even fit in one?"

Rumiko frowned and reached out to key her microphone, when another alarm sounded, this one the insistent, ominous beeping of hostile tracking systems. Lucille's true hearing picked them up at the same time as distant radio pings, finding range from two hundred klicks away, while scrambled electronic transmissions buzzed at each other in the dark.

Lucille's mind screamed as a fresh surge of rage welled up inside him. *How did they figure it out?*

"That's close enough for now, Doctor Stevens," Hara's voice suddenly came through the speakers, dripping with more contempt than Lucille had heard in the entire flight to this point.

Lucille arched an eyebrow, shot a glance to Adept Rumiko, and whispered, "Demand explanation."

Rumiko nodded and hit the mike. "What's the meaning of this, Hara?" she snapped, enhancing the performance with a well-practiced Germanic accent.

"Let's just say our mutual employer knows you too well," Hara replied. "And I'd like to be sure where we stand before you set one dainty toe on *my* ship."

Lucille couldn't help but smirk at that. *Leave it to good, old-fashioned paranoia to ruin a perfectly mundane working partnership!*

"Where we stand?" Rumiko echoed, maintaining her pretense. "You can't be serious! We *stand* in hostile territory, with an enemy DropShip out-massing both of us barreling right this way!"

"A ship *I* can outrun forever, my dear. But I'm willing to lay odds you're just a few one-gee days from fumes in that little tub of yours."

Rumiko turned away from her instruments and favored Lucille with an expression that blended mockery and contempt. Only the slight flicker of reflected cockpit lighting made it possible to see she was rolling her all-black eyes like an exasperated teenager. Lucille gave her a knowing nod and a "move it along" gesture that sent her back with a scowl.

"What do you want, then, *Arschloch*?" she snapped.

"Such language!" Hara deadpanned. "Do you fellate your lovers with that mouth?"

Rumiko didn't even have to fake outrage now. "Oh, you *Mutter Fi—*!"

"Whatever, Stevens! Bellamy here tells me its customary for you explorer types to record all your discoveries on your ship logs, and that you—being the *professional* you are—almost certainly still do so. He also believes that, given your past issues with the company, you are your crew will try and play hard to get with that data once you're all out of danger. Maybe you'd even go so far as putting some kind of kill-switch on those files—you know, just in case."

"Of *course*," Lucille mumbled through his teeth. "Why stop at mere paranoia when one can go all the way to double-crossing?"

Rumiko, her expression now twisted in a mask of pure disgust, closed the mike and turned to him. "Blake preserve us!" she hissed. "To think the Promise is meant to save even dregs like *this* one!"

"At least we won't need to save him in particular," Lucille assured her. His hands were already on the console ahead of him, armored fingers hammering away at the keys with remarkable deftness while he simultaneously paged through the shuttle's utilitarian database. "But he does make an inconvenient request. It would be easy to simply fill a few records with pure gibberish, but these frails will certainly inspect them before they let us close."

"We don't have all day here, Doctor!" Hara's voice crackled through the speakers.

"Say the word, Precentor," Rumiko growled, "and I'll ram this shuttle straight into one of their flight bays before their flyboys know what's happening."

"Not just yet," Lucille said, now typing at blinding speed, eyes glued to his screen. "Keep up the act and stall. They won't shoot as long as they think they can give them something. Perhaps we can bluff them with 'encrypted' files..."

Rumiko grunted.

"And get ready to button up if they call it," he added. "One way or another, we are *taking* that ship."

LEOPARD-CLASS DROPSHIP *KAYLIN*
JARDINE (HERAKLEION) SYSTEM
FREE WORLDS LEAGUE

Ever since the *Kaylin* had separated from her JumpShip, Nathan Bellamy's mere presence on board the DropShip had been a thorn in the side of her captain, Anton Hara. Although he'd tried to leave the IE liaison behind, Bellamy once again surprised him by displaying enough backbone to insist on coming along. It was critical, he declared, that Stevens be "debriefed" by her employers as soon as possible, and he wasn't about to leave *that* job to the hired help.

Bellamy now stood on the *Kaylin*'s bridge, keeping his magslips firmly on the deck while clinging to one of the handholds beside the DropShip's comm station, where he was studying the data scrolling across one of its monitors. The dark gray coveralls he wore in place of his usual suit today gave him an almost respectable look, like someone who actually *belonged* aboard a mercenary spacecraft, rather than a mere passenger. He even kept a sidearm strapped to his hip now, mimicking the habit shared by every one of the *Kaylin*'s bridge and fighter crewmen. Hara had to admit that Bellamy's manner and bearing were finally starting to show some serious acclimation to spacer life.

"Hell," he once thought aloud to his exec in a moment of wry amusement, "another month or two, and that guy might even pick up enough jargon to really blend in here!"

"Perish the thought," Lenard Bryce deadpanned with a semi-scowl. "If that happens, we'll need to kill him lest he evolves any farther."

While Bellamy continued to study the comm station screen in silence, Hara and Bryce stood near the bridge's central hub, where an all-purpose display table was installed that normally served as a navigational display. Right now, however, the scratched and age-worn screen projected a tactical map of the surrounding space a scant 500 kilometers around the *Kaylin*. At this scale, the DropShip itself appeared as a fat green oval with wings, anchored to the map's center. Adjoining arrows and telemetry data showed its present velocity, heading, and relative position within the planetary system.

A little less than 100 kilometers to the DropShip's port and trailing a bit behind was a smaller red circle icon representing Brooke Stevens' K-1 DropShuttle. Its own telemetry and heading arrows described a course that currently ran roughly parallel to *Kaylin*'s, give or take five to ten degrees. Between the two vessels drifted a pair of slightly smaller wedge-shaped icons. Painted in the same shade of green as their mother ship, these fighter markers currently maneuvered to close with the shuttle while simultaneously keeping pace with both ships.

The fighters would be in firing range soon, waiting on orders from Hara to either go weapons free or assume an escort position. Orders that right now were being held up by the silent liaison still hovering over the comm station.

Bryce cleared his throat softly, drawing Hara's attention long enough to throw him a look and a palms-up gesture that said it all. *What the hell are we waiting for?*

Hara nodded and turned around. "Mister Bellamy," he called out, "talk to me. Is this what we're here for or not?"

Bellamy seemed reluctant to turn away, but when he did, his expression telegraphed his annoyance. "No," he shook his head. "I don't think so. It looks more like gobbledygook to me."

"Could it be a cypher?" Bryce suggested.

Bellamy glared at him. "If so, it's nothing like anything IE uses."

"I'd presume Stevens doesn't exactly play by all the IE rules," Hara said. "Otherwise, she'd still be wearing your logo, right?"

Bellamy's face didn't even redden. Instead, he shrugged and said, "Maybe, but I've seen coded transmissions before, and this one looks more like what you'd see if you set brain-damaged toddlers at a keyboard. My gut says she's pulling a stunt."

"Bitch move," Hara grumbled, then addressed the crewman seated beside Bellamy as he moved toward the comm station. "Jacoby, get her back on the line for me. Len, tell our boys to get ready for a warm-up."

Jacoby gave a curt "aye" and went to work, tapping open the mike at his station and patching it into the nav channel that already connected *Kaylin* and Stevens' shuttle. A secondary channel, beaming to the two *Lightning*s of Fyre Wing, shunted from the comm station to the tactics table, allowing Bryce to relay commands out of earshot.

Bellamy stepped aside, once again demonstrating his growing intelligence by not questioning anything.

"Stevens," Hara barked into the mike, "do you really think you can bullshit us?"

"Why, what*ever* do you mean, Captain?" came the woman's snarky reply.

"You know damned well what I mean. Do I really have to have my pilots explain to you that we're not messing around?"

Stevens' voice turned ice cold. "You wanted my files," she said, "you got them, *Saftsack*. Did you really expect me to give up all my cards so easily? Let us dock, and I'll hand you the code key."

"Bellamy here doesn't think—"

"*Cap!*" Bryce suddenly hissed loud enough to be heard. Hara whipped his head around. "Something's off! I've got gun-cam images from Fyre here; that shuttle's pristine!"

"Pristine?" Hara echoed. For a moment, he wondered why that would matter—but only for a moment.

"What does that mean—?" Bellamy started to ask, but Bryce drowned him out.

"She's flipping, sir!"

"Weapons free!" Hara snapped back as he shoved himself violently away from the comm station and spun toward the table. "Signal weapons free! Sound red alert!"

"*Captain Hara!*" Bellamy shouted, mere moments before all the bridge lighting switched from fluorescent white to glaring red, and the angry sound of *Kaylin*'s combat alarms blasted throughout the ship.

"Stevens supposedly crash-landed on that planet, Mister Bellamy," Hara yelled back, "but that shuttle out there is undamaged! I don't know who's ship that is, but I know a trick when I see one!"

On a plume of plasma fire several kilometers long, the K-1 class DropShuttle blasted forward the moment its broad nose cap fully swung about. Lighting its engines for maximum thrust, the 200-ton small craft shot from relative-zero velocity to three-gee acceleration in under a minute, while jets of extra maneuvering thrust set its ovoid hull into a corkscrewing roll.

As soon as the shuttle came into range, the two *Lightning* aerospace fighters approaching it opened fire, unleashing streams of high-caliber shells and bolts of coherent energy in near-perfect unity. All but invisible in the void, the weapons tore through space and raked the shuttle's hull. Shards of armor blasted apart and vaporized under the assault, but the craft forged along, unhindered.

Halfway to its target, the whirling shuttle let loose with its own weaponry. A spread of missiles and lasers shot forth, lashing out at *Kaylin*'s aftward flank. The long-range warheads and medium-grade missiles all struck home, but against the superior armor of the 1,900-ton DropShip, their impact was barely a nuisance. Instead, the larger ship lit up its own maneuvering thrusters, rolling and twisting about to face its attacker.

Clouds of missiles, lasers, and bolts of high-energy particles flashed from *Kaylin*'s weapon bays, all aimed at the incoming shuttlecraft. A sudden blast of thrust from the DropShip's main engines added new momentum to her course, throwing it out of the barreling craft's direct trajectory. In mere seconds, explosions of armor splinters, briefly illuminated by flickering bursts of red and blue light, blossomed across the shuttle's broad, blunt nosecone.

And still, the smaller ship came on, turning just enough to match *Kaylin*'s movement.

By the time the fighters—now racing up from behind—could bring their own weapons to bear again, nothing in the universe could stop what came next. But that didn't stop them from trying anyway.

The collision came amid another furious volley of weapons fire from both the *Lightning*s and their mothership. Although the tiny K-1 craft weighed barely more than one-tenth of *Kaylin*'s mass, it plowed into the DropShip at over 6,000 kilometers per hour, striking the broad side of her hull just a meter shy of her aft-starboard launch bay.

As the shuttle disintegrated, *Kaylin*'s hull nearly crumpled from its impact. The ship immediately went into an awkward tumble, spewing atmosphere and wreckage from the rents in her outer hull where whole spans of reinforced armor had been mere moments before. Flashes of cerulean light and glimpses of orange fire flickered amid the expanding cloud of debris, but quickly vanished as the last of the air bled out into space.

The *Kaylin*'s thrusters sputtered out, and even her running lights went dead for a few moments as the fighters of Fyre Wing coasted past above her, but only for a few moments. Then the thrusters fired again, and the lights returned as the carrier DropShip began to stabilize herself—mangled, but still very much alive.

Klaxons blared and alarms wailed throughout the *Kaylin*'s command center, while several monitors blanked out or flashed warning messages in blinking crimson. Clinging to one of the handrails affixed to the central table, Hara pulled himself up from the deck and found Bryce already standing across from him. Bryce held a hand over his nose and mouth, and blood dripped from a cut on his right eyebrow. His glasses were nowhere in sight, but that didn't prevent him from taking note of his captain's questioning look and nodding curtly.

Assured of Bryce's health, Hara swept his eyes around the rest of the bridge, finding the rest of his crew still alert at their stations. Jacoby, at his comm station, pressed one ear of his headset to his left ear, while his right flicked across the panels in front of him. Beside Jacoby, Bellamy looked dazed, but still managed to seize the nearest handhold and pull himself away from the storage locker he'd been thrown against.

"Damage report," Hara called out.

"Still updating!" Jacoby shouted back. "Multiple hull breaches on starboard side! Flight Bays Starboard Baker and Starboard Charlie are gone! Heavy damage to aft dorsal and lateral thrusters! Emergency bulkheads and fire suppression systems engaged! Pressure seals in place and holding! Engineering reports we still have main drives and reactor integrity remains nominal, but we have blown power conduits all over the ship! Backup lines are handling the load, but just barely! No casualty figures yet!"

"Cut power to all primary weapon bays; lighten our energy load! And kill the alarms!"

"Aye!" Jacoby snapped.

"Calling Fyre Wing back to escort positions," Bryce announced just as the collision alarm fell silent. His voice sounded stuffy, and Hara looked over to see his brown-skinned exec had taken his hand away from his face so he could fetch the small, wired comm mike he now held close to his mouth. Above the comm, Hara could see just a slight trickle of blood coming from the man's nostrils.

Hara nodded, resisting the urge to try and check his own nose for signs of breakage. "Any sign of that shuttle?"

Bryce looked at the table, then sniffed and glanced over to the crewman on the sensor station—a pale, thin, blond-haired and blue-eyed young man named Vogel. Vogel, sensing his attention, shook his head without turning away from his own screens.

"Nothing," Bryce said finally. "The craft must have broken up on impact."

"The hell was Stevens *thinking*?" sputtered an incredulous Bellamy.

"Stevens?" Hara echoed with a scowl. "No, I don't think that was Stevens at all."

"What are you talking about? You were *speaking* to her, Captain!"

"I spoke to a woman with a Steiner accent, but none of those messages were on-vid. Damage, they said. Damage I didn't see on that shuttle before it came at us."

Bellamy practically bristled. "Who else *could* it have been?"

"Probably the same assholes driving the *Union* half a day behind them, maybe?" Hara snarled, feeling his patience collapsing as he met Bellamy's gaze head-on. "Or did you forget about *that*?"

Whatever defiance the IE liaison had left in him evaporated at that point. His mouth opened for a retort, but closed just as quickly.

"Right," Hara said. "Helm! Set course for our Jumper! We're out of here as soon as Fyre gets back on board."

"We'll have to use the port side bays for recovery, Captain," Jacoby called out. "I'm still not getting any response from the starboard crew, and power's still sketchy there."

Hara locked eyes with Bryce again. The exec nodded before relaying the captain's commands.

"We're just *leaving*?" Bellamy said.

"IE didn't pay us to die here, Mister Bellamy," Hara said. "This mission's a bust. Wherever your wayward girl went, we won't find her by loitering in a hostile system.

"So yes, you fool. We *are* leaving!"

In the chaos of *Stiletto-7*'s final moments, an outside observer could be excused for failing to notice how the small DropShuttle tumbled around once last time, and fired its engines at full blast, as if to halt its own suicide run just before impact. It would be even easier to forgive the same observer for failing to spot several much smaller *somethings* that tumbled out of the craft while it did so.

Landing a thousand-kilogram suit of battle armor on the hull of a moving spacecraft—while simultaneously trying not to be killed by the cloud of exploding debris from a ship-on-ship collision near your landing point—was a rather difficult thing. Indeed, by the standards of any military, mercenary, or major intelligence agency in the Inner Sphere, it might even be considered a benchmark of insanity.

But the Master's Hands weren't like any military, mercenary, or major intelligence agency in the Inner Sphere. Theirs was a calling greater than all others: the redemption of humanity, at any cost. Suicide tactics weren't just a last resort; to protect the Promise, they could even be considered standard procedure. And so it was that, mere seconds before impact, Adept Rumiko willingly sacrificed herself to soften their wild charge into the enemy DropShip, in the hopes that at least one of her eleven comrades would survive to complete the mission.

Her death would not have been in vain had even one of the troopers survived to board the *Leopard*, so Precentor Lucille considered it Blake's own providence that he managed to link up with four other Domini in all. Their suits were battered, to be sure, but most remained fully sealed and combat-ready. Only Adept Warren's Longinus had suffered major damage to its systems, having bled out its entire oxygen supply after losing half of its (and Warren's) right arm just below the elbow. Despite this, Warren remained mobile, and had simply held his breath until he could scavenge an emergency oxygen tank from the ruins of the depressurized flight bay he'd found himself in. When Lucille found him, the warrior had just finished rigging up a makeshift apparatus that fed air into his suit straight through the stump where his arm had been.

They now stood in the dark, vacant remains of a mid-ship corridor, just outside one of the ship's emergency bulkhead doors. Lucille's helmet sensors and true vision alike could feel the heat from the other side, and a pressure indicator on the door itself confirmed the presence of breathable air as well. As he reached his armored hand for the emergency crank that would open its locking mechanisms, savoring its icy feel as transmitted to his true senses by his Purifier's neural interface, he turned to face his team one last time.

"Remember," he told them, "sweep and clear all frails on sight, but check your fire for shipboard systems; we need this ship functional enough to rejoin her transport. Adept Kano, you shall proceed aft to secure engineering. Adepts Nonehe and Sakov, take the flight bays and mid-ships. Adept Warren and I shall take the bridge. Maintain radio silence and jam all transmissions once we're inside. Understood?"

"By Blake's Will, it shall be so!" Kano intoned.

"Blessed be," said Nonehe and Sakov.

"For Jardine," Warren snarled ominously.

Lucille gave a nod his armor obediently replicated and started to turn the crank. "For the Master, and the Promise!"

The stench of ozone hung heavy in the air, the latest in a series of annoyances that followed the false Stevens' suicide run. For perhaps the ten-millionth time in his entire life as a spacer, Anton Hara cursed the ever-unreliable nature of thirty-first century circuit breakers. The fire that erupted from beneath the nav table was easily enough extinguished, but it killed Bryce's communications with the DropShip's flight deck just as the fighters of Fyre Wing were coming back on board. And—of course!—just as the *Kaylin*'s exec moved to work with Jacoby at the primary comms station, all ship-wide intercoms went down.

And so, for the moment, *Kaylin*'s crew were basically coasting along, but at least the burn back to their JumpShip was underway. Hara took solace in that after the news finally came in from Engineering. In the meantime, Jacoby and Bryce continued their efforts to reach the rest of the ship's personnel using personal devices.

Nathan Bellamy, likely hoping to maintain his own relevance now that he had nothing else to do, stood at the darkened table, staring blankly at its scuffed surface. His low-voiced musings continued, even as Hara did his best to ignore them.

"She *could* still be planetside," he suggested aloud. "Captured, maybe. Or killed, but with her record, that's a bit doubtful. It would explain how they knew enough about her to try and dupe us, but why?"

Hara sighed.

"Right," Bellamy said, as if finding an answer in that. "To protect their secret, they'd be trying to capture any JumpShips waiting for her before they can escape..."

Hara turned to the liaison with an expression of bland irritation, but said nothing.

"But who are *they*?" Bellamy asked. "If Stevens' people knew, they didn't bother to tell us..."

"Fancy that," Hara said flatly.

Bellamy shot him an annoyed glare. "Perhaps we would have gotten some more answers if you'd allowed them to dock, or shot them apart *before* they hit your precious ship, and scavenged the wreck."

"Neither of which was going to happen, Bellamy, as I'm not an idiot."

Bellamy scowled. "I fail to see how any of *this* is better," he grumbled back, waving vaguely at the table.

"You *fail* to see a lot," Hara snapped. "We're in a system you explorer-types have been trying to find for over a century, and someone clearly went through all that time trying to *keep* it hidden. Someone who has at least a fleet of DropShips and fighters to spare on suicide runs like we saw at Shasta and here. Someone who doesn't have any problem attacking JumpShips, Ares Conventions be damned. Whoever they are, they aren't your run-of-the-mill bandits, I can tell you that. We're looking at some House-level operation, of the black variety."

"What, like SAFE?"

"Hell if I know! And to be blunt, I don't really think I *want* to know at this point, because whoever it is has probably marked us already. Your Stevens kicked over a hornets' nest, and now they have our scent too."

Bellamy broke into a smile that Hara instantly wanted to punch off his face. "So *that's* why you're running, isn't it?"

Hara leaned toward the man, coming close enough to make his stupid grin evaporate as he edged cautiously back. "As I said," he snarled through his teeth, "unlike *you*, I'm not an idiot!"

"*Captain*," Bryce suddenly cut in from across the bridge, his voice tense. "We've got trouble!"

Hara straightened himself and turned about, ignoring the flash of rage that registered on Bellamy's face. Bryce was standing just left of Jacoby's chair, his eyes half-squinting, but whether that was from worry or the absence of his spectacles, Hara couldn't be sure. Bryce held his personal communicator at his side, but Hara could see a flashing glow of red coming from the device.

"Something's jamming us," he said without waiting for a prompt. "We can't reach anyone on the ship."

"What?" Hara said, incredulous. In two deliberate steps, he stood over the sensor station. Instinctively, Vogel looked up at him from the seat and gestured silently at the displays. The radar screen showed a cloud of random static, while the external and internal sensor screens appeared completely blank. Reaching over and switching through their inputs changed nothing. "Where is this coming from?"

"Unknown," Vogel said. "Everything's too overloaded with noise for me to even triangulate."

Hara glanced around the bridge to find everyone's eyes on him. Even Cadence—the ever-silent brunette at the ship's helm—had turned back from her flight control boards with a look of concern. Bellamy's expression had also given way to worry. A cold feeling grew in the pit of Hara stomach and his mouth ran dry. They all realized, as he did, that anything close enough to jam the *Kaylin*'s systems was close enough to be an imminent threat.

But nothing else had even been on the radar once that shuttle rammed them...

"*Son of a Canopian whore!*" Hara hissed under his breath. Pointing at the aftward hatch, he locked eyes with Bryce and barked, "Lockdown the bridge! That shuttle wasn't a kamikaze! We've been boarded!"

Bryce moved swiftly, but before he even reached the door, it swung inward with a heavy, ominous *thud*. Before anyone else could react, a hulking monstrosity ducking into the bridge through the opening. The hulk was a one-armed beast of a man clad in a badly dented suit of battle armor painted in a mix of bloody red and deathly black. The trooper within wore no helmet, exposing the visage of a bronze-skinned man with vaguely Asian features in what appeared to be a black, skin-tight hood. Although the man's left eye was readily visible under the bridge lights, the other seemed to be covered by a chrome-ringed, green-lensed monocle. Stranger still, his lips curled back to expose what looked like a mouthful of jagged, metallic teeth.

But what truly chilled Hara to the bone was the symbol he saw emblazoned on the right side or the armor's broad chest, scratched up, yet still clearly visible: a downward-pointed broadsword on a field of black. It was a symbol most familiar to anyone who lived or worked among the peoples of the Free Worlds League for the last fifteen years:

The insignia of the Word of Blake.

Before Hara could blink, Bryce reached for the pistol at his side and slid it from its holster. In that same amount of time, the one-armed trooper turned and raised a metallic claw toward him. From a weapon concealed somewhere inside the suit's armored palm, a hail of bullets erupted, impossibly loud within the confines of the bridge. Blood splashed across the cabin as each round tore through Bryce's thin frame, nearly cutting him in half. In an instant, the man who'd served as Hara's first officer for more than a decade—a man he'd come to trust with his deepest secrets and his very life—was gone.

"*Len!*" Hara's cry was automatic.

"Jesus Christ!" Bellamy yelled out, diving forward to put the nav table between him and the monster.

The trooper turned again, his feral snarl unchanged as he stepped further into the command center, and swung his arm about to spray another burst of shells at the forward end of the cabin. Hara flinched and ducked as the shots flew past, only to hear a scream from Cadance somewhere behind him. The pinging of missed rounds echoed about the bridge, punctuated by a loud cracking Hara couldn't immediately identify. As the shooter paused briefly, Hara also became aware of an ominous hissing, but his instinct to assess the damage was overridden as he saw a second form lumbering through the hatch.

The second warrior wore armor that looked more eerily human-like than the first, armor that moved with a terrifying fluidity. Weirder yet, parts of the thing appeared to be blurring, with colors shifting and flowing across several of its more prominent surfaces in surreal patterns. The rest of the battlesuit was bloody red, and its trooper's face hid within a helmet looked more like a green-lensed gas mask.

As the first Blakist fired again, ripping Jacoby apart where he sat, the second raised a weapon of its own, a giant muzzle that seemed to take up its entire forearm. In horror, Hara realized this cannon was pointing his way, and he pushed himself forward, scrambling toward Bellamy's hiding place. Crimson light flashed overhead, close enough for him to feel its blistering heat, and a sickeningly wet *pop* nearby marked the end of Vogel's life.

A strange, almost dreamlike silence descended upon the *Kaylin's* bridge, marred only by the buzzing of half-ruined electronics and the persistent hissing of a breached line somewhere near the pilot's station. Hara pulled himself into a seated position next to a wide-eyed Bellamy who—against all his past estimations of the man—now clutched a Magnum autopistol in his hands like someone who actually knew what he was doing. Glancing about while he fumbled for his own sidearm, Hara struggled to comprehend how everything had gone so wrong so quickly. His entire command crew was dead, his ship wrecked and boarded, days away from any safe haven—even if they *could* call for help.

None of this made sense!

"What do we do, Captain?" Bellamy whispered through his teeth.

Hara blinked at him incredulously.

"You surrender," an amplified voice declared before Hara could find any words. *"Or make peace with whatever god you profess to believe in."*

Bellamy sat frozen, his mouth agape. Hara pulled himself into a crouch, turning away from the IE liaison so he could keep an eye on his side of the nav table. In his mind, the tactical situation was finally starting to crystalize, and it was a bad one. Two battle-armored troopers stood now on his bridge, waiting for him or Bellamy to give up or do something even dumber. While both of their suits had looked damaged to Hara, only one trooper—the one with a missing arm and exposed head—could possibly be felled by the weapon in his hand. That warrior, Hara knew, had moved closer to the starboard side of the command center when his friend came in—which meant he might be standing just around the corner from where Hara now huddled. Give or take a half meter or so, it was possible Hara could peek around and squeeze off a clean shot at that monster's head. If he hit, the Blakist might fall, but if he missed...then what?

Hell, Hara told himself, *even if I* hit, *what next? Try and bull-rush the* other *one-ton battlesuit standing between us and the nearest escape pod?*

"W-who are you?" Bellamy called out without warning. Hara nearly jumped at the sound.

"We are the Guardians of the Promise, frail soul," answered the amplified voice. *"We are the bloody hands of Justice, the bane of the Clans, and the bringers of truest peace. We are the salvation you House-spawned children so desperately need."*

Hara winced as he heard a single *thump*, accompanied by a heavy vibration in the decking. It felt close to him. The starboard trooper was moving again. Had to be!

"I don't understand," Bellamy nervously shouted.

"Your understanding is not required," came the reply. *"Suffice to say, we are the warriors who will save mankind from the shadows, your unseen protectors."*

"Our protectors? If that's true, then wh-why are you attacking us?"

"Because you have trespassed. Your presence here threatens the Promise."

"Our presence here?" Bellamy repeated. "Where's 'here?' We just jumped into this system to—"

"Do not try lying to me, Frail!" the voice boomed now. *"You were in league with the intruders who set foot on our world, even if you* did *ultimately hope to betray them."*

Another *thump*, another vibration. That same trooper, creeping along in his armor, was moving closer. Cautiously, Hara tilted his head just far enough to catch a glimpse of where Bryce's corpse lay, stretched out upon the floor. Directly above the body, ominously glaring right back at Hara, stood the one-armed man.

"Okay, okay," Bellamy was saying, his voice cracking. "You're right, okay. B-but this is—I mean, maybe we can cut some kind of...deal here?"

Hara heard and felt two more *thumps*, and realized the warrior who was speaking was now on the move, likely circling along the chamber's port side, toward Bellamy. In his mind, he could almost see it. The aft hatch, wide open, now unguarded, less than ten meters away. *If* he could act before the wounded trooper did, *if* he could land the shot right, and *if* he could bolt fast enough while the talkative one was still dealing with Bellamy...

"*A deal?*" the unseen trooper asked. "*Do you truly believe you're in any kind of a bargaining position here?*"

"There has to be *something*!" Bellamy pleaded. Hara could practically taste the man's terror now, the bleeding edge of hysteria that made his every word sound breathless and small. "Something your people need! M-money? Information? Con-connections? I—I know people! All over the Sphere!"

"*Are* you *this ship's captain?*"

Hara's eyes widened and he snapped his head around. He still couldn't see the other trooper, but he could see Bellamy glancing back his way, slack-jawed, his face frozen with fear.

"*Oh, shiiit!*" Hara growled. In that instant, nothing was clearer than the next few seconds ahead, the certainty that Death itself was reaching out for him.

Without another thought, Hara spun back toward the first trooper, raised his weapon, and fired. He was up and running before he could even tell what he'd hit, his eyes on the aft hatch as if nothing else in the universe existed. The blood rushing in his ears all but drowned out the sound of alarmed cries, a shouted command, and the air-splitting *pop* he felt in his chest. Somewhere in all that came a nova of angry red light, which lasted for less than a moment.

Suddenly, his nostrils were overwhelmed by the stench of burning metal. Hara gagged, and found himself on his knees with no memory of falling. Just half a meter ahead of him stood the open hatchway. On the corridor wall beyond that, he noticed a blackened scar he'd never seen before, surrounded by a watery ring of the darkest red. That was when he realized he couldn't breathe, couldn't speak, and couldn't even feel his legs anymore.

Hara reached a hand up to his chest, and looked down to find the ashen edges of an impossibly large hole in his shirt. His fingers, half numb by the time they reached the wound, came away bloody. As he tried to turn around, gripped by a final compulsion to look out at the stars from the *Kaylin*'s viewports one last time, his vision swam, and the cold, black fog of oblivion closed in all around him...

MERLIN-CLASS DROPSHIP _AGRAVAIN_
RETROGRADE INTERCEPT COURSE (ADRIFT)
JARDINE (HERAKLEION) SYSTEM
FREE WORLDS LEAGUE
10 NOVEMBER 3067

The *Agravain* was dead.

Her fusion heart was cold and inert, her atmosphere-recycling lungs empty and still, while the plasma thrusters that served as her wings and legs sat limp and lifeless. And for all their expertise with spacecraft systems, there was nothing Brooke or Tibor could do about it.

The Blakist DropShip became a Flying Dutchman within minutes after the bridge fell—undoubtedly in a last act of spite ordered by her doomed captain. A powerful rumble announced the destruction of the reactor's containment chamber, and though Brooke was certain that they'd all perish an instant later, the all-incinerating nova she and the others braced for simply never came.

Tibor, still clutching the fresh laser wound in his thigh, managed to *laugh* about it. "A fusion plant that actually scrams itself right!" he exclaimed. "The interstellar safety code strikes in our favor for a change!"

But now, a day later, he and Brooke finally had to admit defeat. The damage done to the engines and power plant was simply beyond their abilities. The only consolation left was that however many Blakists were on board after they'd taken the command center, all of them had either died or fled the ship soon after. Amid the floating ruins of Engineering were two more bodies than had been there during the stowaways' last visit, both shredded by shrapnel from whatever they'd exploded in there. The jettison of a life pod—the second, and last, of the two the ship had been equipped with—followed by the launch of some kind of small craft from the hangar bay, not only carried away whoever else remained, it left Tibor, Brooke, and Alahni with just one other means to escape the dead ship.

"It's a heavy fighter of some kind," Tibor said. "Damned if I recognize the type, though."

"Looks brand new," Brooke admitted. "And sleek. But still..."

They were in the launch control station of *Agravain*'s flight bay, a dimly-lit side-chamber in a large, round, and otherwise wide-open deck. Beyond the station, the bay was occupied by little more than a few giant retrieval mechanisms, some empty stowage gantries, two fighter catapults, and a single, large, red-and-black craft with back-swept wings and a semi-circular tail wing assembly lacking any apparent vertical stabilizers. One of the bay's two wide space doors was already opened to vacuum, its corresponding catapult sprung and empty, while the strange aerospace fighter sat slightly off-kilter on its own catapult, facing the closed door.

With the rest of the DropShip's atmosphere bled out the day before, entering this area didn't cause the same windstorm of changing air pressure they'd experienced when seizing the bridge, but that fact did little to reduce the strange sensation of mixed panic and exhilaration everyone felt upon coming in. Alahni, in particular, nearly hyperventilated in her vac suit and grabbed the nearest handholds for dear life when she saw the yawning void beyond the opened bay door, the starfield beyond silently and lazily drifting by in an endless loop as *Agravain* idly tumbled through space. It took more than a few assurances from Brooke and Tibor to get her to relax and trust the magnetic slips on her feet enough to shuffle-step into the control room.

Emergency batteries kicked in throughout the DropShip within minutes of its engine's demise, casting much of the ship's interior into an eerie red twilight. Most of the computer systems were off-lined instantly, but Tibor found his E-console was still able to reactivate some of them—however briefly— as they explored the derelict. But opening doors was another matter, as the depowered hydraulics for every major hatchway required a lot of hand-cranking to spring them. Even under the microgravity that followed the loss of continuous thrust, the working of these various mechanical door controls, not to mention the constant need to alternate between reliance on magslips and handholds for travel, made for an exhausting day's work.

The lack of sleep and food wasn't helping either. Brooke felt her eyelids drooping and her stomach growled softly. It took her a few moments to realize she just trailed off mid-sentence while she stared blankly at the parked aircraft through the control station windows.

"I know," Tibor said. "It's still a fighter. No fuel expansion system."

"What does that mean, again?" Alahni nervously asked. Brooke turned to her and found the girl's eyes remained glued to the station windows, staring incredulously at the open bay door, and the stars beyond it. Had she not spoken up, it would have been easy to imagine that Alahni wasn't listening to them at all.

"It means," Brooke began, "that—unlike a shuttle or DropShip—this fighter will burn a good part of its reaction mass every second the engines are lit."

"Which means it'll be pretty fuel-expensive to slow it down," Tibor added. "Depending on how much that thing carries, the tanks will most likely be emptied out long before we've decelerated from the speed this ship's already moving at."

"Slow down?" Alahni asked. "Why would we need to? The Guardians must surely still be chasing us!"

"Once we get out there," Tibor said through a stifled yawn, "we can start feeding telemetry to the *Sacajawea* to come and meet us part way with one of her other shuttles. But shuttles and fighters aren't really built to dock with each other, so the goal will be to match speeds as we get close. It's dangerous and tricky, especially if you try to do it under fire or in too much of a hurry. But it's doable. So, it's safer the lower you can get your velocity."

Alahni blinked and finally managed to tear her gaze away from the void outside. "But if we still can't dock," she started, "how would we...?" Abruptly, her eyes widened.

"*Ja*," Tibor said. "Exactly. So be careful with that vac suit."

"Well," Brooke muttered, "the sooner we launch, the better. I just hope there's room for all three of us in that thing's cockpit..."

Close to an hour later, after manually cranking open the second launch door to reveal more open space beyond, the last three living souls on the *Agravain* prepared to climb into the confines of a technological marvel none of them had ever seen before. Although designed with up to two occupants in mind, room for a third body in the rear co-pilot's seat was discovered in the form of several redundant control systems that proved remarkably easy to remove.

"Aha!" Tibor exclaimed through their shared radio channel when he found the release mechanisms. "Modular tech! State of the art! I think I've heard of this fighter type after all."

"So this is an OmniFighter?" Brooke asked.

"*Ja*," he replied as he pulled the last power cables free and yanked the secondary gunnery station up from its mounting. "I think it's a joint project the League and the Word started cooking up ten years ago or so. Shame we couldn't secure this thing before they purged this deck; we might have been able to swap out the guns for some more fuel tanks."

"Without a tech crew who actually knows what they're doing?"

Together, Brooke and Tibor hurled the bulky console away, aiming for the far side of the flight deck. Between the microgravity and the DropShip's tumble, the weightless console flew across the flight deck in a way that looked utterly unnatural. Noiselessly, it eventually bounced off a support beam near the empty flight bay's ceiling and ricocheted into a dark recess far out of the way.

"A guy can dream, can't he?" Tibor said. Peeking back into the passenger area, he gave a short nod. "Well, it's not a lot of room, but if I take Alahni on my lap, we both hold the harness straps, and brace with our legs—"

"Whoa, there!" Brooke cut in. "If *you* take Alahni on your lap?"

"What's wrong with that?"

"*You're* the better pilot here, Trouble. It's going to be difficult enough launching from a dead ship without a functioning catapult."

Tibor gave Brooke a wary look that was rewarded by a crooked scowl from her. "Alright," he said with a sigh.

She turned back to Alahni, whose suited form was re-emerging from the launch control station, and gave a short, awkward wave to catch the young girl's attention. "How went your search over there?"

"I finally found what appears to be standard ration packs and some spare emergency ox-canisters in a couple of storage cabinets back there," Alahni replied. "Will there be enough space in that thing?"

Tibor glanced into the fighter's open cockpit once again, then looked back at the Jardinian, who was holding up a narrow metal cylinder the size of a personal coffee thermos in one hand, and a pair of small, foil-wrapped packages in the other. "It'll be really tight," he said, "especially in the back with you and Brooke. But we *should* be able to make it work..."

Once the passengers and provisions were secured, Tibor dogged the canopy and spent the next few seconds hunting and pecking at the various control switches to begin the process of starting up the fighter's power plant and life support systems. A soft whooshing—merely felt at first, and heard only as the internal air levels climbed closer to breathable— filled the cockpit.

"Right," he began, "nobody crack their helmet seals until we're free and clear of the ship and I give the okay. This launch will probably get a little bumpy."

"Bumpy?" Alahni nervously repeated. "How bumpy?"

"The DropShip is actually in a slow tumble right now," Tibor explained. "And its normal catapult launcher is useless without a flight deck officer helping us out, so we'll be relying completely on jets and maneuvering thrusters to keep us aligned with the opening. And since there's basically no gravity with the DropShip, because it's adrift—"

"Trouble," Brooke cut in, "can we *not* discuss this right now? You've got this, and you know it."

"In other words," Tibor said with a smirk, eyes and hands still darting across his instruments, "stop scaring the girl. Got it."

"I *can* still hear both of you," Alahni protested. "You know this, right?"

"Can't be helped. I mean, sure, we could keep quiet, but that would probably make it harder to keep you distracted before I do *this*—!"

Slamming the main thrust control forward, Tibor kicked the fighter's gear release and triggered the fuel ignition systems in concert. Instantly, the 85-ton OmniFighter went from a low, idling thrum to the full-blast of three-gee acceleration. Alahni gave a squeak that nearly pierced Tibor's eardrums despite the filtration of his helmet speakers, while he and Brooke each let out audible grunts of their own.

In less than an eyeblink, the fighter vaulted off the deck, through the open bay door, and straight out into open space.

But it didn't do so cleanly. A loud *bang* and a hard slewing of the craft to the right added to the chaos of the moment. Tibor felt himself thrown hard to the left, his helmet rapping against the armored canopy with an ominous *crack*, and Brooke's "*Scheiße!*" at the same time told him he wasn't the only one. His eyes dropped immediately to the damage monitor, where an alert beeped for his attention and a wireframe image painted the forward half of the fighter's right wing in blazing red.

"Trouble?" Brooke called out.

"We clipped the exit!" he shouted back, killing the main throttle with one hand while his other struggled with the flight stick. "Forewing took the hit, but I think we're still in one piece!"

"May God and Blake preserve us!" Alahni's voice mumbled in the background, nearly lost to the din of warning sounds and the firing of maneuver thrusters.

Beyond the canopy, stars swirled about as they continued to spin through the void, their lights outshone only by the occasional flare of Jardine's distant sun and the reflection of the

Agravain's derelict hull. Tibor grumbled a few choice curses of his own as he pulled at the controls and feathered the thrusters, but over the next full minute or so, he finally managed to bring the massive war machine back under control.

Killing the damage alarm took another minute after that, by which time Tibor swore he had a migraine coming on.

"Trouble?" Brooke called out again, with wary relief in her tone.

"Is everyone back there alright?"

"I think so. You?"

"Nothing seems broken," Tibor said with a sigh. "At least, no more than it already was."

"We're okay, then?" Alahni asked. "Truly?"

"Heh," Tibor said, finding more joy than he expected in the way she asked. "Yes, *mein Liebling*. We're okay."

"Don't worry, Alahni," Brooke said. "We're in good hands now. You can open your eyes now."

"Oh my god!" Alahni said a few seconds later. "The stars... There's so many!"

"Beautiful, aren't they?"

Tibor felt a smile cross his face as he listened to their conversation, and looked up through the canopy at the eternal night of open space. All at once, it seemed, the tension and fear that had tensed up his every muscle over the past few days just melted away. A sense of immense relief washed over him that he could barely believe possible just minutes ago, as if the weight of an entire universe had finally come off his shoulders—if only for the moment.

"Yeah," he whispered, even though he knew Brooke wasn't really asking *him*. "They are."

EPILOGUE

To: Bertram Habeas, Asst. Ed., HART, Chekswa School of
   Literature
From: Leuchtend Wahrheit, Dir. of Comms., Dobless
   Information Services
Re: Alliance Handbook Project, Data Correction
Send Date: 5 Dec 3067

Greetings, Professor Habeas,

It has been brought to our attention that the first edition publication of your abridged almanac, entitled The Lyran Alliance Handbook, has already begun its statewide electronic dissemination. That being said, I regret to inform you that, upon reviewing the final drafts your team sent our way, they appear to contain minor cartographic errors which we have only been able to verify, in their entirety, in the last few days.

Miraculously, it appears we would have missed these errors ourselves, were it not for an astute amateur cartographer who sent us a written request to verify our own interstellar maps. It was only then, upon cross-referencing our charts with the CCS-produced maps included in your team's publication, that we noticed the errors at all. ComStar's historical gremlins strike again!

For the sake of historical accuracy, I am including data files for the specific maps affected: Post-Age of War (2571), post-First Succession War (2822), and post-Second Succession War (2864). I highly recommend that these *updates be incorporated into your electronic distributions of the* Handbook *at your earliest convenience.*

If you have any inquiries regarding this or any of our other academic services, please feel free to address them to my office. It has been a pleasure corresponding with you.

—LW, DoC, DoBInf
Ludwigdhafen

EXPLORER-CLASS JUMPSHIP *SACAJAWEA*
ZENITH JUMP POINT, LORIC
LYRAN ALLIANCE
12 DECEMBER 3067

Strapped into a gee-chair, Alahni shook as her mind and body fought back the intense nausea and dizziness they had yet to grow accustomed to after four consecutive trips through hyperspace. She had found it helpful to keep her eyes squeezed shut throughout the process, though, and while she knew it was completely unnecessary, whispered a thanks to Jerome Blake every time she returned to normal space. This time, her prayer was doubly emphatic, as the jump didn't carry with it the same nightmarish visions of cyborgs and fire that came with the last three.

In the days between each leap, Alahni reflected often on the oddity of Jerome Blake. From childhood, she had been raised to revere him as a savior of mankind, the visionary who foresaw humanity's End Times, and worked to save those he could from the terrors to come. Brooklyn Stevens told her that, to a certain degree, most of that was true, but the story was far more complex than that—so much so that many historians felt the Sainted Blake may have done more to accelerate the Succession Wars than shield anyone against them. Nowhere was this more apparent than in the news reports the *Sacajawea* had picked up after its last jump, with rumors of chaos that seemed to rattle Brooke and Tibor, even after all they'd been through.

It was all enough to make Alahni wonder why she still whispered prayers to Blake at all.

As she felt the last ripples of jump-induced confusion fade away, she opened her eyes to find that she was, in fact, still strapped in her seat, within the simple shipboard quarters Doctor Stevens had provided her. Gray-painted walls of metal surrounded her, broken mainly by a simple hatchway facing the ship's main grav deck corridor, and the porthole-simulating monitor affixed to the opposite wall. Lit by a quartet of bright yellow pseudo-fluorescent bulbs recessed into the ceiling, the chamber came with thin, deep blue, wall-to-wall carpet, a pair of simple-yet-comfortable fold-out single-sleeper cots on the aftward side, and the utilitarian computer desk which Alahni now sat before. A second door to the chamber, fashioned from some form of synthetic, laminated wood, stood closed on the room's forward side, beyond which was the washroom she shared with the cabin next door.

Brooke's cabin.

Ever since their escape from Jardine, the first Lost Ones Alahni ever met had been nothing but protective and considerate. But while both Brooke and Tibor did their best to keep Alahni safe and help prepare her for the realities of a life beyond her Wayward tribe, the attentions of the former often felt more like the doting of a mother toward her child. In fact, during the first week after their first jump, Brooke's visits to her cabin "to check up on her," started to feel almost smothering—until Alahni finally asked if Doctor Stevens had any kids of her own. The older woman seemed almost ashamed at that, and her visits declined noticeably in the days that followed. And while her warmth toward Alahni never truly waned, when she did come by, she maintained a certain distance away, as if there was now some form of invisible barrier between them.

All in all, it was a little bit awkward at times.

Tibor Mitternacht, meanwhile, had assumed more of a mentoring role, answering Alahni's questions about history and technology in the Inner Sphere while also showing her around their wonderous jump vessel. He also filled in some of the blanks about how the various Succession Wars and the Clan Invasion had unfolded while Alahni's people lived their lives off the map. His explanations were remarkably candid, neither praising nor condemning the horrors of history, and those who brought them about. His dry accounts simply told her how things happened and why, so far as he understood them. They were certainly less dramatic than her own versions of the past, as she told them to entertain or educate the youth of the Shrouded Forest. (But she tried not to dwell on that too much now—at least not outside of the quiet moments, when she had the time and privacy to grieve for those left behind.)

Reaching up to her sternum, Alahni pressed the release on the chair's harness, and pulled the straps off her sides. Retractable cords pulled the harness the rest of the way, minimizing their presence by coiling the straps along the chair's back and underside, where they'd remain until needed again.

Clicking the heels of her mag-shoes together, Alahni felt her feet being tugged toward the metal plating beneath her quarters' carpets, and gently pushed herself away from the chair. For her, learning to stand and move in microgravity had been a crash course ever since those days spent on the *Agravain*. But then again, she had to admit it was a lot less stressful than relying on sheer adrenaline, fear, and willpower to keep herself running around, climbing ladders, and fighting hostile Guardians on a ship burning hard enough to make her feel like her weight had doubled. Thanks to some patient tutelage from Brooke, Tibor, and the rest of *Sacajawea*'s crew over the last month, she could now maneuver comfortably in the null-gravity conditions that perpetually characterized JumpShip life outside of a spinning grav deck.

These newfound skills enabled her to rise from the desk chair and half-walk, half-float to the outer wall, and its window to eternal night. (Indeed, although all of *Sacajawea*'s living quarters occupied the bulk of the ship's grav deck, and thus approximated 0.7 gravity most of the time, Tibor had explained to Alahni early on that Captain Pohl always kept the rotational systems disengaged for half an hour before and after each jump, as a safety precaution.)

Projected on the porthole-monitor was a universe of stars, not a single constellation of which Alahni could identify. As beautiful then as it was when she truly stared out from the cockpit of that stolen aerospace fighter, the darkness of the void nevertheless also chilled her to the bone. For weeks she had marveled at the view beyond *Sacajawea*'s windows, often transfixed by sights these Lost now took for granted. Jardine, her home, was about sixty light-years away by now, but even though she knew what that meant on a technical level, it still boggled her mind to think about it. For most of her life, Alahni's whole world had been a tribe in a patch of forest barely twelve kilometers across, hiding in the shadows of the City of Hope.

But all of that was gone now...

"Welcome to Lyran space, Alahni."

Brooke's voice broke through her concentration, but it still took several seconds to tear her eyes from the view. She stared blankly for a moment, briefly wondering how long the Lost woman had been standing there, and how she missed the sound of either of the doors opening behind her. The strange distance Brooke had maintained over the last two weeks was still there, but Alahni could also sense something else—sadness, or worry, perhaps—just barely evident in her brownish-green eyes.

"This is the Loric system," Brooke went on after a moment, nodding toward the faux porthole. "Home to almost two billion people."

"Are they friendly?" Alahni asked.

Brooke shrugged with a faint smirk. "If one has the money, I suppose."

Alahni blinked. Money was a concept she understood only in the abstract; neither the Guardians nor the Waywards used currency as such. The Guardians received any resources they didn't already have from the other worlds of the Five, while everyone else back home saw to their own needs through their own sweat and muscle—bartering among themselves for everything else.

"You look nice today," Brooke murmured. "The outfit, I mean. Looks good on you. Glad it fits."

Alahni frowned and glanced down at herself. The wardrobe that came with her new quarters included a selection of casual and work clothes that belonged to one of the *Sacajawea*'s former crew. While the synthetic fibers and machine stitching took some getting used to after a lifetime spent wearing handmade garments of hide and spun furs, she couldn't deny their appeal, both in comfort and their colorful variety. Moreover, they even *smelled* different from her old tribal wear, carrying a vaguely floral scent Alahni first took to be from whatever perfume their previous owner favored. (Brooke eventually explained that the fragrance actually came from the chemical soaps used in the shipboard laundering system.)

Just before the jump, Alahni had chosen to wear a soft blue vest over a pale gray blouse, with pleated black trousers. But as she took in Brooke's uniform—loose-fitting khaki coveralls, cinched at the waist by a black cargo belt, over a neck-hugging black undershirt—she started to feel strangely overdressed for the day.

"Thank you," she replied after a moment. "It does. Your friend Marissa truly had good taste, I take it?"

Brooke smiled a bit sadly and nodded. "She did, but she didn't show it off nearly as often as you might think. I wish you could have met her."

"She sounded nice."

"She was," Brooke said with a sigh. "She really was..."

An alert echoed throughout the JumpShip, a noise different from those Alahni already identified with the hyperspace jump procedure. It didn't seem particularly urgent, as Brooke didn't tense up or bolt from the room when it sounded, and it faded quickly away, like a single toll of an electronic bell. Brooke's eyes did turn away from Alahni, however, her attention shifting back to the porthole screen. Following the older woman's gaze, Alahni saw what looked like a long metal rod, floating in space, dim lights of red and green pulsing at both ends. It's presence there alarmed her; that JumpShip surely wasn't there before, was it?

As they watched, a flicker of silvery...something started to emerge from one end of the vessel, gradually unfolding like a strange, metallic flower bud. In minutes, Alahni knew, it would form a large, reflective parasol—a jump sail. Now she understood the alarm; it was a signal to the *Sacajawea*'s crew that another ship had jumped in nearby.

After a long silence, Brooke let out a sigh without looking away from the distant craft. Something new had just blinked near the middle of the JumpShip, a yellow spark of light that moved ever so slightly downward before vanishing a second later.

"Looks like our *friends* are here," Brooke said at last, with an unmistakably sardonic emphasis on the word "friends." "Get ready to steel yourself for this."

Alahni nodded hesitantly and turned to find Brooke's eyes on her again, but this time there was a new fire in them. It was a look she hadn't seen since Jardine.

Outside the airlock to the small craft bay, each clad in a light duty flight suit, Tibor Mitternacht and Lawrence Pohl stood in a state of semi-attention. Above the heavy steel doors, the air pressure light glowed a dull, angry red, while a steady hum from somewhere beyond the walls droned on. They'd only been there for a few seconds now, but already, Tibor could sense the unease in Lawrence's breathing. So, he wasn't surprised when the gray-haired JumpShip skipper glanced his way just a few heartbeats later.

"You holding up alright, Trouble?"

Tibor looked back at him with a shallow, half-hearted smile. "As well as I can," he said. "You?"

"Still in shock, to be honest," Lawrence said. "I mean, nukes on the Triad? Luthien gone dark? War on Outreach? What the hell is happening out there?"

"I'm afraid to find out."

The journey from Jardine to Loric had been made under complete EMCON. For each jump, the *Sacajawea* stayed off the communications grid, selecting uninhabited systems along a seemingly random course until they reached Lyran space. It wasn't even until their last stop over Giausar that they dared send a message packet to Loric via the local HPG station, so the Interstellar Expeditions agents awaiting them there knew they were finally en route.

Other messages also went out at that time, of course— each one a calculated risk, given the very real possibility that the Word was undoubtedly still looking for them. But the real shock came when they picked up several news packets while waiting for the *Sac*'s jump drive to recharge.

It sounded like the entire Inner Sphere was going straight to Hell. And the Word of Blake was at the heart of it all.

"You don't think we—?" Lawrence began.

"No," Tibor snapped, waving a cautionary hand between them. "Don't even suggest it. This was...something else, something they planned, way before we even took this job."

"Still..."

"Still," Tibor repeated with a nod. He understood all too well. "We're marked. We saw a secret they've been hiding for generations. And something they haven't unleashed yet. Something maybe the rest of the universe doesn't know about."

"That's why Brooke asked you to send the worm?"

Tibor nodded again. Of the data packets they'd sent back at Giausar, that bit of code he put together was probably the biggest gamble of them all.

Lawrence sighed and gave a weak shrug. "Then I hope it gets where it needs to go."

"So do I," Tibor admitted. "So do I."

With a faint hiss and a heavy *clank* of metal on metal sounding from somewhere inside the walls, the air pressure light flashed a cool green, signifying that the bay beyond finally reached the right pressure and oxygen content to safely enter. Tibor gave Lawrence a stern nod, and saw it returned in kind.

Their game faces came back on just as the door opened, revealing two men in identical black coveralls. Each of their uniforms was adorned with the simple "*IE*" logo of Interstellar Expeditions, stitched into the outer fabric on each shoulder.

Behind the two men sat a plain, gray, S-7A shuttlecraft "bus," securely clasped and held to the deck by the bay's retrieval boom. Aside from a simple registry of seemingly random numbers and letters stenciled just behind its forward canopy shields, the craft was unmarked. Tibor figured it for a rental.

The man who approached Tibor first was easily recognized between his ultra-short blond hair, pastel blue eyes, fair skin, and a face so broad it was almost flat. Doctor Henry Croft's expression was pensive, almost sheepish, as he extended a hand toward Tibor...who left him hanging for an uncomfortably long time before he accepted it.

"Mister Mitterschmidt, Captain Pohl," Croft began, "on behalf of Interstellar Expeditions, please accept my profuse apologies for the behavior of Doctor Bellamy and the mercenaries under his command. You and Brooke, of all people, surely must understand how the lure of the unknown can sometimes drive some of our field personnel to foolishness."

"Foolishness like that should be fatal," Lawrence snarked.

"I'd say that in this case, it possibly was," Croft said. "We have not heard from Bellamy, Captain Hara, or any of their expedition since we become aware of your situation."

"Small comfort," Tibor deadpanned. "I'm sure Doctor Stevens and myself would've loved to *thank* your boys personally for all their little stunts."

"Their stunts at Jardine, I take it?"

Tibor gave Croft an empty smile, but held his tongue and gestured for both men to follow him and Lawrence to the grav deck. At this point, Croft would just have to wait to see Brooke if he wanted the details.

As the four men half-walked, half-floated through *Sacajawea*'s corridors, Croft tried to make small talk with Tibor and Lawrence several times, while his own companion—a dark-haired, middle-aged, and slightly heavy-set man wearing tinted glasses—remained utterly silent. After getting only the briefest possible replies, he finally gave up halfway along.

The conference room Brooke had selected for this meeting was smaller and blander than the one usually reserved for mission planning. Instead of a table for ten surrounded by just that many synth-leather chairs, with bookshelves and starmaps lining the walls, this chamber housed a small, metallic, wood-veneer table flanked by four metal seats covered in faded black fabric. There were no bookshelves in here, beyond those hidden behind the doors of a small row of cabinets just as dull and gray as the otherwise unadorned walls. Off-center on the table stood a small trideo projector, held in place by magnetic feet. The air in this under-used room smelled a bit stale, with hints of ozone and the dry odor of dusty, neglected heating elements.

At the far end of the room, closest to the holo-projector, stood Brooke Stevens and a young woman whose strangely exotic Polynesian beauty and intensely curious stare clashed with Brooke's comparatively more mundane Anglo-European features and the perturbed expression she turned Croft's way as soon as he entered.

"Doctor Croft," Brooke began sharply, "I hope you realize how easily we could've blown you out of the stars before your shuttle even docked here."

"Absolutely, my dear," Croft managed with a mirthless smirk. "But you've never been one to blow a deal at the last moment."

"And who says we even have a deal anymore? Those flunkies you sent along to help us made some pretty underhanded plays out there."

"And, as I have already told Tibor and Lawrence here," Croft gestured vaguely toward the two men, who now stood off to his left, "I apologize for that, both personally and on behalf of IE. In fact, prior to our jump to this system, I managed to convince upper management to authorize a doubling of your payment and even an offer to cover any repairs your ship requires at this time. Of course, that's all provided you have evidence of a mission accomplished."

"Heh," Brooke scoffed. "We picked up their radio chatter, you know. Your mercs tried to scare my crew off by broadcasting their position in a system they knew to be hostile, so they could try and take me and our data at gunpoint."

"You and I both know greedy men only get that bold when they see a prize in reach, Doctor. You can't tell me you *didn't* find Jardine."

Brooke stared at Croft for a long moment, then allowed herself a crooked smile. "Oh, you're too good for IE, Henry."

Brooke pulled one side of her coveralls open and reached inside while Croft's eyes intently followed her every move. From an inside pocket, she withdrew a data chip, flourished it briefly, then set it into the projector.

With a soft *beep* and a nearly inaudible hum, the device sprang to life, and the glowing, holographic image of a star system materialized above the table. Text call-outs flashed quickly in the field, spilling out solar data, highlighting jump points, and flagging the various warning buoys before, finally, one world flashed in brilliant green, and suddenly exploded in size until it dominated the entire field. Beneath and alongside the slowly rotating orb, statistics on everything from axial tilt and orbital distances to atmospheric composition and magnetic field ranges scrolled by on rings of text.

"Jardine," Brooke said simply. "Right where we left it."

"And where might that be, exactly?" Croft asked after a moment. "For that matter, how can you be absolutely sure it *is* Jardine?"

Brooke tilted her head and arched an eyebrow before reaching out to switch off the projector. Ejecting the chip, she tucked it back into the same inner breast pocket it came from while a thin smile crossed her face.

"We lost a crewmember, a DropShuttle and a *Possum* landing on that planet, and I can't count the number of times some bionic psychopath nearly killed Trouble and me both. But you can verify the log data we compiled in this chip from the *Sacajawea* and the DropShip you guys lost on Shasta. Not to mention the detailed navigational data we managed to salvage from the Blake DropShip we snuck aboard in order to get off-world. I can also offer our full vid-statements, giving you complete accounts on everything we found there, to verify that, yes, that *is* Jardine.

"But the hardest evidence we have is staring you right in the face right now," Brooke finished, with a gesture toward the young girl beside her. "Doctor Henry Croft, meet Alahni, Keeper of Tales for the Shrouded Forest Tribe on Jardine. Alahni...?"

Alahni nodded to Croft without saying anything, her expression apprehensive. Brooke reached into another pocket on her jumpsuit and withdrew a syringe and extended her free hand toward the girl. Alahni raised her right arm and pulled back her sleeve, exposing even more of her flawless brown skin.

"This won't hurt a bit," Brooke whispered to her as she expertly found a vein and poked the needle into it. Alahni winced and frowned. "Whether they do anything to us or not," she began while she worked, "most of the micro-organisms found on any life-bearing world get into us as early as the womb. That's basic xenobiology..."

After filling the syringe with Alahni's blood, Brooke fished a small bandage from her pocket to cover the wound, and gave the girl a reassuring smile as she did so. Turning to Croft, she popped the now-filled vial off the needle, and casually flicked it toward him. All eyes in the room watched as the vial, granted the unnatural weightlessness of microgravity, tumbled slowly and strangely through the air in Croft's direction.

Although Brooke's aim wasn't perfect, Croft barely needed to even stretch his arm out to capture the incoming missile. Once he had it, he shook the tiny vial and watched as the crimson fluid inside sloshed about, before making a non-committal "hmm" and handing it to his companion. By the time he looked back, Brooke's gaze already on him.

"I'm sure John will be able to verify that Alahni's blood will show markers unique for microbes indigenous to Jardine. Check any records you like, though I'd recommend you avoid anything sourced by ComStar or the Word."

Beside Croft, "John" let out an inquisitive "hmm?" at the sound of his own name.

Croft smiled, but only for a moment. "I know your rep, Brooke," he said. "I don't doubt what his tests will find. You're no con artist."

"Then you also know full well that I won't be giving you this data chip, or even one scrap more about that world until you agree to a bit more than a pay boost and ship repairs for me. If Hara or Bellamy hadn't managed to get themselves killed before, they'd be able to tell you what I'm saying right now. The planet's hot, hotter than IE can probably even imagine."

"I'm definitely getting that impression right now," Croft conceded with a sigh. "Alright, Doctor. What's it going to be?"

"First, it's going to be *triple* my standard fee, not double, and I want half up front. Second, your people will fix my JumpShip, free of charge. Finally, I want a ship sent to Donegal by no later than next week—"

"Donegal?" Croft blurted out. "Haven't you heard—?"

"—*There*," Brooke went on with intensity, "it will meet a shuttle, whose occupant will tell them where to go next. We will meet your ship at that second destination. Do not ask that individual any questions beyond that, and don't try anything shifty."

"We're not a taxi service, Brooke."

"You are now, because only *when* that's all done, will I hand over this data. Trust me; it's *that* important."

"And after that?"

"After that, you pay my crew the rest of the money you owe us, and we part company."

Croft hesitated, but never broke eye contact with Brooke. "The deal," he said at last, "was for Jardine and *all* evidence of its existence. We'll also want the girl."

An outraged gasp escaped from Alahni's lips and she took a reflexive step back away from the table, her eyes darting back and forth between Brooke and Tibor. Brooke laid a reassuring hand on her shoulder and narrowed her eyes on Croft.

"She's not property, Doctor," Brooke snapped, "and I'll not subject her to your likes. You have all the evidence you need in that blood sample and the data chip I'll give your people at the rendezvous. Take it and be happy."

Croft sighed again, lowering his eyes a moment, his mind clearly racing for an answer. A bland smile found its way to his face by the time he looked up again. "Counterproposal," he said. "I'll do all you ask, and even *quadruple* your pay for this mission, if you and your crew come back to the fold. You found Jardine; I don't need John to finish his analysis for that. IE could use a woman like you, and I think you'll find our new long-term employment options much better than those you left behind."

Brooke gave him a lopsided grin and shook her head slowly.

"Think about this, Doctor," Croft cautioned. "In case you haven't heard, the Word has gone mad lately. They're on a warpath, and no borders or treaties seem to be stopping them outside of Marik and Liao space. If they really do have the stake in Jardine you're implying, you're surely on their radar as well. With IE, you'll have more protection."

"Takes a lot of nerve to offer that after what we've gone through, Croft," Brooke said coldly. "The deal stands as I phrased it. Full repairs, triple pay—half now, and half when we rendezvous with my...associate. Botch this, or sell me out to the Blakists, and not only will you never see this data, but I'll see to it that you and everyone you care about find yourselves floating in the void.

"Take the deal, Henry, or screw you guys. We're going home."

A tense silence hung over the room and lingering. Alahni, her eyes still wide and worried, glanced at Brooke, comparing her defiant glare to Croft's sour expression while the two fought their wordless battle of wills. Finally, after what felt like an eternity of seconds, the older man blinked, and tipped his head in defeat.

"You're playing a dangerous game, Brooke," he said, "but fine. Have it your way. And may God have mercy on your soul."

"One way or another," Brooke told him, "I figure we'll see soon enough."

My dearest Tyler,

I hope this message finds you well. I have so missed you in these past many weeks, and as I write you now, I can only beg for your forgiveness over and over. I have been away for so long—too long. I don't dare say more at this time, but I beg you now to pack your things. Call it excess paranoia if you will, but while I may take my chances with my life, I refuse to do so with yours.

So, while I know this is going to come as a great inconvenience—and I can hear your outraged "I told you so!" from here—I think it's time for that little contingency we talked about. Take only what you need, Love, and whatever you need to handle the trip, wait for me at the rendezvous. I will find you there soon.

And when I do, please set an extra place for dinner. There's someone I want you to meet...

(signed) Brooke

SCOUT-CLASS JUMPSHIP *BROKEN KNEE*
ZENITH JUMP POINT, SKYE
LYRAN ALLIANCE
12 DECEMBER 3067

So many promises, so many dreams, now lay in ashes. Ashes Apollyon could virtually taste as he regarded the holoprojector in front of him. There, rendered in faithful, high-resolution detail, floated the image of his greatest friend and mentor.

His Master.

The man, who once bore the surname of a House Lord, who'd eschewed his throne for the truer power of knowledge, whose foresight had helped guide the faithful through some of the darkest days of this new era, sat behind a desk of polished obsidian, in a chamber of dark gray shadows. His face was a mask of scars not unlike Apollyon's own—most earned from the treachery of his own kin—and what remained of its original, frail flesh was weathered and worn by age. From the ruddy, warped half of his face, where no hair grew, his true right eye blazed in angry red from a socket of gleaming titanium, while its more expressive companion, reinforced by implants far less overt in nature, stared into the camera with no less intensity beneath a grey eyebrow now arched low in frustration.

With his hood of his bone-white robes thrown back, the Master's half-head of wispy, silver-gray hair was clearly visible, mostly swept back in neat formation, save for the few errant strands that scattered about here and there of their own accord. Thin cables peeked out from somewhere behind his right ear, before snaking back again to disappear somewhere within the collar of the red-and-gold tunic he usually favored these days. A faint, warm glow showed near the right side of his chest, betraying activity from the filters of his true lungs. Though his sullen, pensive speech had been unimpeded by their efforts, the first of the Master's Hands knew when his liege was struggling to breathe. It pained Apollyon to see him this way.

"My friend, rest assured that I am well and unharmed. The treacherous Dragoons never breached my sanctum grounds, and none of their number escaped our wrath. Nevertheless, I have enacted our most prudent contingencies. We shall ensure these Clan-spawned curs pay the ultimate price for their hubris."

Apollyon clenched his fists as a new wave of rage passed over him. The Wolf's Dragoons were among the first worries he'd expressed when the Master chose to journey to Terra. But the true heart of the Word would not be swayed for such petty concerns. Even with their ill-gotten homeworld a scant two jumps away from the sacred havens of Terra, the Dragoons could pose no credible threat to the Master or the Promise—at least, none the Word was well prepared to encounter, now that the time of the Third Transfer was nigh.

But then that foolish relic on Outreach had to go and slip his leash too soon. Had Wayne Waco not managed to get himself killed taking out the hated Jaime Wolf, Apollyon would have commanded his finest to do the deed himself. And now, years of careful planning to deal with the Inner Sphere's Dragoons problem as surgically as possible had been scattered to the winds—at the very *worst* possible moment in history!

"Because of this, and the crises brought down upon us at the capitals, we are forced to reallocate our assets for the time being..."

Another wave of rage crashed down on Apollyon as he fought to keep his focus. Another fool, closer to the Word's heart, heralded these "crises" his Master spoke of. Cameron St. Jamais and his Sixth of June had long impressed the Word's true leadership with their fierce loyalty to Blake's legacy—but even in these traits, Apollyon always knew they paled in comparison to the selfless dedication of his Manei Domini. St. Jamais gave him pause, in fact, for his obvious and overt ambition. Where the Hands served for nothing greater than Blake's Promise itself, St. Jamais's efforts to climb the Word's ranks were crass and vulgar.

But even Apollyon could not believe it when the Word's Precentor-Martial managed to foul up *everything* when it mattered most, and sent the Promise itself careening into the pits of chaos!

That the Master did not immediately demand St. Jamais' head on a platter at first confounded Apollyon. But when he eventually sensed the reason such a fool had been left in the very visible position he'd so brazenly sought, his confusion gave way to prayers that he would live long enough to witness the man's inevitable reckoning.

"Your hunt for those who violated our paradise has raised attentions elsewhere, my friend, and for this reason, you must see it through to the end. I have, in the interim, sent orders new orders to the rest of our Shadows, which you will find in the data file I'm attaching. I have also sent orders to Erinyes, whom you shall rendezvous with once you have ensured your mission's success. As much as it pains me, my brother in Blake's Wisdom, the Karpov Protocols must be observed if any of the Promise is to survive."

Apollyon's mouth went dry and he felt his own breath catch in his lungs. The Master's words, though anticipated, were like a vibrodagger to his gut. He closed his eyes—true and frail alike—and instantly envisioned the fires that would soon engulf everything he once held so dear. But where the orders and the image might have brought another man to tears, Apollyon simply let out a long, controlled, regretful sigh, and willed his heartbeat to slow down again.

It would be done. For the good of all, it would be done.

When Apollyon opened his eyes again, the Master's image was gone, replaced by the glowing broadsword insignia of the Word of Blake. He blinked sadly at the image, unable to remember any of the Master's final words before he'd signed off on this message. Had he said anything at all after confirming the dreaded Karpov Protocols? For the first time in decades, Apollyon felt unsure of himself. There was so much he wanted to say to the man in the holovid, but they would need to wait. There was too much that needed done right now, and the Master's Hands would need to be ready.

Apollyon ejected the chip from the holovid reader and closed his frail hand around it. With one more deep breath and a moment of silent meditation, he forced his mind to re-center itself before he finally reached over the communications panel beside the holoprojector.

"Precentor Lucille," he called into the device.

Damien Lucille replied instantly, as if he'd been hovering over his speaker all along. "Yes, Precentor?"

"Stow the sails and initiate jump calculations."

"Acknowledged, Precentor," Lucille said. "Our course?"

"Unchanged," Apollyon grimly told him. "Our course remains unchanged."

Lucille's response came after the briefest of hesitations, but his voice resonated the same gravity as the orders he'd been given. "Understood, sir."

GRIFFIN
MEDIUM—55 TONS

NEXUS
LIGHT—25 TONS

OWENS
LIGHT—**35** TONS

RAIJIN
MEDIUM—**50** TONS

ROCK POSSUM
MEDIUM—40 TONS

MORE BATTLETECH FICTION BY HERBERT A. BEAS II

If you enjoyed this *BattleTech* novella, you can find other stories by Herbert A. Beas II in the following books:

THE HUNT FOR JARDINE
(FORGOTTEN WORLDS, BOOK ONE)
BURIED IN THE ASHES OF WAR...

Freelance explorer and treasure hunter Dr. Brooklyn Stevens has made her career finding lost artifacts from Inner Sphere history, but during the waning days of the FedCom Civil War, a job offered by the academic organization known as Interstellar Expeditions affords her the chance to pursue the find of a lifetime: a missing planet, one lost in the ravages of the brutal Succession Wars.

But the world of Jardine did not only die in fire—it was erased from stellar maps entirely, and Brooke's employer wants to know why.

She must hunt down the only known link to this forgotten world: a dangerous predator native to Jardine, whose initial discoverer was silenced under mysterious circumstances. Someone wants this planet to remain buried—and they will go to any lengths to ensure that Brooke's quest to uncover the truth of Jardine's disappearance ends in tragedy.

FINDING JARDINE
(FORGOTTEN WORLDS, BOOK TWO)
UNCOVERING THE SECRETS OF A LOST WORLD...

Interstellar explorer and freelance treasure hunter Dr. Brooklyn Stevens has made the find of a lifetime—an entire planet thought lost for centuries. Jardine was supposedly wiped off the maps of the Inner Sphere during the hard-fought Succession Wars, but the verdant forested world she and her adventuring partner just crash-landed on tells a much different story.

And so do its inhabitants. Dr. Stevens and her partner soon find themselves between two very different groups: one whose members are an unholy amalgamation of man and machine, the other a hardy group that lives off the land. Both groups are soon after Stevens and her knowledge about Jardine—one side to protect the planet from those that would seek to reclaim it, the other intent on killing anyone who knows of its existence. Caught between both sides, Brooklyn must uncover the mysteries of Jardine...and stay alive long enough to tell the universe about it...

WEAPONS FREE
(BATTLECORPS ANTHOLOGY VOLUME 3)

This volume features "Growing Up," in which the would-be Baron Hasseldorf must win a duel on Galatea to earn a command position in Kirkpatrick's Bandit Killers.

FIRE FOR EFFECT
(BATTLECORPS ANTHOLOGY VOLUME 4)

This volume contains two stories by Herbert Beas. The first, "Case White: To Serve and Protect," is set during the climactic Case White operation, where a TerraSec officer learns the difference between upholding the law and fighting a war. The second story, "Forgotten Worlds: The Hunt for Jardine," follows treasure hunter Brooklyn Stevens in her quest to locate one of the Hidden—rumored secret planets controlled by the fanatical Word of Blake.

BATTLETECH ERAS

The *BattleTech* universe is a living, vibrant entity that grows each year as more sourcebooks and fiction are published. A dynamic universe, its setting and characters evolve over time within a highly detailed continuity framework, bringing everything to life in a way a static game universe cannot match.

To help quickly and easily convey the timeline of the universe—and to allow a player to easily "plug in" a given novel or sourcebook—we've divided *BattleTech* into eight major eras.

STAR LEAGUE
(Present–2780)

Ian Cameron, ruler of the Terran Hegemony, concludes decades of tireless effort with the creation of the Star League, a political and military alliance between all Great Houses and the Hegemony. Star League armed forces immediately launch the Reunification War, forcing the Periphery realms to join. For the next two centuries, humanity experiences a golden age across the thousand light-years of human-occupied space known as the Inner Sphere. It also sees the creation of the most powerful military in human history.

(This era also covers the centuries before the founding of the Star League in 2571, most notably the Age of War.)

SUCCESSION WARS
(2781–3049)

Every last member of First Lord Richard Cameron's family is killed during a coup launched by Stefan Amaris. Following the thirteen-year war to unseat him, the rulers of each of the five Great Houses disband the Star League. General Aleksandr Kerensky departs with eighty percent of the Star League Defense Force beyond known space and the Inner Sphere collapses into centuries of warfare known as the Succession Wars that will eventually result in a massive loss of technology across most worlds.

CLAN INVASION
(3050–3061)

A mysterious invading force strikes the coreward region of the Inner Sphere. The invaders, called the Clans, are descendants of Kerensky's SLDF troops, forged into a society dedicated to becoming the greatest fighting force in history. With vastly superior technology and warriors, the Clans conquer world after world. Eventually this outside threat will forge a new Star League, something hundreds of years of warfare failed to accomplish. In addition, the Clans will act as a catalyst for a technological renaissance.

CIVIL WAR
(3062–3067)

The Clan threat is eventually lessened with the complete destruction of a Clan. With that massive external threat apparently neutralized, internal conflicts explode around the Inner Sphere. House Liao conquers its former Commonality, the St. Ives Compact; a rebellion of military units belonging to House Kurita sparks a war with their powerful border enemy, Clan Ghost Bear; the fabulously powerful Federated Commonwealth of House Steiner and House Davion collapses into five long years of bitter civil war.

JIHAD
(3067–3080)

Following the Federated Commonwealth Civil War, the leaders of the Great Houses meet and disband the new Star League, declaring it a sham. The pseudo-religious Word of Blake—a splinter group of ComStar, the protectors and controllers of interstellar communication—launch the Jihad: an interstellar war that pits every faction against each other and even against themselves, as weapons of mass destruction are used for the first time in centuries while new and frightening technologies are also unleashed.

DARK AGE
(3081–3150)

Under the guidance of Devlin Stone, the Republic of the Sphere is born at the heart of the Inner Sphere following the Jihad. One of the more extensive periods of peace begins to break out as the 32nd century dawns. The factions, to one degree or another, embrace disarmament, and the massive armies of the Succession Wars begin to fade. However, in 3132 eighty percent of interstellar communications collapses, throwing the universe into chaos. Wars erupt almost immediately, and the factions begin rebuilding their armies.

ILCLAN
(3151–present)

The once-invulnerable Republic of the Sphere lies in ruins, torn apart by the Great Houses and the Clans as they wage war against each other on a scale not seen in nearly a century. Mercenaries flourish once more, selling their might to the highest bidder. As Fortress Republic collapses, the Clans race toward Terra to claim their long-denied birthright and create a supreme authority that will fulfill the dream of Aleksandr Kerensky and rule the Inner Sphere by any means necessary: The ilClan.

CLAN HOMEWORLDS
(2786–present)

In 2784, General Aleksandr Kerensky launched Operation Exodus, and led most of the Star League Defense Force out of the Inner Sphere in a search for a new world, far away from the strife of the Great Houses. After more than two years and thousands of light years, they arrived at the Pentagon Worlds. Over the next two-and-a-half centuries, internal dissent and civil war led to the creation of a brutal new society—the Clans. And in 3049, they returned to the Inner Sphere with one goal—the complete conquest of the Great Houses.

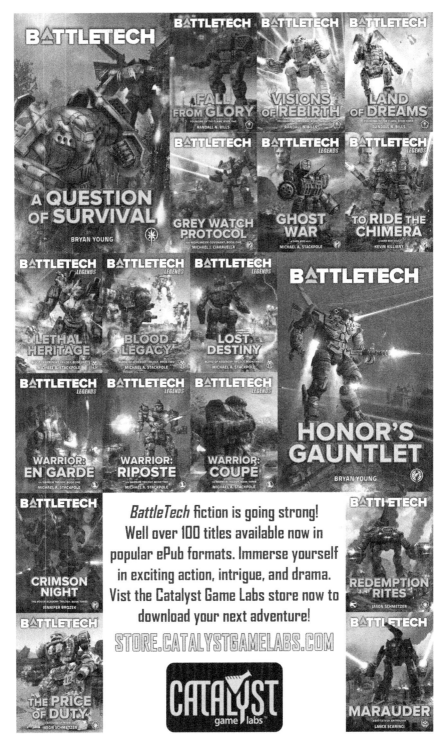

Printed in Great Britain
by Amazon